Reader Comments on the Cherish Novels:

"Compelling novels about life's struggles and victories and God's unfailing love and grace."
—Mary Lou McKean

"Brought me into that town [Cherish] and those people's lives. Very inspiring!"
—Vickie Woodrum

"Love the books!"
—Terri Oakley

"Got the [second] book on Sunday and finished it on Monday. Love it!"
—Joan Bateson

"Oh, my goodness. I reread your first book so I could refresh my memory… Finished it and began the new one... I LOVED the new one [second book] so much. Tears were flowing in places. You have a wonderful God-given talent for telling a wonderful story. I can hardly wait for number three."
—Debbie Baker

"We both just finished book two. It was great! Looking forward to book three!"
—Steve and Renee Dunmead

"I just finished reading your book [book two], Debby, and loved it!!! Are there more books coming?"
—Amy Thomsen

Other books in the Cherish series by Debby L. Johnston:

Cherish: A Still, Small Call

Cherish: Behold, I Knock

CHERISH:
CREATE IN ME A CLEAN HEART

Number Three in the Cherish Series

Debby L. Johnston

WESTBOW PRESS®
A DIVISION OF THOMAS NELSON & ZONDERVAN

Veterinary consultant: Dr. Roger St. Clair, DVM.

Art Credits:
DLJ logo by Kate Frick (*Frick.chick.designs@gmail.com*)
"Cows" sketch by Maddie Frick (*Made Line Designs*)
"Adam and the Snak" drawing by Heather Ann West
"Irises" watercolor by Debby L. Johnston
Photo of Author by Scott Johnston

WestBow Press books may be ordered through booksellers or by contacting:

WestBow Press
A Division of Thomas Nelson & Zondervan
1663 Liberty Drive
Bloomington, IN 47403
www.westbowpress.com
1 (866) 928-1240

ISBN: 978-1-9736-1153-0 (sc)
ISBN: 978-1-9736-1154-7 (hc)
ISBN: 978-1-9736-1152-3 (e)

Library of Congress Control Number: 2017919384

Print information available on the last page.

WestBow Press rev. date: 02/08/2018

CONTENTS

LETTER FROM THE AUTHOR

Dear Reader,

Writing the *Cherish* series is like weaving a tapestry. In this installment, the individual stories of characters you've come to love (and some you will meet for the first time) converge to reveal the beautiful pattern the Master Designer has had in mind from the beginning. In the closing chapter of the previous *Cherish* story, Mac Garrett (Reverend Andy Garrett's father) responded to an altar call and invited Jesus into his life. Now, in this story, Mac falters and fears he cannot live the life he has been reborn into. Follow his progress, as Mac learns how God not only began a good work in him but continues to work in transforming him into something he never imagined he could be.

Create in Me a Clean Heart, from this book's title, echoes King David's prayer in Psalm 51 for forgiveness and restoration. David recognized his inability to be free of sin without the help of God. Centuries later, God's Son, Jesus, opened a new way to forgiveness—a way that assures sinners they can be *"holy and blameless, in His sight"* (Ephesians 1:4). As part of the new life Jesus died to impart, God, Himself, takes up residence in the hearts of His children, and He journeys forward with these individuals in order to perfect their walk with Him. Paul tells us in Philippians 1:6 that *"He who began a good work in you will carry it on to completion until the day of Christ Jesus."* It is my desire that this third *Cherish* story will encourage you as God transforms you, too, by the power of His grace.

God bless you, my friends!

Debby

OUR ETERNITY WAS YOUR PLAN ALL THE TIME

As the sun in softness stroked the earth with morning,
Your tender hand drew up a clump of clay.
You turned and shaped and formed it to your image;
In its barren soul You blew the dust away.
Then everlasting filled the spaces where no life had been,
And thoughts and dreams first woke the virgin mind.
And eyes anew beheld and wholly worshipped You,
And in that place, there was no end to time.

For our eternity was Your plan all the time,
Our eternity in Your presence divine—
Our every day and every thought and in between.
Your company's what my soul was designed for,
It's my destiny You came down to die for.
Love so amazing, love so astounding,
Love everlasting—it overwhelms me.
Your love is everything. Through all time, I'll walk with Thee.

You've promised new life everlasting;
This clay we bear, though marred, will be new.
And 'round Your throne our crowns we'll be casting,
And forevermore we will walk in love with You.
Love so amazing, love so astounding,
Love everlasting—it overwhelms me.
Your love is everything. Through all time, I'll walk with Thee.

Your company's what my soul was designed for,
It's my destiny that You came down to die for.
Love so amazing, love so astounding,
Love everlasting—it overwhelms me.
Your love is everything. Through all time, I'll walk with Thee.

DEBBY L. JOHNSTON

Dedicated to my wonderful husband, Scott,
and to all my readers. All praise to Jesus Christ,
the Author and Finisher of our faith!

PART ONE
SEARCH ME, O GOD

CHAPTER ONE

SKUNK (JANUARY 1981)

"Oh, my!"

Reverend Andy Garrett hadn't seen a single skunk since coming from Chicago to the small Illinois town of Cherish almost two years ago. And he had forgotten how pungent they smelled—until today. Now, he and the church secretary, Opal Reese, got a whiff of one coming down the hallway.

When it appeared, it turned into Clifford Myers.

The farmer who sauntered into the office of the First Baptist Church and casually dropped off a bag of clothes for the aid closet (per his wife's instructions) didn't seem to be aware of his odor.

"Thanks," Opal managed to say while holding her breath.

Because she would have to breathe soon, Opal barely acknowledged Clifford. Her fingers kept rhythm at the typewriter, and she nodded only briefly when the farmer tipped his hat and turned to go. Andy, however, made the mistake of asking what had happened. Clifford's head shot up, and he stalled at the door.

Opal rolled her eyes. "Excuse me!" she said. "I have to get something from the sanctuary." She leaped from her desk and would have bowled Clifford over, but she couldn't take the chance of brushing against the odor-bearer. She glared at him until he got the message and moved from the doorway.

"Sorry, ma'am. 'Scuse me," the farmer mumbled.

Andy took shallow breaths. The smell was worse at close range than when it had first wafted into the room. Andy couldn't hide his distress.

"Can you still smell it?" Clifford asked. "I figured it was gone by now. It was strong at first, but I guess I've got to where I can't smell it anymore."

Andy wondered how that could be.

"My hunting hound tangled with a skunk before dawn this morning," Clifford explained. "I locked the dog in the storage shed 'cause she smelled so bad."

"Well," said Andy, as politely as he could, "the dog must have rubbed up against your coat, because"—Andy breathed through his mouth—"you've got it all over you, Clifford. And you stink!"

Clifford laughed. "What do you know? I s'ppose I'll have to get Louise to wash it out."

Clifford made no move to leave, however. And Andy could stand it no longer. He took a chance and grabbed the clueless man by the sleeve. "Clifford, you can't stay in here. Come back when you've got rid of that smell."

The farmer looked surprised. "Wh-why," he stammered, "s-s-sure, Pastor. I'll see you later."

The odor lingered and trailed the retreating figure down the hall.

Andy smothered a "Lord, help us!" and ran to the bathroom. Then he hurried back to the office and used up the entire can of odor spray he'd borrowed. Unfortunately, it made the room smell like skunk and flowers, which was almost worse. He ended up opening every window, even though it was a cold day.

And then he went in search of Opal.

"We can't work in there for a bit," Andy said when he found her.

"Really?" Opal replied. "Can you believe that man couldn't smell himself? And he's contaminated that bag of clothes, too." Opal's nose wrinkled in disgust.

Andy said, "I feel sorry for Louise. She'll be the one to have to clean him up, and I can only imagine how Clifford's truck will smell for weeks."

"And his house!" Opal declared. Then she muttered, "I will never understand why everything has to happen to the Myers family."

It seemed true, Andy thought. The Myerses did tend to have more than their share of trouble.

At the office door, neither Andy nor Opal made a move to enter. The smell trapped in the hallway was bad enough, and they knew that the reeking bag Clifford had brought for the aid closet still lay inside.

Opal finally set her mouth, sucked in a breath, and rapidly twisted the knob. In one swift motion, she thrust her arm into the unfortunately scented interior and snatched her coat off the hook behind the door.

"I don't know about you," she announced, "but I'm taking an early lunch!" She punched her arms into the coat sleeves and disappeared down the hallway.

Andy intended to follow suit. But first, he had to lift the bag of clothes and set it out on the sidewalk. He wondered if it would ever be fit to bring back inside.

CHAPTER TWO

FIVE IN A PARSONAGE

Minutes later, at home, Andy regaled his family with the story of the "skunk in the office." A trace of his brush against Clifford and the offending bag of clothes confirmed the tale and made it necessary to change his shirt before lunch.

"You don't need to hold your nose," he chided his wife. "It's not that bad!"

"Mm-huh." Abbey ignored him and held her nose anyway on her way to the washing machine.

Winston followed her but caught a whiff of the shirt and backed away with a snort. Unable to identify the penetrating smell and its unpleasant effect on his senses, the bulldog sneezed.

"We don't like it much, either," Andy said with a laugh, and the brindled pet lumbered back to the kitchen in search of more pleasant odors.

Little Emily was in the kitchen, too, and Winston knew that the exuberant four-month-old could be counted on to fling wonderful items from her high chair to the floor. Indeed, just then, Emily squealed, and her pacifier flew across the tray and onto the linoleum. Winston's eyes zeroed in on its flight, and his feet scrambled to follow. But the dog stopped dead in his tracks as bombs of "*Don't you dare!*" exploded overhead.

Winston ducked, tucked in the tiny twist of his tail, and scurried into the living room.

Andy rinsed and returned the pacifier to Emily's tray and stooped to make a face.

"Did you miss your favorite uncle?" he asked. In reply, Emily thrashed her arms and swept a spoon to the floor.

There was no need to retrieve this utensil; it would be collected after the meal, along with several other fallen objects destined for the kitchen sink. Andy ignored it and squeezed into his chair at the tiny dining room table.

Emily and her parents—Andy's sister, Molly, and brother-in-law, Paul—had expanded the number of occupants in the First Baptist parsonage to five. With its two bedrooms and one bathroom, the little one-story house barely accommodated them all. But the crowding was temporary. A brand-new double-wide mobile home awaited the Doakses—next to the charred remains of their burned-out farmhouse. The displaced family would move in as soon as their broken bones had sufficiently healed.

The injuries had occurred on a rainy night, not long after Thanksgiving, when flames had claimed the Doakses' stately, century-old, two-story house. Molly's leg had broken in her escape from an upstairs window, and Paul's leg and arm had been casualties of heroism and a collision with a discarded lawn mower. Only little Emily had escaped intact, thanks to her Grandpa Mac, who had caught her as Molly had dropped the little one into his arms. Andy reflected, now, that if Mac had not extended his holiday visit, he would not have been there to catch Emily. Nor could Mac have driven the rest of the family to the hospital.

Andy was grateful that his father had been there, and he was grateful for the lives that had been spared.

Andy was still amazed that he and his family were here, together. It wouldn't have happened if he had not decided to accept the call to this small rural community. He had seriously questioned God's leading. (What did he, as a city boy, know about farm country?) But now, he could see the wisdom of God in placing him and Abbey here. Andy treasured the nearness of his family, and he marveled at the generosity of his congregation.

Andy and Abbey had learned quickly that everyone in a small town is not only a neighbor but also a friend. Church-member friends actually lived beside them and down the street, and they were always looking for ways to help—like today.

When Andy answered a knock on the front door, next-door neighbor Sylvia Potts greeted him with a large, generously frosted sheet cake. Before he could exclaim, she chirped, "Just a little something to brighten your day." At her elbow, four-year-old Lizzie smiled, as if to say she had helped.

Andy whistled his approval and shouted back into the house: "Chocolate sheet cake!" A chorus of thank-yous echoed in reply.

Sylvia called back, "I hope you're having a good day! We're keeping you all in our prayers!"

Andy smiled at Sylvia, and he swatted at Winston. "Get back!" he ordered. Sylvia ignored the command, and as the dog backed away, she transferred the cake to Andy's arms.

From behind his master, Winston continued to growl. His eyes never left the big yellow tomcat suspended in a stranglehold in Lizzie's little arms. Although Butter and Lizzie were regular visitors to the parsonage—the two had an open invitation to afternoon cookies and milk with Abbey—Winston never failed to register his objection to the cat.

Lizzie knew that the growling dog was all bark and no bite. She lingered to lisp, "Thay hello to Misto Mac."

Andy grinned. "Of course, Lizzie. Mister Mac isn't here, right now, but I'll tell him hello for you when we see him. Okay?"

Lizzie nodded and swung Butter in a half-circle to lug him down the steps. The cat never tensed. His body hung limply, and his plush tail swept the ground.

Andy watched for a moment as Lizzie and her cat retreated, and he marveled at how Butter put up with the abuse.

He also pondered on how Lizzie had fixed her friendship on "Mister Mac." It had seemed an unlikely bonding. Andy's dad had never been remotely child crazy, not even with his own children. But Lizzie had somehow exercised a peculiar charm over the man during her visits—a charm that had softened Mac's gruff responses. Of the various Garretts Lizzie had met at the parsonage, she had, for some reason, singled out Andy's dad for her attentions—and Mac had reciprocated.

Lizzie now caught up with her mother. And Andy heard Winston blow a satisfied snort at their backs, an apparent statement on the fact that the cat had not been allowed in. On a trot through the living room, Winston roughly snatched up his favorite toy and savagely shook it as if to say, "Take that, and don't come back."

Andy howled at his dog's put-on bravado. "That's right, Winston. You're one tough dog!"

Oblivious to his master's sarcasm, Winston acknowledged his praise and waddled over for a pat on his square head.

Later, Andy promised everyone, "I'll pick up more milk from the farm, tomorrow."

He lingered at the table over a piece of Sylvia's cake and washed it down with a generous glass of milk—one always had to have a tall glass with chocolate cake.

Even without the cake, milk disappeared quickly now that Emily was with them. It was a reversal of provision. For nearly a year and a half Andy and Abbey had been getting milk and produce from the farm, but now they were providing milk and meals to the farmers.

Two years ago, Paul's dad had retired and moved to town, and Molly and Paul had come from up north to occupy the Harmony farmstead. Andy had expressed apprehension about the move; he had wondered how Molly would make the transition from city girl to farm wife. After all, he and Molly had grown up in Herndon, a suburb of Chicago, with no reason to foresee a move any farther south than the Eisenhower Expressway, or perhaps Aurora—certainly not to the middle of the state and miles of cornfields. But Molly and Paul had moved, and Molly had blossomed on the farm.

Then barely a month later, Andy and Abbey had ended up mid-state, too—and Andy had been the one to adjust more slowly.

Happily, the move had brought a welcome surprise. When Andy had telephoned Molly to share that he was taking a pastorate in Cherish, she had shrieked into his ear that the town of Cherish was only thirty minutes from their farm in Harmony.

And the proximity of their moves had allowed brother and sister to continue to support one another, even to the point of gathering, now, around a too-small dining room table and sharing a single bathroom for weeks.

It was inconvenient, but it was family.

The disaster-enforced crowding helped the Doakses accept, and even look forward to, their upcoming move to the mobile home—a mass-produced and sterile thing, devoid of the farmstead's character and history. It would be a far cry from the home that Molly and Paul had lost, but it would serve until they were able to rebuild.

Phillip Doaks (Paul's father) and MacAndrew Garrett (Andy and Molly's dad) had already moved into the two back rooms of the four-bedroom mobile home, to be where they could milk the cows, feed the livestock and chickens, and keep up other chores until Paul could put them out of business. The otherwise retired seniors were glad it was winter; there was nothing to be done in the fields.

CHAPTER THREE

MAC

Mac's muscles ached as he rested against the vanity in the double-wide's back bathroom. He winced and frowned. In his prime, he had been able to put in long hours of physical exertion without consequence, but now he creaked and hurt and couldn't wait to drop into bed. Phillip no doubt felt the same. After all, the farm's previous owner had retired for a reason.

Mac looked away from the mirror. If only he could turn back time! What had once been sleek muscle was now slack and wrinkled. The thick, wavy hair of earlier years had gone missing or turned gray, and the time he'd spent in the out-of-doors had deepened his squint lines.

"Ow!" Mac winced again. He cut short his tasks at the sink and turned toward the bed. *Just a few more steps*, he told himself. Then he willed his body under the covers and was soon fast asleep.

In spite of his daily fatigue, Mac was glad for the work. It made him feel useful again. He was no farmer, but it was good that he had come to the farm and that he had been here when things had fallen apart. No one could have anticipated how much he would be needed. His arrival had saved his family and the farm.

At the parsonage, late in the afternoon the next day, Andy collected the pieces of his dad's forwarded mail and grabbed his car keys. Andy had become the go-fer between his sister's family and the farm. His car practically knew the route by heart, so there was no danger of wrong turns. He turned up the radio, and as he cruised down the highway, he belted out the words to *Sail On* with the Imperials. He ignored the strange looks from the few cars he passed.

With the volume still cranked, Andy pulled into the farmyard and parked in front of the barn. He nearly ran over Phillip, who rushed out of the barn door with arms waving. Phillip smacked the hood of the car with his palm.

"Hush! Keep it down!" Phillip hissed.

Andy fell back with a "Huh?" The farm was in the middle of nowhere, with no neighbors to hear. But Andy complied and twisted the dial to off before he killed the engine.

"Sorry," Andy said.

"Shhhhh!" Phillip shushed, again.

This time, Andy whispered, "What's up?" and held out his palms, in question.

Phillip didn't answer. Instead, he grabbed Andy's arm and led him on tip-toe into the barn. Straw and dirt muffled their footsteps, and Andy wondered who or what they were sneaking up on.

Behind the cow stalls, Phillip stopped. There, the two of them crouched in the shadows. Through the rough wooden slats Andy now spied his city-bred father hunched on a tiny milk stool and hesitantly gripping the teats of a stanchioned cow. Andy wondered if this was his dad's first attempt at milking.

As they watched, unseen, Mac's forefingers tweaked the teats in high expectation. But nothing happened. The calm Jersey, slowly chewing her feed, ignored the man at her side, and she refused to release anything to the unfamiliar hands at her udder. Mac heaved his dissatisfaction.

Then, Phillip casually emerged from his hiding place—leaving every impression that he'd just arrived.

"How's it going? Any luck?" he asked.

"See for yourself," Mac growled. He exhaled in disgust and kicked the empty bucket. Then Mac spun off the stool and relinquished it to Phillip. "You'd better do this," he muttered.

Phillip lowered himself and calmly bent to the task. When warm milk spat into the pail, Mac uttered an exasperated epithet.

"I did exactly what you're doing," he protested, and Phillip chuckled.

"These gals are picky," Phillip drawled. "But you wait. You'll win them over! You have to remember, I've been doing this for forty-some years. And some of these cows still remember me."

Mac's frown deepened, and he shook his head. He was clearly irritated that a cow had just shown him up. He was even more irritated when he realized that Andy had seen the whole thing; Andy had finally shown himself.

"Hi, Dad."

Phillip covered Mac's embarrassment with some easy banter. As the milk continued to hiss between Phillip's knees, Andy marveled to see his dad let the matter go.

"Brought your mail," Andy offered.

"Thanks," Mac said, without looking up. "Guess I forgot it. Bunch of bills."

Phillip interrupted, "That's all I ever get, anymore." Then Phillip asked Mac, "Hey, you wanna try this, again?"

Mac looked doubtful, but Phillip offered some coaching. "Just a little squeeze, top to bottom," he said, and he demonstrated.

This time, Mac had some success. In triumph, he crowed, "Hmmpf! I knew it couldn't be that hard!"

Andy couldn't get over the give-and-take between the two men. Mac had been a know-it-all, all of Andy's life, and the chip on his dad's shoulder had often led to unpleasant exchanges with anyone who had set out to, or who had inadvertently bested him. The fact that Mac had deferred to Phillip's expertise in milking—and other farm chores—was a wonder.

And the even bigger wonder, according to Paul, was that Phillip had reciprocated. Evidently, his father was no pushover, either. Paul had told Andy that his farm-born dad tended to be prickly, especially when it came to city folk. For him to have patiently schooled Mac was (as Paul said) "just short of miraculous."

Yes, thought Andy. *It's a marvel to see these two proud and take-charge men somehow manage to strike up a working relationship—maybe even a friendship.*

The needs at the farm after the fire had thrown Mac and Phillip into an unnatural collaboration. In other circumstances, these two hardheads might never have connected. In light of the circumstances, it was good that they had. Both of them had been needed to keep the farm going. Separately, neither of them could have handled the work. Together, they were able to preserve the farm and maintain Paul's livelihood.

"Grab a pitchfork."

Mac tossed the words over his shoulder to Andy. "We'll put you to work. Build some callouses on those book-readin' hands."

Andy laughed. "Can't. Got to get back for supper. Promised Abbey."

Besides, Andy wasn't sure he could work beside his dad.

Phillip walked Andy to the car and gave him the usual carton of eggs, a jug of milk, and some news: "Be sure to tell Paul that the Wion's dog just had puppies. If he wants, I can reserve one to replace Skipper. The farm needs a dog."

Seven-year-old Skipper had been hit by a car not long before the fire. With everything that had happened, Andy doubted that Paul had given a second thought to another dog. "I'll tell him," he said.

"And hug that little Emily for me!" Phillip charged him. "Give her a kiss, right here." (Phillip pointed to the back of his neck.) "That's the sugar spot."

"Will do." Andy promised. "See ya' soon."

On the way home, Andy thought about Phillip and Mac and about all of the changes the Garretts and Doakses had experienced in the last couple of months—upsets that had changed all of them, especially his dad. Andy grinned to recall the image of his father on the milk stool. Mac Garret on a farm! Who would have guessed that his dad would be chasing chickens and tossing feed bags, especially at this stage of his life?

Andy had never known his dad to shun hard work. But Mac was a product of the city. In recent years, he had ruled a heating and air-conditioning business from an office, and he had retired well. His hands had known success and had long ago lost the callouses worn by manual labor.

Mac had always been a proud man, and Andy chuckled at what his dad's country club friends would think if they knew that the high-and-mighty, self-made businessman Mac Garrett was down here forking hay and mucking cow stalls.

City boy! Andy thought.

Grannie would have had choice words, too, about Mac in a barn.

"Nothing wrong with farm work!" she would assert. "It's as good as all that so-called *tough stuff* you do in that fancy, city office."

"Besides," she would add, "Rachel wasn't always a *city girl*."

Grannie had never let Mac or her daughter, Rachel, put on airs around her, even after Mac had made his first million. She knew their background—a background in poverty, like hers.

A spitfire from the backwoods of Kentucky, Grannie had never had much, but she had always been down-to-earth and real. Andy still missed her stories, her ruby lipstick kisses—and her love of televised all-star wrestling.

Grannie had always been a breath of sanity. It was Grannie who had single-handedly put the pieces of the Garrett family back together every time it had fallen apart. As quickly as Mac and Rachel could rip the household to shreds and demoralize their children with their nonstop fighting, Grannie could sweep in and reestablish bedrock.

And when Andy and Molly had grown up, Grannie had continued to encourage them. Only Grannie, out of his whole family, had appreciated Andy's decision to enter the ministry. "Praise the Lord!" she had cried when he had told her his plans, "The boy has got the call!" Once, over the phone, Andy had heard her repeat the news to her senior-high-rise friends. Grannie had been proud of him.

But Grannie had died, and now only her memories lived on.

Other changes to the family landscape had followed Grannie's death.

Andy's mother had died unexpectedly of cancer. Rachel had ignored the pain in her abdomen and had told no one until it was too late. And Mac, who had always been larger than life and harder than steel— and who had bickered away nearly forty years in a loveless marriage— had shriveled up. It had made no sense to Andy. His dad hadn't said two kind words to his wife when she was living. So why had the man whose voice had thundered gross unkindnesses throughout Andy's childhood—often to the sound of knick-knacks crashing against the walls—crawled into his recliner and shut himself off?

Surprisingly, Andy's mother had anticipated her husband's reaction. Before she had died, Rachel had made her children promise to pray for him and help him. "He's not as strong as he puts on," she'd said. "He doesn't know it, but he needs God. And although I finally opened the door and let Jesus into my life, it will be much harder for your father."

It had been true. Mac, who had always shaken his fist at the world and God, had given up when Rachel had died, and he would not leave his house. Andy believed his dad would still be there if Molly had not drawn him out and invited him to the farm for Thanksgiving.

Mac had sternly qualified his visit to the farm by insisting that it was "just for the holiday." He had been adamant that he would not stay a day longer. But he had stayed. And the food and activity of the farm had somewhat revived him.

Even so, Mac had remained hard, and his mind had stayed messed up. His dark dreams and nightmare screams had awakened Molly and Paul, more than once. And Mac's torments would surely have followed him to an early grave except for a chance discovery that had unexpectedly explained everything.

The discovery had come shortly after Thanksgiving and before the fire. That's when Molly had finally opened the three large boxes Mac had brought from home. Each box had contained armloads of Rachel's clothes, shoes, purses, and more—things that Mac had yanked from the closet and swept from their bedroom.

When Mac had carried the boxes into the farmhouse, he had told Molly, "You take these. I don't want to see this stuff, again."

Under the packed memories, Molly had found her mother's jewelry case. When she'd lifted it, to set it on her dresser, she had spotted a hidden newspaper clipping. The yellowed headline had declared: *MacAndrew Garrett Acquitted in Death of Infant Son.* Molly had read and re-read the lines before she had assembled the family and asked her father about it.

"No!" Mac had shouted when she held up the paper. And then he had shocked the family by insisting that he HAD killed the baby!

The story he related was tragic. The death had happened one night, shortly after their first baby, Little Mac, had been born. Rachel had been ill, and although Mac had been working long hours, he had shouldered the responsibility of Little Mac's nightly feedings. In response to the infant's Midnight cries, Mac had risen from an exhausted sleep. He had rolled up a towel and set it so the baby could take his bottle without being held. And although he had not meant to, Mac had dozed off. In the short time he had slept, the baby had choked and died.

"So, you see," Mac sobbed, "I did kill the baby! I did kill him!"

Mac's attempts to revive Little Mac had left bruises on the tiny body, and Mac had been charged with manslaughter. But in a surprise verdict, the jury had acquitted him.

"I wish they'd hanged me!" Mac had spat bitterly as he'd finished the story at the Doakses' kitchen table. It was clear that he had never acquitted himself.

Rachel had borne blame, too. She had known how worn-out her husband had been that evening, but she had selfishly rolled over and ignored his request for help. And so, after the baby's death, Mac had blamed her, and she had blamed him. And over the years, they had bludgeoned each other with their shared guilt.

"I know it doesn't make sense," Mac had told his listening family, "but it was our fights that kept us going. Without the fights, we would have buried ourselves, long ago, in our pain."

"And," he had added, "we didn't want to mar your lives with this, so we agreed to keep the story secret. I'm just sorry you had to learn about it, now."

Andy had gritted his teeth at Mac's last statement. By keeping the secret, his parents had pursued a damaging course for their children. Without knowledge of the tragedy, Andy and Molly had endured years of seemingly senseless parental fighting and hatred.

And only after Andy had heard the story had he begun to make sense of the cold reserve that had always existed between him and his father. Before the revelation, Andy had always assumed the fault had been his—that his lack of mechanical ability, or some other shortcoming, had been such a disappointment to his dad that it had warped the father-son relationship. But after the unveiling of the secret, Andy had seen a different truth. It was his father who had been flawed.

Andy knew, now, that his dad had been emotionally crippled by an event that had blinded him, long ago. And because of that dreadful event, Mac had never been able to see Andy. Mac had seen only his dead son; his living son had been invisible to him—blocked by the ghost of a lifeless, blue body.

CHAPTER FOUR

THE PAST GIVES WAY

The unveiled secret also explained why, even after Mac and Rachel had clawed their way to financial success, they had not changed. Mac had gained wealth and respect in the gas furnace business, but the Garrett domestic battles had continued to rage. As a result, as soon as they were able, the Garrett children had fled beyond their parents' reach: Molly by marriage, and Andy by bartending in Chicago.

Thankfully for Andy, however, Chicago had not been outside of God's reach. God had revealed Himself to the runaway and had impressed on him the need to change his life's direction. As only God can do, His Spirit had led Andy from the dim interior of an Old-Town Chicago bar to the brightly lit halls of a nearby Christian college, and then to seminary. Andy's beautiful Abbey had been part of God's plan, and, together, he and Abbey had come to serve their first church, in Cherish.

Not long after their move, God had set out to work in the lives of the rest of the Garrett family.

Andy had rejoiced when Molly had begun to attend Paul's childhood church in Harmony and had come to know the Lord. Next, Andy's mother had accepted Christ's grace, shortly before the cancer had taken her away. Only Mac had been left.

And then the fire had happened.

The fire had stoked Mac's anger even hotter against the God he had always said he didn't believe in. How could a loving God take away a man's infant son—and then his wife? How could a loving God allow a fire to destroy Molly's home—and threaten her baby? How could a loving God leave them all with broken bones—and cripple the Doakses' livelihood? If there was a God, why was life so empty, and mean, and meaningless?

Mac had raved, on and on, about God's failures. And his family—stuck in the little parsonage and unable to escape his tirades—had suffered in silence. But one day, Andy had had enough. When Andy had spiritedly challenged him, Mac had drawn back, in stunned silence. Andy had bored in and had passionately listed the many times God had blessed his father, even though Mac had refused to acknowledge the gifts.

"You're right," Andy had said, too loudly, in interrupting Mac's never-ending verbal assault, "We can't erase the fire, and we're still working on healing from the broken bones. And we can't bring Mom back."

Andy had paused before adding, "And you can't bring back Little Mac."

Mac had snorted at the admission of God's failures, but Andy had persisted: "But, Dad, you also can't say that God doesn't care. God has always been right there, in the middle of the troubles, with you."

Mac's eyes had narrowed to slits and his jaw had set, but Andy hadn't stopped. "God has always been there, for all of us. And He has identified with us. While on Earth, God, in the person of His Son, Jesus, was born poor—just like you and Mom—and He was wrongly accused, and beaten, and put to death for crimes He'd never committed. But Jesus broke through, Dad! He came back to life and broke a hole in Heaven, just for us."

Mac had looked away and clenched his fists, but Andy had not been intimidated. Instead, he had finally appealed with an example he knew his father could not ignore. Andy had said, "In the same way that your love reached out and saved Emily when she dropped from the second-floor of the burning farmhouse, God holds out His arms to save you from a bitter, pointless existence. He's waiting to catch you, Dad; and in the same way that you didn't fail to catch little Emily, He won't fail to catch you. You just have to let go; you've got to make the jump, Dad. You have to let go of the past and trust that God's able to give you a new future."

Andy had doubted that his words had penetrated the angry, stony figure before him. He'd said more than he'd expected to. But he had been glad he had tried.

And then, the next morning—Sunday morning—Mac had unexpectedly shown up at Andy's church. He had sat quietly through the service, and he had bowed his head during the prayer. Andy had never seen his father pray, and he had wondered if Mac had lowered his head out of simple courtesy. But then, Mac had stepped out from his pew, and during the altar call, he had walked down the aisle to profess his faith in Jesus.

That Sunday morning had been two weeks ago. In that span, Christmas had come and gone, and the New Year had begun. And Mac was still coming to grips with the idea of forgiven sin and undeserved blessing.

Mac had always assumed and expected condemnation from God. He had always been ready for judgment—but never for forgiveness. Forgiveness had surprised him. Andy (yes, Andy, the son he had always called his *idiot boy*) had said that God loved him and had sent His Son to die for his sins so he could have EVERYTHING. Andy had said that nothing was truly lost, that everything was held in God's Hands for blessing, now and in the life after, if we would only receive it.

Mac had not realized how much he had needed that hope. His whole life had been a scramble to achieve on his own terms. But like sand, the things he had treasured most had slipped through his fingers. There had been nothing left to hold onto, nothing he could count on, until now. Now, Mac had realized that God was that something—that SOMEONE—who would not disappoint. And because of Jesus, God would not hold his sins against him.

Mac had nearly run down the aisle of the church, that day, because he had been afraid he would miss it. It was his moment, his last chance. He had cried as he had run: "O, God! Don't let me be too late! I need You! I need Your saving!" And then Mac's heart had nearly drowned in the Love!

Awash in a warmth and tenderness he had never known, Mac had stood at the front of the First Baptist Church and wondered, *is this what Andy has been experiencing all these years?*

CHAPTER FIVE

SIEGE

Filtered sunlight from the stained-glass window in the pastor's study fell over Andy's shoulder as he prayed, *Thank you, again, Heavenly Father! Thank you for drawing my dad to Your salvation and for working to heal the brokenness in our family.*

An unexpected rap on the door interrupted his prayer.

Because Andy had been thinking about his father, he thought the visitor might be his dad. But it was not. Instead, Opal introduced a stranger.

"Dr. C. G. Logan," she said. "He's asked if he could meet you."

Opal ushered in a slight young man in his mid-thirties with a smooth, ruddy face, bright blue eyes, and just-past-blond brown hair. Dr. Logan extended a strong hand, and from the expression on his face, Andy could tell he was surprised to find that the pastor was close to his own age.

"Good to meet you, Dr. Logan," Andy greeted him, and he motioned for the visitor to sit.

"*Dr. Logan* sounds a bit stiff," the man said with a smile. "I'd feel better if you would just call me *Siege.* That's what my friends call me. It's a kind of shorthand for *C. G.* Or you could call me *Logan.* I get that a lot, too."

"Okay. *Siege*, it is. How may I help you?"

"I don't mean to intrude," Siege apologized, "but I was on my way to an appointment, and I had a couple of minutes. Since I was passing by I thought I'd introduce myself. I'm new to Cherish, and I'm a Baptist."

"Praise the Lord!" Andy grinned, and Siege countered with an "Amen!"

Siege continued, "I imagine you knew Doc Gilman?"

"The veterinarian?"

"Yup. I'm his replacement. I've taken over his practice, now that Gilman's retired."

Aha, thought Andy. *The doctor is a vet.*

Andy immediately pictured his bulldog, Winston, trembling on the shiny, cold examination table in the little veterinary practice on the edge of town. Andy recalled how Doc Gilman had gently probed and spoken calmly in the dog's ear before slipping him a rabies shot.

"Great!" said Andy. "You'll probably meet Winston one of these days. Bulldog. Scared of vets."

Siege laughed. "They all are. Comes with the territory. I do better with large animals."

Andy knew little about veterinarians or farm stock, but he did know that Doc Gilman's practice had included both large and small animals. And Gilman had had farm clients all across the county, some as far away as Harmony. Andy wondered, now, if Gilman had been to Paul's farm.

Andy also recalled that Doc Gilman had been a Presbyterian. It was nice to have a Baptist replacing him.

"Married?" Andy asked before he noticed that Siege's ring finger was bare.

"Not that lucky, yet. Keeping my eyes open, though."

Andy murmured a "good for you." He couldn't imagine Siege escaping the attention of the single women of Cherish for long.

As they chatted—Siege declined a cup of coffee; he couldn't stay that long—they found themselves laughing over several interests they held in common: "You like bluegrass, too? What do you think of the DeLorean DMC-12? Did you watch Mister Roger's Neighborhood as a kid?" Andy realized he'd met a kindred spirit.

"It'll be good to have you in church on Sunday," Andy said. "And tomorrow night we have midweek Bible Study and choir practice."

Siege shook his head. "Sorry to disappoint you, but I probably won't be a regular for the midweek stuff. Too many late-night calls." But then he threw up a hand as if he were swearing in, in court. "But I should be in church on Sundays—unless an emergency arises."

As he brought his hand down, Siege checked his watch. He scooted his chair back and stood. "I hate to leave so soon," he said. "This has been great. But I have to get to my appointment."

"No problem," Andy assured him. "But we should get together again when we have more time."

"Definitely," Siege agreed. "Let's do that. And I'm looking forward to hearing a good sermon on Sunday."

"They're all good!" Andy bragged good-naturedly. And Siege shot back, "I'm sure they are; at least the subject is always top-drawer."

"The best!" Andy replied, and he stood to walk Siege to the outer office door.

"So, I've come here to see you at work," Siege quipped. "Now it's only fitting for you to bring Winston in to see me."

"Uh-huh," said Andy. "And why would I want to ruin a perfectly good master-pet relationship?"

Siege laughed. "I'll be gentle," he promised. "Bring him in sometime when he doesn't need a shot. I'll just give him a treat. We can get off to a good start."

Then Siege tipped his hat to Opal, and he set off down the hall.

"Looks like you two got along well," Opal observed. "Nice guy."

"Yeah," said Andy. "He's the new vet. And he's a Baptist!"

Opal raised her brows in approval, and when she did, it struck Andy, for the first time, that although her hair had recently become blond, Opal's eyebrows had remained brunette. He had never noticed it, before, even though it had been several months since Opal's flyaway, spiky hair had changed color.

Now that he'd noticed the discrepancy, Andy had a hard time ignoring it. He decided, however, that although the disparity was curious, it wasn't unattractive.

It didn't really matter, though. Opal's value wasn't in her looks. What Andy appreciated most about her was her knowledge of the church and her mastery of the office equipment. The mimeograph taunted him whenever Opal took a vacation to visit her daughter, Brenda, and first granddaughter, Zephyr. Maybe one day he'd get the hang of it.

Today, Opal finished scrolling something out of her typewriter, and she slid it across the desk for Andy's attention.

"Is this for the newsletter?" he asked, with a quick look at the title on the page.

Opal smiled her reply.

Andy already knew it was one of her pithy poems. Opal's rhyming humor regularly found its way into the monthly church newsletter, and Andy enjoyed the privilege of first review.

He gripped the sheet with both hands and dutifully read the lines. Opal watched for his reaction.

THINGS ARE JUMPIN'
By Opal Reese

I opened up my eyes and saw
A frog hop on my floor.
I opened up my cupboard
And a frog jumped in the door.
I opened up the ice box—
A frog was in the meat.
I sat down at my table,
But a frog was in my seat.
I poured a drink of water and
A frog was in my glass.
(I tried to fish him out of there,
But he just kicked and splashed!)

I am so tired of frogs today—
This is no more a joke.
If Moses doesn't shoo them soon,
I think I'm gonna croak!

At Andy's groan, Opal smiled and said, "I thought you'd like it."

Then she twisted a spike of blond hair and turned back to her work with a satisfied grin.

CHAPTER SIX

BULLS-EYES

Overnight, it had snowed about a foot and a half—big heavy flakes that accumulated quickly and canceled school and work the next day.

Four empty breakfast plates had been pushed to the center of the kitchen table where the Garretts and Doakses leisurely sipped their morning coffee.

"Some people say snow is silent," Andy remarked philosophically, as he watched the cream swirl in his cup. "But to me, it sounds like kids playing. Every Cherish child is going to be outside, today, making snowmen and snow forts. At least that's what I would be doing, if I were still young."

"You ARE still young," Abbey retorted, pulling her robe tighter against the little chill that signaled the furnace had kicked in again.

Molly laughed. "That's the truth. Andy's never truly grown up. I'm surprised he's not out there, already, making a snowman."

"I haven't even brushed my teeth, yet!" Andy protested.

"Or got out of your pajamas," his sister countered.

Andy had to admit that he was enjoying playing hooky. He was sure that teachers, like Stu Darrell and Danny Hart, were just as excited as their students to have the day off, too.

That thought had barely formed in Andy's mind when the telephone rang. Abbey answered and identified the caller as Erica Hart.

"Sure, Erica," Abbey said. "Are you sure you want company on such a nice day off? Hang on, and I'll ask."

Abbey polled the bath-robed trio: "Erica has invited all of us to come to their house. Danny has new snow tires on the station wagon, and Erica says he'll be happy to swing by and pick us up. The neighborhood kids are making snowmen in the yard, and we can watch their progress from inside, over hot chocolate and peanut butter bars. What do you say?"

Paul and Molly had not hazarded many trips outside the house since coming to the parsonage, except for physical therapy trips to Harmony in the back of Mac's Lincoln. They looked at each other, now, and Paul said, "Sure! I think it's time we started trying to get out more. And why not try it on the worst day of the year for a couple of crutch-dependent invalids?"

"We're hardly invalids," corrected Molly. "But I agree. Let's do it! We're tough country folk. Besides, it's only a half-block away."

Abbey told Erica to give them time to dress. "We'll call when we're ready for our ride," she said.

The minute Abbey hung up the phone, the lethargic morning took on new energy. The pajama-clad quartet wove in and out of the parsonage's bedrooms and one bathroom. And once they were ready, Andy gave Danny a call.

"Come and get us!" he cried.

With only one tense moment, Danny's new tires cut neat, deep tracks in the snow. The tracks led straight into the garage where there was a single step to climb to get into the house. And, aside from their groans at the effort to get out of the car, Molly and Paul managed well.

Erica threw open her arms. "Welcome to winter wonderland!" she cried.

The smell of hot chocolate drew the newcomers to the dining room table, and through the picture window they could see the backyard. There, Jack and Tory Darrell, Ben and Luke Hart, and Lizzie and Stevie Potts had already stacked two large snowballs and were rolling a third for the snowman's head. The Darrell's terrier, Roxy, yapped at the children's boots. Andy tapped on the window to say hi.

It was cozy to watch the wintery play from the warm indoors and to enjoy the company of close friends.

After only an hour of relaxed adult conversation, however, the indoor peace gave way to a noisy invasion. Cold little fingers and nearly frozen toes came inside to thaw, and full little bladders demanded to be emptied. A soggy mound of coats and mittens collected inside the back door, and the garments' hosts noisily overran the dining room.

"Did you see my snow doggy?"

"I put the hat on the snowman all by myself."

"Can I have a carrot for the snow baby's nose?"

"Tory knocked my snow boy's head off!"

"Why can't I take my drink outside?"

"I have to go to the bathroom, again, please."

Peanut butter bars and glasses of milk disappeared between trips to the bathroom, and every minute was punctuated by giggles and shouts and little running feet. But then, the pile of limp coats and mittens resumed its lively arms and legs, and an army of rubber boots beat a retreat to heed the siren call of the snow.

A full minute of silence followed the last slam of the storm door.

Andy broke the quiet with, "How do you teachers do it? My head's still spinning from all the commotion."

"Oh, the classroom is seldom like this," Stu replied. "This kind of pandemonium is reserved for recess. There are rules in the classroom for when to speak and when to listen. You have to raise your hand."

Then Danny interjected, "But, of course, there's always that ONE student who tests the rules."

Molly immediately laughed and pointed at Andy.

Stu fell back in mock surprise. "You?" he asked. "I never would have guessed!"

Andy's classroom antics were well-known, even in Cherish. As part of his testimony about God's work in his life, Andy had shared some of his most outlandish classroom pranks, from kindergarten through high school, and the congregation had laughed. But then, Andy had had a hard time outliving the tales. The stories preceded him, wherever he went. After all, in a small town, it was one's stories that defined as well as entertained.

Even now, Andy found himself mumbling, "I'm so sorry!" as if Stu and Danny had been his teachers.

"That's okay," Stu reassured him. "You're the success story that gives us hope."

Andy hung his head. Stu's comment reminded him of the look of astonishment he'd caught on the face of his former sixth-grade teacher when the man had seen Andy in a guest-pulpit, one Sunday morning, up north.

At the close of the church service, Andy had cringed when Mr. Franklin had introduced him to his wife with, "THIS is the student I've told you all of those stories about." Mrs. Franklin's mouth had gaped, and she had gasped, "And he's a minister?"

"Looks like it," said Mr. Franklin. "Hard to believe, isn't it?"

Mrs. Franklin had shaken her head and replied, "I guess miracles do happen!"

Andy felt better when the morning's conversation turned to hunting and the ladies retreated to Erica's sewing room to ooh and aah over the progress on her latest quilt.

"I still do a little duck hunting," Danny said. "I usually get one or two ganders from a blind down at Tarr's Marsh. I'm no Hal Morgan, of course. But then, with birdshot it's not too hard to hit what you're after."

At the mention of Hal Morgan's name, Andy sat back and sighed. He resigned himself to being in the spotlight, once again.

Sure enough, Stu's eyes widened. "Nobody's as good as Hal Morgan," Stu declared.

And Danny disagreed. "You're forgetting about Pastor."

Andy smiled self-consciously, now. He wondered, *What will Paul think?*

Out of the corner of his eye, Andy could see Paul waiting for the punchline. Paul was the only person in the room who didn't know the story. Andy sheepishly shrugged his shoulders, as if to say, "What can I tell you?" Stu was going to tell the tale, anyway.

It didn't matter that the incident had occurred nearly two years ago. The story was now part of Andy's Cherish persona.

Andy had been pastor in Cherish for less than a month, when Hal and Sharon Morgan had invited him and Abbey for a visit. Andy had felt apprehensive about the house call because he had been warned that Hal loved to give new ministers a hard time. Andy could recall every detail of that day. Stu's version—the legend—paled beside Andy's vivid memory. So, Andy stopped listening and started remembering it, exactly as it had happened:

He felt out of place and insignificant on the sofa, beneath the gigantic bull moose head that towered over his shoulder. The moose—like dozens of other lifeless animals that hung stiffly on the Morgan walls—was proof that Hal seldom attended church. Instead, the man spent his weekends hunting and fishing.

Seated next to Abbey, Andy balanced a plate of Sharon's sour-cream coffee cake on his knee and listened as Hal dominated the conversation with blow-by-blow descriptions of tracking, shooting, and dragging in game from the wildest parts of every state in the country. Andy hoped he was showing proper enthusiasm for the array of marksmanship ribbons that Hal flashed, and the collection of trophies that filled his display cases.

Then all of a sudden, Hal suggested, "Why don't you and I let the women stay here while we go out to the shooting range behind the barn?" He nudged Andy. "We can pull off a few pistol rounds."

Andy panicked. Was this the start of Hal's humiliation of him as the new minister? Andy had never held a real pistol or rifle, and he didn't like the idea of handling guns in front of a marksman like Hal. But Hal refused to take no for an answer. Clearly, he wanted to show off.

At the door, Andy insisted, "I don't have a license to shoot a gun."

"You're okay for target practice in my yard, this once," Hal bullied. "No worry. Let's see what you can do!"

Outside, Hal popped cartridges into a couple of pistols and handed one to Andy. After giving Andy a slap on the back, Hal stepped away. Andy nervously eyed the bulls-eye posted yards ahead, in front of a pocked maple. The pistol was definitely heavier than the Roy Rogers cap gun he had played with as a kid. Finally, Andy steadied the gun, took aim, and squeezed the trigger.

"Whoa!" Andy yelled at the unexpected force of the recoil. Hal slapped his sides in laughter and then trotted over to check the target.

Hal was slow in returning, however, and was shaking his head in surprise.

"Beginner's luck, man," he said. "You nailed it!"

"You mean I hit the bulls-eye?" Andy asked in astonishment.

"'Fraid so!" said Hal, who now took aim and squeezed off a shot on the same target.

Eager to see his own success, Andy followed Hal to the tree, but just as he got there, his terse host ripped the paper bulls-eye from its pins and said, "Let's try for a longer distance, okay?"

Hal posted a new paper a few yards past the first.

"I'll start this time," Hal said, and he carefully aimed and re-aimed before pulling the trigger. Andy took the next shot, with little finesse—just aimed, steadied, and squeezed.

When they checked the target, they found two nearly dead-center shots.

Hal managed a, "Well, I'll be! You sure you don't go to the practice range?"

Though he was thoroughly flabbergasted, himself, Andy played it cool. "I haven't shot anything except a cap gun as a kid and a BB gun when I was nine. Guns don't hold much fascination for me."

Hal wasn't listening, however. He had stepped inside the shed and brought out a plastic soft-drink bottle that he'd filled with water. A length of clothesline hung from a nearby tree, and Hal slipped its loop around the top of the bottle and tightened it. Giving the bottle a shove, he set it swinging in a wide arc. Hal hurried back to where Andy was standing.

"Let's see how you do on a moving target," Hal said. He motioned for Andy to take a shot.

Andy shrugged, and without any real heart in it, he squeezed the trigger. Instantly, water spurted in a stream from the plugs on both sides of the bottle and sprinkled an eight-foot path along the ground. Andy turned to smile in surprise at Hal, but Hal was already on his way back into the shed. Andy wondered what was coming next.

This time it was a compound bow.

"Ever shoot one of these?" Hal asked, abruptly, while taking a quick shot at a target he had tied to several bales of hay. Hal missed the center by an inch.

"Nope. Never have," Andy answered, hoping there weren't larger and more complex weapons yet to come.

Hal curtly handed him the bow and then chuckled at Andy's awkwardness until he finally got his stance and bow position set.

"Okay, let her rip!" cried Hal. Andy eyed the target, pulled back, and released.

Hal's eyes bulged, and the muscles in his neck twitched when Andy's shot hit dead center of the bulls-eye. Hal brusquely marched over to retrieve the arrow and started back to the house. Through clenched teeth, he managed to say, "I think Sharon has more coffee brewing."

Although pumped by his success, Andy felt bad about the distance it had created between him and Hal. When he saw a foam-target practice deer next to the fence, Andy thought he'd try a little humor to soften up his host.

"There's the big buck, now!" Andy whispered loudly, like the announcer of a field sports program. "And the great hunter decided to try his trick shot!"

Andy clumsily pulled the bow down between his legs and, without looking, let an arrow fly. But the ploy backfired. The arrow hit its target right between the eyes!

Hal groaned and disappeared into the house, leaving Andy to retrieve the arrow.

Andy set the bow outside the back door and humbly prayed, "Lord, I'm so sorry for embarrassing Hal. I had no idea! But then, You know that. I pray he'll not be too upset and that we haven't gotten off to a bad start."

Hal talked little for the rest of their visit. But he did grudgingly shake Andy's hand when they said goodbye. Andy wondered if Hal would ever talk to him again, or if he'd ever come back to church. Andy would definitely be praying about that.

Although Andy intended to keep the day's activity a secret, he did enjoy recounting his success to Abbey on the way home. She made him feel like a hero. "Wow! I'm impressed, honey!" she said. "I can't believe you beat Hal!"

She pecked him on the cheek. It felt good.

He and Abbey vowed not to speak of the shooting match to anyone. First of all, no one would believe it. (Andy barely believed it, himself.) Plus, they didn't want to embarrass Hal.

But on Sunday, Danny Hart greeted Andy with, "I hear you've been hiding one of your talents from us."

"And what might that be?" Andy asked, in case Danny wasn't talking about their visit to the Morgan's.

"Well," said Danny, "the way I hear it, Hal's telling all the men of the church that you're a dead shot and 'not to mess with the preacher if you know what's good for you!"

Andy was incredulous that Hal had mentioned it, and Danny wanted to hear the whole story. Andy gave him the short version, and Danny said, "Well, whatever you did, Pastor, you certainly made an impression on Hal. He has embarrassed every preacher we've ever had with how they 'don't know their head from their butt when it comes to shootin!' And if you've impressed him, you've really arrived!"

Andy shook his head at the memory. And he listened, now, as Stu finished narrating and embellishing the popular version of the tale. As usual, Andy always came out the star.

The guys in the Hart dining room all looked at him, and Andy hung his head and smiled humbly.

But as always, Andy felt guilty. He felt badly that he had never interrupted to correct the story and make sure the listeners knew that the real hero was God. Andy couldn't shoot his way out of a paper bag! But as usual, he let it ride. After all, it didn't really matter much, did it? And he did enjoy his little moment of celebrity. It was one time the guys didn't tease him about being a city boy.

When Stu finished the story, Andy felt a nudge. It was Paul. "I never knew that about you!" he said.

Andy blushed and basked in the new regard he beheld in his brother-in-law's eyes—until Paul suggested, "When I get my leg back in shape, maybe you and I could do some pheasant hunting at the farm, and you could give me some shooting pointers."

Uh-oh. Andy laughed nervously. *This was it.* He had wondered when this day might come.

Andy had not touched a gun since he had held the pistol at Hal's. Nor had he sought any occasion to retest his marksmanship. He had known better. Whatever prowess he had enjoyed at Hal's had been a one-time gift from the Almighty to humble Hal into respecting God's servants and to prompt the hunter to come to church more often. It had not been a gift for Andy to pursue further. The object had been to lionize God, not Andy. And Andy knew he needed to correct the legend, now, to give God the credit He deserved.

It was humbling, but Andy knew he had to do it.

He mumbled to Paul, "You know I'm no hunter! I've been called to be a fisher of men, not a hunter of animals."

Even as he said it, however, Andy knew it sounded pious. And he knew that this halfhearted, seemingly humble, denial was not enough to give God His due. Andy was ashamed that he did not want to let "Sure-Shot Andy" bite the dust. He had enjoyed his notoriety.

But he knew God wouldn't let it go. God would get His rightful recognition the minute Andy pulled another trigger.

And so, Andy finally cleared his throat and began to correct the ballad of "Andy Garrett, the Pistol-Packin' Pastor!" It felt good to tell the truth.

CHAPTER SEVEN

CANNED PEACHES, CLOSED BIBLE, AND ANNABELLE

While those in Cherish were enjoying their hot chocolate get-together, Phillip and Mac were more or less snowbound in the country. It would have taken a lot of effort to clear the heavily drifted farm lane for a getaway. And as long as they could get to their chores, there was no need to bother.

Mac, who had never worn snow-shoes, found them useful on the trek back and forth to the barn, the chicken coop, and the field fence where he and Paul tossed feed for the bull. The work was more tiring than usual because of the snow, but the day passed well.

Mac's biggest worry was meals. What would they eat? If they couldn't get out, how would they get to the nearby Bennett farm for the meals Sheryl Bennett prepared for them each day? Paul had arranged for Sheryl to cook for them while they worked the farm in his absence.

Mac's stomach growled with worry as he did the early chores. *Will we get to eat, today?*

Mac finally asked Phillip about it, and Phillip told him not to worry. Phillip sounded calm, but Mac could not reign in his imagination and a picture of the two of them reduced to skin and bones and discovered around an empty table.

After the early chores, Mac followed Phillip back to the mobile home. There, to Mac's relief, Phillip whipped out the pancake turner, heated the griddle, and prepared eggs, bacon, pancakes, and fried potatoes—everything Mac had been dreaming of. Mac ate his fill and stopped worrying.

"You're a good cook!" he said.

But then, at lunchtime, Mac found eggs, bacon, pancakes, and fried potatoes on his plate, again. It seemed that Phillip could cook only these four items, and nothing more. After eggs, bacon, pancakes, and fried potatoes for dinner, too, Mac began to hate eggs, bacon, pancakes, and fried potatoes. He frowned but said nothing.

And then he learned that Phillip felt the same way, because after supper Phillip donned his snow shoes and disappeared for a few minutes. When he returned, he held up jars of home-canned peaches and strawberry jam. Mac danced a happy jig, lifted his hands toward Heaven, and cried, "Thank you, Lord!"

Phillip said, "I just hope the Lord protects us from Molly; she'll kill us if she finds out we've raided her precious canning cellar. But I figure this is an emergency."

"Definitely an emergency!" echoed Mac. "Besides, she might not even notice."

"Not likely," announced Phillip. "But we'll hang together."

Then, setting aside all thoughts of their future demise, the two men emptied the jars before going to bed.

The next day, Mac praised God for a clear sky. The sun would make short work of the snow, and he and Phillip would soon get back to their usual routine—including meals at Sheryl Bennett's. In the meantime, Mac was grateful for canned peaches and jars of jam, which broke up the monotony of eggs, bacon, pancakes, and fried potatoes. A thaw would make the day's chores less difficult, too, and reduce some of his aches and pains.

Unfortunately, the sun would not change the closed Bible on his dresser. Mac kept the Bible there because it showed that he had become a Christian. But he avoided looking at it because it had also become a symbol of failure. He had not touched it for many days.

It hadn't been that way, at first. After opening his heart to Christ, Mac had eagerly begun to read a few chapters in the Bible, each evening. And then his excitement had waned. His excuse had been the fatigue from the work, and then the snow. But in reality, it had been due to his stubbornness. Andy had known that his father wasn't much of a reader, so he had suggested that his dad begin reading in the book of John. But Mac had not paid attention. He had stubbornly started reading at the beginning of the Bible, instead. After all, he had thought, that's what you did with books. You started at the beginning and read through to the end. That way, you didn't miss anything.

But Genesis, chapter five, had made him rethink his strategy. Was the whole book going to be one long genealogy? This wasn't what he had expected the Bible to be. The first few chapters had been interesting, but the genealogies had stopped him, cold. After Genesis five, Mac had decided to skip ahead, so he had fanned his way through several pages in hopes of finding something more readable. But the book of Chronicles had been more of the same. And then the book of Jeremiah had thoroughly confused him.

Too proud to ask Andy for help, Mac had never made it to the New Testament. His nightly reading had simply ended.

On Saturday morning, Phillip carefully milked Annabelle so he wouldn't make her problem worse. He had to empty her so he could alleviate the heaviness of the milk in her bag. The weight pulled on her wound.

Somehow, overnight, Annabelle had snagged her udder on something, and there was a tear. It was large enough that Phillip knew it should be stitched. But when he called Dr. Gilman's office, the new voice on the other end of the line startled him. It took a minute for him to process that the old vet was no longer practicing. Phillip finally told Dr. Logan to come.

"Do you need directions?" Phillip asked Siege.

"I don't think so," came the reply. "The Doc left pretty clear directions printed on all of his farm records."

To reassure the farmer, Siege read back the notes his predecessor had provided for driving to the Doakses' farm, and Phillip was satisfied.

Phillip sighed as he hung up. *Everybody's getting old,* he thought. *Old and retiring. Now it's Doc Gilman.*

In less than an hour, Siege made the turn down the lane identified by the Doaks' mailbox. He pulled his truck into the farmyard, and his eyes took in the burnt rubble that had once been a farmhouse. Next to it, a new double-wide mobile home had been installed.

A man waved to Siege from the barn. Siege pulled in front of the open door and parked. After he climbed out and collected his bag, there was a handshake and a quick "Dr. Logan" and "Phillip Doaks" by way of introduction. Then it was straight to business.

Under the watchful eye of Phillip—and another man whose name Siege hadn't yet learned—Siege examined the Jersey's tear and rummaged in his bag for the silk and needle he needed. He deadened and disinfected the area and began to suture the wound. Annabelle barely noticed.

When he was done, Siege set out some Betadine to leave with Phillip, but he saw that the farmer already had some and knew how to use it. Siege put his supplies back into his bag.

"Good job," Phillip told him. "Sorry to lose Doc Gilman, but glad to know somebody competent has taken his place. Where are you from, son?"

Siege replied that his family was from Kentucky but that he'd studied at Auburn University in Alabama. "I finished school five years ago and worked in a southern Indiana practice for three years. Then I heard about this opening (Doc Gilman was a friend of a mutual acquaintance at the University). And here I am."

Siege sensed that Phillip liked him, even though, at first, the farmer's eyes had narrowed to find him so young.

"You grow up on a farm?" Phillip asked.

"You bet," Siege said. "Most large animal vets are farm kids. Not many city guys want to get their boots muddy, these days!"

Phillip laughed at that, and he jabbed Mac in the ribs. Tipping his head in Mac's direction, Phillip told Logan, "This here's a city guy! But he's all right. This is Mac Garrett, by the way."

Mac extended his hand. "Nice to meet you."

Siege shook hands and then cocked his head toward the burned-out house. "What's the story, there?" he asked. And Phillip told him about the fire.

"Burned just before Christmas," Phillip said. "My son and his family barely made it out. We've got Mac, here, to thank for their rescue. He was visiting for a few days from up near Chicago and ended up being a hero!"

Mac nodded humbly, and Phillip continued. "My son is still knitting from some busted bones. Mac and I are keeping things together until Paul can get back on the job. Sure hope it isn't much longer, though. We're both too old for this!"

"It's a big job," Siege acknowledged. "Just be glad it's not summer and you have the field work to do, too."

"You've got that right!" agreed Phillip. (*The kid knows his business,* Phillip thought.)

Siege rummaged for his keys and said he'd better get going. He added, "Let me know if you need anything else." Phillip nodded, and a moment later the vet's truck engine rumbled to life.

As Siege put the vehicle in gear, he leaned over and hollered, "I suppose that's the city guy's Lincoln, over there?" He pointed to Mac's car and grinned impishly. Parked between the barn and the mobile home, the luxury vehicle stood out like a ballerina at a hoedown.

Phillip laughed, and Mac shook his head at the two of them.

Still flashing his grin, Siege waved goodbye. He spun the wheel around and headed back the way he'd come.

CHAPTER EIGHT

SEIGE COMES FOR DINNER

The veterinarian caught the surprise on Mac's face on Sunday. Just inside the church entrance, Siege walked over to shake Mac's hand.

"How's that fancy car?" Siege quipped, and Mac snorted.

"Gets me from here to there," Mac said amiably. Then he added, "Didn't expect to see you here."

"Vets go to church, you know."

"Yeah, but I didn't know any of 'em were Baptists!"

Siege laughed. "You got me, there!"

Andy saw the two men talking, and he came to join them. That's when Mac learned that Andy and the vet already knew each other.

"Hey, Doc," Andy said, "My wife and I were wondering if you'd join us for lunch at the parsonage, after the service. My dad'll be there, too." Andy tipped his head toward Mac.

"I never pass up free food," Siege said—and he revised his mental card catalog to reflect that Andy had called Mac *dad*.

Winston had no idea that the object of his welcoming slobber for Sunday dinner was a veterinarian. Nothing in the visitor's

Sunday shoes and suit gave him away. Siege was enjoying the civilian freedom to rough the dog's ears and pat his broad back. Winston even winningly showed his tummy. Siege shrugged a "what can I say?" when Andy spied the two of them getting along so well.

"Don't tell him," Siege whispered loudly.

"It'll break his heart when we have to bring him in for shots," Andy whispered back.

During the rest of the introductions, Siege pieced together the Garrett and Doaks family ties.

Paul confirmed, "Yeah. That was my cow you stitched up. My dad said you did a good job—as good as Doc Gilman. He said you looked young, though. (Of course, he says that about everybody, anymore). But he was satisfied that you knew what you were doing. If you impressed my dad, you must have done okay!"

Siege nodded a "Thanks." Then he said, "I saw you had a fire, out there."

"Yeah," Paul said. "And we kinda got busted up gettin' away. But we should be back there, soon."

Siege interjected, "I hear you're letting this city fella run things until you get back." He lifted his chin in Mac's direction, with a twist of a grin and a wink.

"Hey, I'm putting in some quality time, out there!" Mac protested.

And Paul agreed. "He sure is! My dad says he's a great righthand man. Mac got a little more than he bargained for when he came for Thanksgiving dinner and stayed around. But we're mighty glad he's here. He's been a big help."

"So," said Siege, turning his attention to Andy, "I take it you're the only guy who's never lived or worked on a farm; is that right?"

Andy shrugged, and his dad laughed. "Yeah!" Mac said. "He's never lifted a finger on a farm. At least I know how to milk a cow—in a dire emergency!"

"I wouldn't say you're an expert at it, yet," Andy quipped back.

"But I've got more experience in a barn than you have," Mac challenged.

Siege interrupted. "I just asked because I wondered if Andy would ever want to come with me on a couple of farm calls."

Andy looked surprised, and with everyone listening, Siege could tell that Andy felt compelled to say "Sure!"

"Great!" said Siege. "I'll give you a call the next time I have a calving or a farrowing. I can always use the company—and an extra hand."

Siege observed the little smile that escaped and played across Paul's face; and the smile, along with the uncertainty in Andy's voice, made Siege wonder if farm calls might be too uncomfortable for Andy. Maybe Andy was too much of a city boy. Siege hoped not. He enjoyed Andy's company, and he looked forward to some laughs and some theological discussions while they were on the road.

I'll have to take it easy on Andy, Siege noted. *Time will tell.* And then he secretly slipped Winston a bite of biscuit under the table.

CHAPTER NINE

THIS LITTLE PIGGY

"This is a kid's book!" Mac protested when Abbey handed him her childhood Bible storybook.

Mac knew the gift was in response to his announcement, at dinner, that in Sunday school "they always talk about stuff I've never heard of." It was true. Just this morning, Mac had made a fool of himself when one of the class members had commented about the plagues in Egypt, and Mac had thought they were discussing a current event from the news.

Mac hated not knowing things, and he toyed with the idea of skipping Sunday school from now on. It didn't help to have Abbey now hand him a children's book. He didn't say it, but his manner showed that he was insulted.

"You're right. It is a children's book," Abbey hurried to explain. "But it is also the fastest way I know for you to gain a lot of the basic Bible knowledge. It's quick reading, and nearly every story is in here, in an order that's easy to follow. And each story has a Scripture reference, so you can go to the Bible and find it there, too."

Before Mac could object, Andy interrupted. "I never would have made it through seminary without that book. I was going to quit before Abbey gave it to me to read."

Mac didn't understand. "A children's book?" he asked. Why had Andy needed a children's book for graduate school?

"Yeah," Andy replied. "I got to seminary and found that I didn't know anything about the Old Testament—and not much about the New Testament, either. I didn't have years of Sunday school lessons to draw from, like the other students had; I was too new as a Christian. And when the class would discuss topics that drew on various Bible characters or basic themes, I couldn't participate. So I was ready to quit school."

Mac was surprised. "I never knew that!"

Andy nodded. "It's true. And the only thing that saved me was Abbey's Bible storybook. Without it, I could never have learned the basic stuff fast enough to keep up. That little book gave me the boost I needed. It may appear simple, but it's mighty!"

Still doubtful, Mac thumbed through the pages. There were a lot of pictures, and the stories were short. And he didn't see a single genealogy.

"It's not a substitute for your Bible," Andy said. "It's just a supplement to help you catch up. You won't need it forever."

Abbey added, "And you don't need to take it to church. Nobody needs to know you have it. You can read it on your own, at the farm."

That helped. But Mac still frowned. *A kid's book!*

But he took it with him when he left.

Andy had just finished his evening prayers, turned off the light, and pulled up the covers to go to sleep when the phone rang. He glanced at the clock: its hands pointed to eleven.

It was Siege. Andy groaned inwardly.

"I just got a call to help deliver a litter of pigs," the wide-awake voice said in his ear. "How about if I swing by and pick you up in ten minutes?"

"Uh-h-h-h," Andy breathed. He wasn't sure about this, and he had to shake off the idea of going back to sleep.

Finally, he said, "Sure. That'll be fine. I'll be waiting for you."

He hung up, and this time he groaned outwardly. *What am I getting myself into?* He knew that farmers and veterinarians always had their hands in places he wasn't comfortable with. But he was committed now.

Andy explained to Abbey what was happening, and she encouraged him. "How exciting!" she said.

But Andy had been more excited about going to bed. Why had he told Siege yes? And why did it have to be so late at night?

Abbey dug out a pair of old blue jeans, a sweatshirt, and some wool socks, and Andy added an old winter coat and some boots. At the sound of the truck in the drive, Abbey sent him off with a kiss and a "have fun!"

Andy sighed as he went out the door.

In the dark, Siege maneuvered down the unlit gravel roads as if he'd been there a thousand times. He kept up a lively discussion of his favorite bluegrass songs and singers, and within less than a half hour, the truck was bouncing over the frozen ruts of a farm lane. Andy could see lights, and Siege pulled up next to the barn.

"Ho!" someone hollered. "In here!"

Siege grabbed things from his truck and led Andy from the cold February wind into the relative warmth of the barn. A heat lamp warmed the farrowing pen, and Andy could hear the heavy breathing of a distressed sow.

"It's 'er first, and somethin's wrong," the farmer explained.

Siege asked a few questions and checked the pig's vital signs. Then he quickly washed his hands with soap in a bucket of water the farmer had provided. After lubricating his hand, Siege made a manual examination of the birth canal.

As he did so, Siege spoke in a low tone, explaining to Andy that difficult farrowing's were pretty rare "but they do sometimes happen. I suspect that we've got two or three tangled piglets trying to come down the canal at the same time. I'm going to try to fix things so they come one at a time."

After a moment, a triumphant "YUP!" let Andy and the farmer know that Siege was right. "Come on, little guy," Siege said as he slowly removed his hand.

A little snout appeared. Then a second snout quickly followed. And a third.

The sow seemed to relax, and her breathing became more normal. The farmer collected the piglets and rubbed and warmed them. Once they were dry, he set them next to the sow to nurse.

"I think things are going to be okay, now," Siege announced. "We'll know in a few minutes when the next one comes down."

While they waited, the veterinarian introduced Andy to the farmer.

"Oh," said the man, in surprise. "I thought you were in vet training or somethin'. Nice to meet you, Preacher."

Andy told the farmer where he pastored and that he was originally from near Chicago. The man slapped his overalls and hooted, "Ha! A city boy!" Andy wondered if every farmer had the same opinion of outsiders. Then Andy hurried to ask if he knew Junior Harris, the farmer who ushered at Andy's church.

"Why, sure," said the farmer. "Me and Junior go 'way back. Tell 'im Charlie West says 'hey.' Junior and me went to school together, and we fancied the same girl. Only, Junior married her! I married her sister."

Andy hadn't known that about Junior. He would definitely say 'hey' from Charlie on Sunday.

"Ho! Here she goes again!" called the farmer. And as they watched, a fourth piglet popped out onto the straw.

"Now that's how things is s'pposed to be!" said Charlie. He was satisfied that his sow was out of danger.

Siege agreed, but before they left, he and Andy decided to wait until a couple more piglets were born.

Andy was clearly tickled at how easily the rest of the piglets made their way into the world. "They just spurt right out!" he exclaimed with excitement. And he had fun helping to dry and warm them.

Charlie and Dr. Logan discussed other farm business while Andy hovered over what he called the "fresh babies."

Finally, the vet said, "I think we're done, here, Pastor. The sow's doing fine. We can pack up and head home."

Andy gave the nurslings a final stroking and reluctantly followed Siege to the truck.

Abbey heard Andy come in, and she shook off her sleep. She knew her excitable husband would be wound up and ready to tell her everything about the night's experience. She was right.

"Baby pigs are the cutest things!"

Without a hint of sleepiness, Andy described every birth and how he had helped to rub and dry the piglets.

"And Siege says I can go with him, again, sometime!"

"And look at what you're learning about farm life that will help you connect with farmers in the congregation," Abbey declared.

Still caught up in the night's experience, Andy said, "I just wish pigs didn't grow up to be so big and ugly."

Abbey smiled. She was glad they did grow up big and ugly. Otherwise, Andy would be bringing home a piggy every time he went with Siege. Abbey didn't want a pig in the house—or the yard.

After only a few hours of sleep, Andy repeated his saga of the piglet births for Molly and Paul.

Paul laughed and said, "I may have to get me some pigs, this spring, just so you can spend the night when my sows start to farrow. Between you, with the sows, and your dad, with the cows, I'll hardly have to lift a finger with the livestock!"

Junior Harris tried to stifle his laughter, aware that his guffaws were drawing glances and smiles from other patrons of the Star Diner. But he couldn't help it. He was caught up in Charlie West's colorful description of the vet's visit with his *assistant.*

"Never saw a city guy get so excited over pigs in my life!" Charlie chuckled. "I'm thinking of naming one of them after him and sending him pictures as it grows up."

"You do that," giggled Junior. "Just make sure he never finds that pig on his dinner table! City folk don't handle that well, you know."

After they left the diner, Junior continued to giggle. He couldn't wait for Sunday when he could tease his pastor about his veterinary expertise.

Junior knew that an obvious grin on his face throughout the sermon would stir Andy's curiosity and drive him to rush to the back of the sanctuary after the service. And he was right. The minute Andy pronounced the benediction, he turned and charged down the aisle to buttonhole the usher.

"Okay, what's going on, Junior?" Andy demanded. "More bats in the building?" (Andy mentioned bats because last year a tiny bat hanging above the pulpit had tickled Junior into giggling throughout the service like he had today.)

"Nope," said Junior. "No bats." He grinned. "This time it's pigs!"

Andy knew, then, that Junior had talked with Charlie West. "Is your farmer friend telling tales about me?" Andy asked.

Junior suppressed a giggle. "Yup," he said. "Charlie says you got a kick out of those pigs poppin' out like they do. It is somethin' to see, ain't it?"

Andy agreed. "Never seen anything like it. I had a lot of fun the other night. Doc Logan tells me he'll call me again when he gets an interesting call."

"We might make a country boy out of you, yet," Junior teased, and he slapped Andy on the back. He liked it that Andy was visiting the farms. *Andy's a good pastor,* Junior thought. *Even if he is a city boy!*

CHAPTER TEN

STUCK

Even though his father never mentioned it, Andy could tell that Sunday school had gone better for him. And on the way home from church, Abbey confirmed it. She told Andy that his father must have read far enough in the Bible storybook to know about the parting of the Red Sea, because she had observed him nodding and following the morning's lesson without difficulty.

Andy didn't bring it up to his dad. He knew better than to press his father about reading his Bible. Andy could say it from the pulpit but not over the dinner table.

Mac seemed to melt around Lizzie Potts, and Andy was amazed.

After Sunday dinner the little girl rang the parsonage doorbell, and the minute she saw Mac she cried "Misto Mac!" and ran into his arms.

Mac returned her hug and led Lizzie into the living room. There, Lizzie perched on the sofa with her little hands folded like a tiny adult set for some serious conversation. Mac followed suit and nodded his head like a gentleman and a good listener. Lizzie then launched into a description of the dime the tooth fairy had left under her brother's pillow. A whole dime! Lizzie stopped to test several of her teeth, and she frowned. How did one lose teeth, she seemed to wonder?

Andy heard Mac gently suggest, "I think you have to be a little older before your teeth can come loose and you can put them under your pillow."

Lizzie sighed in resignation. "I wish I'd grow up faster."

It did seem to be unfair that Stevie would always be bigger. But Lizzie accepted Misto Mac's pronouncement. He was her friend, and she trusted that he must know.

Now she told him she was going to sing him a song she had learned in Sunday school. Andy saw his father listen attentively and then applaud. Lizzie's eyes sparkled.

To keep his dad from becoming overwhelmed with little-girl attention, Andy invited Lizzie to the kitchen for a cookie. But his plan didn't work; Lizzie refused to come unless Mac would come, too.

To Andy's surprise, his father took Lizzie's hand and said, "Let's go to the kitchen together, shall we?"

In an aside to Andy, Mac whispered, "The ball game hasn't started yet, and I could use a cookie."

Andy marveled. *What has Lizzie Potts done to my father?* But in truth, he already knew the answer.

Prior to the fire, Mac had had little time for babies and small children; Mac had even refused to hold his granddaughter. But after the fire, everything had changed. That awful night, Molly had dropped Emily from the smoking upstairs window into Mac's arms. Paralyzed with fright that he might fail and be the cause of another baby's death, Mac had screamed out for God's help so he wouldn't drop her. And the God that Mac had always said he didn't believe in had sent Emily safely into his arms. The emotional trauma of the rescue had left Mac sobbing; he had nearly come apart at the seams. Paul had brought him back with a bellowed military command that had forced Mac's attention on the present. And Mac had recovered enough to get everyone to the hospital.

But at the hospital Mac had cried again, when from her hospital bed, Molly had lifted Emily for him to take to Cherish; Molly had pointedly said she trusted him with her baby. At the prospect of taking responsibility for the child, Mac's old fear had gripped him. He had frozen. Could he be trusted? Could he overcome the curse? After a long hesitation, he had finally grit his teeth and reached out. With Emily clutched to his heart, he had then broken into sobs. Molly's trust had disarmed him. She had made him recall that only hours earlier he had rescued the baby; he had been responsible for a tiny life that had not died. And Molly was continuing to trust him with that precious infant.

Trust. Trust in an old man who had once let a baby die! Molly had seemed to know the power that her trust would have over him. And indeed, her trust had cracked the tomb of his heart and let in a fresh breeze.

Andy had been there to see it all. And he still counted that moment as the divine beginning of God's work in leading his father to the Cross. The path his dad had walked had seemed impossible, with its steep declines into cold, dark valleys. But the power of just one ray of His Son's Light had pointed the way up, until the grip of Christ's nail-pierced hand had secured Mac's place on the mountaintop!

Changes. There were so many changes. Andy thought about how the old had gone and the new had come.

Today, however, Mac was crushed. He stood, devastated, in the barn. What was he doing? He was a Christian, now. He wasn't supposed to be cursing—cow manure or no cow manure.

"What the…?" had singed the morning air with a string of other raw language. It had happened without thought, in response to a minor accident. Mac had bent over to pick up a dropped pitchfork when his glasses had slipped off his nose and splattered into a pile of fresh cow manure.

His God-blasting outburst had left Mac sick to his stomach. Phillip had no doubt heard everything. Not that Phillip had never heard Mac curse before, but Mac had tried to change since he'd come forward in church, and cursing was one of the things he had set out to conquer.

Mac wasn't sure if Phillip knew of his recent commitment to Christ; Mac hadn't mentioned it to him, yet. But Mac had managed to not curse over the past few weeks. He had been pleased with himself and his progress in living a proper life. But today, the cursing had come tumbling out as if he'd never exerted an ounce of control.

Mac's conviction wasn't because someone had confronted him about his cursing. It was simply something he had felt was right. He had felt convicted about it ever since he had walked down the aisle of the church, and he had tried to change. But now he felt terrible. The gutter words had spewed out too effortlessly. It was as if they had been waiting for the opportunity to escape, and the minute he had let down his guard they had crashed the gate. He had failed.

Mac despised that the words had still been there. He stood holding the soiled glasses, repentant under the great beams of the barn. In anguish, he threw his head back and whispered hoarsely, "I'm sorry! I'm sorry, God."

But the weight of his transgression did not leave him.

When Mac finally joined Phillip at the feed troughs, he tried to avoid Phillip's gaze. But Phillip asked, "Do you have a touch of something? You don't look too good."

Mac didn't feel too good, but he shrugged it off. "Nah. I'm fine."

Mac saw the raised eyebrow; he knew his countenance gave him away. Mac wondered what to say—if he should say anything. Phillip was no saint (he could be nastily grumpy), but Phillip didn't curse; at least Mac had never heard him. Phillip went to church in Harmony, the same church Phillip's son and Molly attended. Should he tell Phillip he was sorry for his outburst?

Mac decided he should say something. He ventured, "Phillip, I understand that you've been a church-goer all your life. I haven't. In fact, I can count on one hand the number of times I set foot inside a church, until recently."

Phillip uttered a brief "uh-huh" to let Mac know he was listening as he spread feed.

Mac wasn't used to talking about this kind of stuff. He exhaled before starting again.

"A couple of weeks ago I went to Andy's church," he said. "And at the end of the service I came down the aisle and told Andy I believed in God and Jesus, and that I wanted to join his church. I know it surprised everybody—but then, you've probably already heard about it."

"I have," said Phillip. "And it was a good decision."

"Well, be that as it may," Mac said, "I'm sure you just heard me swearing, and I want to apologize. I dropped my glasses in some"—Mac decided on the word 'poop'—"and the words just flew out."

"A cow-pie, huh?" Phillip grinned. "Don't worry about it. Apology accepted."

But Mac still felt the weight of it. He had cursed the God he now believed in. He asked Phillip, "How do you do it? I mean, I go to church, now, but I have trouble getting rid of stuff like the cursing. I've talked that way for so long that I don't know how to change it. You just heard me! I know it's a sin against God.

And I'm also afraid that, one of these days, I'm going to say or do something that'll get me kicked out of my son's church!"

Phillip grew serious. "Just be yourself, Mac," he said, with a shrug. "God hears your apology. And those church people are just like you and me. Nothing you can say isn't something they haven't already heard at one time or another. I'm sure they know you're working on it."

It wasn't the answer Mac had hoped for. Phillip didn't seem to have any advice on how to change. And Mac desperately wanted to change. He was used to being in control. The fact that he couldn't conquer the swearing bothered him.

He didn't bring it up to Phillip, again. Instead, he worried about it. And he returned to reading the Bible and the Bible storybook Abbey had given him. But he had not yet reached the New Testament in either book, and what he read in the Old Testament only compounded his belief that it was impossible to live the kind of life the Bible called for people to live. He wondered if he was losing his newfound salvation, or if he was destined to be a second-class Christian.

CHAPTER ELEVEN

I NEED TO HEAR IT AGAIN

In the parsonage living room on Sunday, Andy, Paul, and Mac waited for the ballgame to begin. Andy drifted in and out of a nap. With his eyes closed, he could hear Abbey and Molly washing dishes in the kitchen.

Suddenly, Mac said, "I've been reading the Ten Commandments." Then he followed up with, "I've broken nearly every one of them—and I keep breaking them."

Andy's eyes opened. He wondered, *Why the confession?* It surprised him, and he could see the question in Paul's eyes, too.

Then Mac asked, "Won't God judge me for that? Especially since I can't seem to change? I keep swearing and cursing, just like I always have. I don't know how to be anything but what I've always been. I'm no good at this Christian stuff. I can't be like you. Maybe I'm not really a Christian, at all."

Andy was wide-awake, now. How could he reassure his father without treading too heavily?

He prayed silently. *Dear God, don't let me sound too pious or holier-than-thou. After all, this is my dad! He's never taken well to people telling him what to do, and I'm just that 'idiot kid' he's never had much respect for. But he needs help. Help him to understand Your truth and feel Your love.*

Andy's heart calmed. "The Ten Commandments are tough, Dad," he began. "And they're impossible. Nobody can live up to them, not even me. Romans 3:23 says, *'for all have sinned and fall short of the glory of God.'* We're all sinners and under judgment."

Mac fidgeted and then declared, "But you're not the same as me. You're different. You don't swear anymore, for example. I've cursed God all my life—and I'm still doing it."

Andy interrupted him. "I may not swear, but I commit other sins."

"None that matter much," Mac mumbled. "When I swear, it's against God! It matters. Plus, everybody can hear my swearing. One of these days, I'll get kicked out of your church!"

"You can't compare sins, Dad. Every sin is against God, and nobody's perfect. God doesn't look at sins by degrees. A sin is a sin. Plus, Jesus said that if a person so much as *thinks* wrong things in their heart, they're as guilty as if they had physically committed them. James 2:10 says that *'whoever keeps the whole law but stumbles at just one point is guilty of breaking all of it.'*

Mac threw himself back in his chair. "No!" he exclaimed.

Then he crossed his arms over his chest. "So, what's the use? What's the point of anything? If nobody can do good, why bother? You're better than me—and so is Paul. Neither of you swears or does other sinful things. God should take that into account."

Paul squirmed in his seat. Andy could tell that he was hoping Andy had a good answer.

Andy shook his head and said, "That sounds reasonable to us. But God doesn't evaluate us by how we compare to others."

Before his dad could object, Andy hurried to ask, "Would you agree, Dad, that Charles Manson is worse than you?"

The question caught Mac by surprise. The crazed cult-leader had stirred his followers to commit murders a few years ago, and Manson still drew attention from time to time in the newspapers.

Mac had to agree that he was better than Charles Manson, and he said so.

Andy continued. "Okay, then let's do some supposing for a minute. Let's suppose that, according to how bad we are, we get placed under varying depths of water in a lake. (Of course, this isn't how God works, but we're just supposing, here. Okay?) So, let's put Charles Manson under, say, a hundred feet of water. And let's put you under fifteen feet of water, because you're not as bad as Charles Manson. And let's put me and Paul each under ten feet of water, since you think we're somehow better than you are. So, again: here's Manson one hundred feet down, and here's you at fifteen feet down, and Paul and I are ten feet down. Now, Dad, which of the four of us is drowning?"

Mac blinked and then replied, "All four, I guess."

"Right!" said Andy. "None of us is above water in that example, and it doesn't matter how we compare to one another; all of us are drowning. In the same way, sin is sin, and none of us is sinless. What matters is: have we have accepted Jesus as our Savior? As the Son of God, Jesus is the only one who has ever lived a sinless life, and only He can lift us out of our sin predicament and set us on the high ground that He won for us on the Cross. Jesus brings us close to God and gives us a brand-new life—as Children of God. John 1:12 says, *'Yet to all who received him, to those who believed in his name, he gave the right to become children of God.'*"

Mac frowned. "I may be a child of God, but I'm still messed up. Doesn't my swearing separate me, again, from God?"

"No," said Andy. "Jesus died for ALL of your sin. But you're right that God won't let you get by with continuing to sin."

"I think I'm too far gone," Mac sighed. "I think I'm too old to change."

"Not so, Dad. You forget that you're a newborn! You're not old in God's family. In fact, you've just come down the birth canal and have landed smack-dab in the middle of a new family. You're just a baby in Christ. You can't yet focus properly, and you don't have a complete idea, yet, of who you have become. Plus, you've just met your Heavenly Father."

Mac grumbled, "But I feel like I've driven God away."

"The Holy Spirit hasn't gone away. He's still there, inside of you. Do you know how I know?" Andy asked.

Mac shook his head. "No."

"I know because you told me. You said you felt terrible for swearing. But before you became a Christian, swearing didn't bother you at all, did it?"

"No. I never gave it a thought."

"Well, that's the Holy Spirit in you. You feel bad because you've sinned against Him—after all He's done for you."

Mac hung his head. "I do feel guilty."

"But you can get rid of that guilt," Andy said. "God doesn't want you to feel guilty for the rest of your life. 1 John 1:9 says that *'if we confess our sins, He is faithful and just and will forgive us our sins and purify us from all unrighteousness.'*"

"I do confess, whenever I mess up," Mac insisted. "But I still feel guilty and ashamed."

"That's because you're not believing what God said. 1 John 1:9 says that God forgave you the minute you repented and confessed."

"Okay," said Mac. "But that verse also said something about purifying me. When is that going to happen?"

"In one sense," said Andy, "it's already happened. You were purified the minute you accepted Jesus. Once you became a Christian, your sin was no longer counted against you; God now sees only Jesus, standing in your place. That's called *grace.* And in another sense, the new sins you commit are forgiven and wiped away the minute you confess them."

"But if I keep messing up the same way, over and over, how many times is God going to let me confess that same sin?"

"Well, let's see," said Andy. "John's verse doesn't say, 'if we confess our sins, He'll forgive us up to three times.' It says, *'if we confess our sins, He is faithful and just and will forgive us our sins'*–period."

"But how do I change? How do I get to where I don't curse anymore?"

Andy said, "It's all about love."

"Love?"

"Yes, love."

"I don't get it. What's love got to do with it?" Mac asked.

"Everything," said Andy. "God loves you and wants you to succeed. When you pray to Him and ask for His help, He's going to give it! Pray to Him about it, and turn your heart and your mind to Him and His Word. Don't focus on your failure—focus on Him and His promises. As you do, you'll find that His face and His words will come to you in the situations that anger you and bring on the cursing and the swearing. The Psalmist David learned this lesson. In Psalm 119:11 he says, *'I have hidden your word in my heart that I might not sin against you.'* And when Jesus was tempted by Satan in Matthew four, He also referred to God's words in Scripture to keep Him from sinning.

"When we store God's words in our hearts, we give the Holy Spirit a source to draw from, to remind us of what God expects from us and how He promises to help us. And when we fill up our minds with Him and the good truths of His Word, there's less room for the old sin habits to hide."

Mac nodded slowly.

"You're His child, now," Andy said, "and Your Heavenly Father loves you. And He is determined, like any good parent, to make you a mature child of His. He's not going to stop working on you. Philippians 1:6 says that *'he who began a good work in you will carry it on to completion until the day of Christ Jesus.'* Day by day, as you journey with Him, He will be at work transforming you.

Then one day, you will be complete. 1 John 3:2 says, *'Dear friends, now we are children of God, and what we will be has not yet been made known. But we know that when he appears, we shall be like him, for we shall see him as he is.'*"

As Andy said this, he felt the promise of it in his own heart, and he sighed at the fullness of it.

Then he said, "You aren't the only one being worked on, Dad. We're all being worked on. We're all on the same journey toward maturity. And as Christians, we're all part of the same eternal family that helps each other and prays for each other, along the way. As a Christian, you're never alone. You have God's Spirit in you, and you have a vast family in the worldwide Church of God. That huge Church of God includes the Cherish church family and all of the Christians in the Garrett family. You and I and Molly and Paul and Abbey are family not only by blood, but also by Spirit. And we are to encourage and pray for each other.

"You may not know it, but your immediate family in Christ has been praying for you for a long time, Dad. And God has heard our prayers and has helped you to open your heart to Him. And He's helping you, now, to grow in Him. We'll continue to pray for you, because you're doubly our family! We won't stop. We'll keep praying for you, as you grow."

Mac looked at Paul. Paul nodded. Mac was sobered at the thought of them all praying for him. And he said quietly, "I'll pray for all of you, too."

Then Mac asked, "Would you write down some of those verses for me? I want to hold onto those."

Andy jotted the verses on a piece of paper and gave it to Mac. "There are a lot of good verses in the Bible. And there's a lot of good teaching about Jesus and the Holy Spirit in the New Testament. How far have you gotten in your reading? Did you like the book of John?"

Mac shifted uncomfortably in his seat. "I didn't start reading there, yet," he admitted. "I started in Genesis, and I've been reading straight through. I have a lot more to read before I get to John."

Andy hesitated before he gently said, "Okay. You'll find a lot of good stories and history in the Old Testament. But I think that for now you'll get more spiritual direction if you start in the New Testament, with John or Matthew. That's where the stories of Jesus are and where you can learn more about Him and how to be like Him. The Gospels will help you see who the Holy Spirit is changing you into."

Mac nodded sheepishly. "Yeah. I ran into a lot of genealogy stuff in Genesis, and I got bogged down in some of those other books."

Andy smiled. "It's good to read the Old Testament; it tells about God's promise to send Jesus, and it tells what life was like before He came. But for now, you might want to try reading John."

"I'll start reading in John, tonight," Mac said.

CHAPTER TWELVE

A LOOK AT THE MOBILE UNIT

Daffodils nodded in welcome as Molly and Abbey drove down the lane to the farm. It was Molly's first visit. Paul would come later, when he could better manage the steps.

The flowers were beautiful, but they could not erase the ugliness of the ruins of the farmhouse. Molly looked away. She hated seeing the charred embers and the bare foundation. She shuddered at the memories of the fire.

Next to the rubble stood the new mobile home—metallic and sterile-looking. Without the footfalls of generations of Doaks family members on its doorstep or the echoes of decades of love and laughter in its walls, the double-wide's welcome was hollow, and its assembly-line manufacture would always scream *temporary!*—which Molly vowed it would be.

Phillip hugged Molly and Abbey at the door. Molly was grateful that the men had kept the farm going. Their presence, now, in the offending double-wide's doorway, helped to make entering it feel less disheartening.

Molly walked in, expecting to hate everything she found. But the interior surprised her. It was nothing like she'd pictured. The inside walls were papered, and the doors were trimmed and finished, like in any other home. And the rooms were large and bright. She had envisioned her family living in dim, cramped quarters over the months ahead. Instead, she found the mobile unit to be airy and almost spacious. During Phillip and Mac's guided tour, Molly began to envision curtains here and a sofa there. She made lists in a notebook of things to buy.

She also liked the arrangement of the bath and bedrooms at each end. The men had taken the back end, with a bath between their bedrooms, and Molly and Paul would take the front end, with a bath between the master bedroom and what would be the nursery.

In the double-wide's center, the large living room and dining room dominated, and a nice-sized galley kitchen and pantry/ laundry room took up one side. The back door (near the laundry room and the men's bedrooms) opened onto the farmyard. The other entrance (the front, off the living room) faced nowhere and would seldom be used.

The men had purchased matching recliners and TV trays—the only furniture in the double-wide, outside of their beds, dressers, and a television set. The recliners were angled for perfect viewing of the news or a ballgame.

A new washer and dryer had been put to use. Molly was sure that Phillip must have been in charge of sorting clothes and pushing buttons. She doubted that her dad had ever run a load of laundry in his life.

And then Molly did a double-take. In the kitchen, beyond the new stove and refrigerator, she saw a lineup of empty, washed canning jars—jars from her canning cellar.

Phillip avoided her look; he had forgotten to hide the evidence.

For an instant, Molly's anger flared, but then she stopped herself. What were a few jars of canned goods compared to all that these two men had been doing around the farm? Molly pictured them, exhausted at the end of the day, watching the nightly news and treating themselves to her precious canning stores. She couldn't help but chuckle. She decided she should be flattered that, after Sheryl Bennett's best efforts to satisfy their appetites, her father and Phillip had still craved her peaches and jam!

Molly also guessed that the guys must be feeling as ready as she and Paul for a more settled and normal schedule of work and meals. Hopefully, it wouldn't be long now.

PART TWO

KNOW MY THOUGHTS, I PRAY

CHAPTER THIRTEEN

LOCK-IN

Laughter rocked the hallways of the First Baptist Church. It was nearly midnight, and teens scrambled between classrooms to find clues hidden earlier by their youth director.

Chelsea Mitchell sat, now, able to enjoy a rare uninvolved moment while the kids raced from room to room and up and down the stairs. It was going to be a long night, she thought. But it would be fun. Pizza awaited everyone. And Benjamin and Brooke By-the-Way would be here, any minute, with ice cream and to help with additional games.

In Chelsea's teen years, she had sat up and played Chinese checkers with Erica Taylor (now Erica Hart) and other church kids, until breakfast had been served. Now that she was grown, it was harder to stay up all night. But she knew that a lock-in was a right-of-passage for the youth.

A loud knocking on the outer door interrupted her reminiscing. Chelsea jumped. Hopefully, it wasn't the police. During a lock-in a couple of years ago, a church neighbor had reported that the church was *being robbed*, and the police had come.

The man at the door, now, wasn't a policeman, but he did appear to be worried. Chelsea had met him, somewhere, but she couldn't recall his name. *Has he been in church?* She thought so.

"Is everything okay?" the man asked. "I saw lights and shadows of people running."

Chelsea laughed. *It probably does look suspicious if you don't know what's going on.*

"It's a teen-lock-in," she said, and the man uttered an "aha!"

He said, "I was just getting back from a late farm call and saw the activity inside. I got worried that something was wrong." Then he asked, "Is Reverend Garrett here?"

Chelsea now remembered who he was. "You're the new veterinarian, aren't you?"

"Yeah. Sorry, I should have introduced myself. I've missed several Sundays in church with emergency calls, so I'm surprised you remember me. You're Chelsea, right? I'm C. G. Logan. You can call me *Siege*."

"Okay, Siege," Chelsea said, and she wondered if his eyes always sparkled this pleasantly. "But, no, Pastor Garrett isn't here. He came earlier and had a study lesson with the kids, but we didn't make him stay all night."

"Right," Siege said, and it seemed to Chelsea that he purposely lingered. Chelsea wondered at it, and she found herself asking if he'd like to come in.

"Sure," he said. He stepped inside and grinned at the activity in the hallways. "Crazy kids! We used to do this at our church, too. Now I just party with cows and pigs in the middle of the night and usher their young into the world."

Chelsea laughed. "I stayed with my grandparents at their farm, once, when a cow was calving. We sat up all night in the barn, and I thought it was the most wonderful thing! I'll never forget it."

"It is pretty cool, isn't it? And calves are my favorite," Siege agreed.

For a moment, neither of them said anything. Chelsea finally shrugged and asked, "Would you want to stay for pizza?"

Siege nodded enthusiastically. "I'd like that," he said, "if you have enough."

"More than enough," Chelsea assured him, and she led the way to the fellowship hall where the first group of teen detectives had gathered.

"We found them all; we've got all the clues!" shouted Jimmy Fisher. "We won! Does that mean we get to eat first?"

Chelsea held them off until the last group had finished the hunt. She checked each team's search finds and confirmed that Jimmy's group had won. She handed out giant candy bar prizes and quieted everyone so they could say grace before the pizza. No sooner had she said *Amen* than hands converged from every direction to snatch slices of pepperoni and cheese from the boxes.

Staying awake was a hungry business. And the kids barely noticed Siege.

Game pieces flew everywhere.

Benjamin By-the-Way had misjudged the first step at the church entry. Brooke dropped her sack of ice cream and stooped to help him. Benjamin's pant leg had torn, and he now limped—but he assured his wife that he was all right.

Brooke gathered all the game pieces she could find, and she stuffed them into the sack with the ice cream cartons. Everything would have to be sorted out after they got inside.

"Ice cream!" shouted Eric Mowry, when he spied the newcomers.

Brooke handed Eric the sack, and the hyperactive teen tore down the stairs to deliver the ice cream to the kitchen freezer. The By-the-Ways gingerly made their way downstairs, too, and Ben hobbled to a chair.

"What happened?" Chelsea asked.

Siege overheard Brooke's description of Ben's fall, and he stopped taping the four-square game grid on the floor. "A fall, you say? Mind if I have a look?"

"Sure, Doc," Ben said, and Siege thought it remarkable that Ben didn't follow up with the horse-doctor jokes he usually got whenever he asked a human about his health.

Ben's rolled-up pant leg revealed a large lump, mid-calf, and a cut that had started to bleed. Chelsea appeared over his shoulder with a towel and a makeshift ice pack.

"Perfect," Siege murmured as he placed the ice over the bump. Then he told Ben, "I can't tell for sure, but I don't think the bone is broken. We'll keep an eye on it. Just hold the ice here, for a bit. You should probably get an X-ray tomorrow."

"Thanks," Brooke said. Then she sent Eric to retrieve the sack that had held the ice cream. "We need the game pieces that I shoved into the bag when Ben fell," she explained.

Eric leaped across the room on his errand.

Chelsea laughed. "It's one o-clock and these kids haven't even begun to slow down."

It did grow a little quieter as some of the group gathered around an array of board games the By-the-Ways had brought. Chelsea used the moment to set up the projector for showing a movie, later, and she was grateful that Siege could take Ben's place as four-square referee. Siege had shown up at the right time.

Soon, the four-square ball began to bounce. But the game dissolved, somewhere along the line, into a loose version of keep-away, with Siege and the boys in chase around the basement floor.

"The vet's having more fun than the kids," Brooke observed. "I didn't know he was going to be here, tonight. But he's good!"

Chelsea agreed. "He wasn't supposed to be here, but when he saw the lights on, he stopped to make sure things were okay." Chelsea added, "He looked hungry, so I invited him to have some pizza with us, before he went home. And now I think he's got his second wind."

"Cute guy," Brooke whispered, with a knowing look, and Chelsea shrugged it off.

"I guess so," Chelsea said as if the thought hadn't entered her mind. But even as she denied it, she had to admit that Siege had a certain charm.

"He's not married, you know," Ben whispered, and this time Chelsea blushed.

"Okay, you two. That's enough. We're supposed to be entertaining the kids."

But Chelsea did find herself sneaking peeks at the veterinarian as he scrambled across the floor with the teenage boys in close chase.

CHAPTER FOURTEEN

TWITCH

Phillip set down the milk pail. Mac's question required attention.

"How do you think the kids would react if I sold my house up north and bought a place down here?" Mac asked. "I don't want to intrude, and I hope I haven't overstayed my welcome, already."

Phillip said, "Mac, I think your kids would be thrilled to have you move here. The only thing up north is a big empty house; but here, you have family."

"I know," Mac said. "But I don't want my kids to feel like I'm expecting anything from them. Their mom and I used to push too hard when they were kids. I think that's why Molly and Andy moved away so fast when they had the chance. We wanted them to live our kind of life, instead of letting them live their own lives. So they left."

Phillip nodded. "That's not that unusual for a parent. I always wanted Paul to take over the farm, but he and I didn't see eye-to-eye on everything. I was pretty bullheaded about the way I wanted things done. Paul was more forward-looking than I am. I can admit, now, that I like some of the things he's set in place since he's taken over. He's doing a good job. But back then, it wasn't working for the two of us to work the farm together, so Paul left to do construction up north."

That connected with Mac, and he said, "That's how I was! Oh, how Andy used to frustrate me." But then Mac backed up. "No," he said, more deliberately. "I used to get frustrated about something Andy wasn't responsible for. Andy didn't have mechanical ability, like I do. I wanted to share that part of me with him, but I couldn't. And I couldn't share the stuff he was always going on about, with those books he read. We're just two different people. And it took me a long time to get that through my head."

Phillip said, "Being a parent isn't easy, is it?"

Then Phillip said, again, "I do think you'd be doing the right thing to move down here. Before you came, your kids worried about you, and they fretted because you were too far away. They were relieved when you came here."

"And," he added, "a lot has changed since before Thanksgiving."

"You've got that right," said Mac. "A lot has changed."

Mac would think some more about it before he made his final decision on moving. There was no rush. And he wanted to be sure before he shared his plans with Andy and Molly.

Andy bounced on the seat of the veterinary truck as he listened to Siege explain why they were in such a hurry.

"We're going to an Amish farm to check out a horse with a bellyache. Could be colic or constipation—maybe an impaction," Siege explained. He added, "Depending on the situation, it can be serious for the animal; certainly painful."

Andy figured it must be urgent, because this afternoon Siege drove faster than normal. Picturesque scenes of the countryside they usually admired and commented on flashed by in a blur. And Andy was nervous.

Only a few minutes ago, when Siege had hurriedly collected Andy, Siege had said he *needed an extra pair of hands.* Andy had been confident in his role as an assistant with cows and pigs, and he had expected the call to be routine. But now, Siege had mentioned two disturbing things: horse and constipation. Neither sounded good. Andy knew nothing about horses. And constipation sounded, well, messy! What was Siege getting him into?

The vet seemed unaware of Andy's unease and pointed out a pay telephone booth that had appeared out of nowhere.

"The farmer probably telephoned from there," Siege said.

The booth seemed out of place at the bare crossroad, and its anachronism redirected Andy's attention. Andy knew the Amish didn't have phones in their homes; it seemed they were allowed to use phones but not own them. So, Andy decided that a phone booth at a busy crossroad wasn't really so odd.

Most Amish rules made little sense to Andy. He said so, now, and Siege told him a story about a farmer who also happened to be an Amish elder. The man had entered a drawing at the State Fair, and he had unexpectedly won the use of a John Deer 6620 corn/bean combine harvester for three months. Because the Amish were prohibited from operating motorized, self-propelled vehicles, the farmer had a dilemma. Seeking a ruling regarding his prize, he met with the other elders, and it was conveniently decided that this particular combine could be driven, but "only inside a fenced area." Other tractors and equipment were excluded from the ruling.

The enterprising farmer had then promptly hired an *English* to drive the combine from farm to farm, and he had rented the use of it to all of his friends, including the other elders. Everyone, of course, had fenced fields, and that fall, the harvest was completed in a fraction of the usual time. The only losers were *English* photographers who frequented the Amish countryside to capture Amish harvesters at work with horse-teams in their fields.

Andy was still thinking about Amish customs when Siege turned off the road and swung into a drive. Plain-colored clothes hung on a cold clothesline, and two straw-hatted boys lugged pails of something into a tidy, two-story house. Andy was curious; he had never been on an Amish farm before.

But his nerves kicked in the minute he heard the horse's cries of pain. Siege flew from the truck and thrust a heavy gallon jug into Andy's hands. Then the vet ran with his bag to the barn.

When they reached the distress sound, Andy was shocked. The screaming horse in the stall was the largest animal Andy had ever seen. He had expected the patient to be a carthorse like the dozens of Amish buggy horses that frequented the back roads between Cherish and Harmony. But instead, the animal they were led to was an imposing, giant draft horse that stamped and protested his hurt against the sides of the stall. The suspendered owner hung back, with a nod of acknowledgment to Siege.

Andy watched from outside the stall as Siege filled and quickly administered the pain-killing contents of a syringe. When the horse quieted a little, and with the aid of the horse's owner, Siege bent to examine his patient. When Siege straightened, he asked, "Well, Pastor, it's time to decide. Do you want the front end or the back end?"

Stunned, Andy froze. Everything he had feared about this veterinary visit now loomed before him. He finally stammered, "I-I-I guess I want the front end."

Siege chuckled. "Good choice."

Andy stood, dumbly, as Siege drew out a loop of chain attached to a two-foot wooden bar. Deftly, the veterinarian grabbed the stamping horse's head and whipped the chain around its upper lip with a twist. Siege held it in place with the wooden handle. The startled horse could not move without causing the *twitch* to tighten and create new pain. So now, the animal stood quite still.

It trembled and eyed Dr. Logan down the length of its nose—its massive power held in check by a tiny length of chain.

"Okay," Siege said to Andy, "hold this."

A horrified Andy hesitantly took over the twitch.

Siege didn't have to repeat his terse command to "keep that thing twisted, whatever you do." Andy had already fixed the twitch in a death grip. His eyes were nearly as wide as those of the animal towering above him.

Siege set the gallon jug on the stall floor and uncurled the length of plastic tubing that Andy had also carried from the truck. Then Siege reached up and began to carefully feed plastic tubing into the lower part of the horse's left nostril. Andy imagined the temporarily immobilized animal thinking it was him who was working the tubing up his nose and into his gut. And in a moment, it WAS Andy holding it! Siege had reached the stomach and made the hand-off.

In a commanding tone, Siege ordered, "Hold this end for a moment—AND DON'T LET GO OF THAT TWITCH!"

Siege uncapped the jug and attached Andy's end of the tubing. He raised the plunger on the jug to the ready. "In a minute, I'll tell you when to start pumping," he said.

"Right," said Andy, meekly. "I'll be holding the twitch *and* pumping," he mumbled. "And what will you be doing?"

Siege pulled on a pair of heavy, shoulder-length rubber gloves and walked to the back of the stall. "Unpacking things from the other end," he replied. At that, Andy decided his choice of working the front might not have been such a bad idea, after all.

Andy refused, however, to look at the whites of the huge eyes that glared down at him. And he had to fight everything in his being not to turn and run.

After a moment, Siege called from behind the horse, "Start pumping!" Then he added, "And pump slowly."

So, with the twitch still frozen in his fist, Andy began to pump, and the clear liquid flowed through the tubing.

"What *is* this stuff, anyway?" he asked.

"Mineral oil. It'll calm things and get him loosened up."

"Oh, right," Andy shuddered. "Uh, how much do I give him?"

"The whole thing."

And so, Andy pumped and pumped, and the horse stared and stared. And Andy refused to think about what Siege was doing at the other end.

When he heard the dung begin to spill onto the stall floor, Andy swallowed to think this might all be over soon.

That's when he looked up and caught a glimpse through the stall's slats of the farmer and his two boys, who were giggling at him. Their whispered comments were in German, so Andy couldn't tell what they were saying, but he felt sure that this had been a highly entertaining afternoon for them.

Finally, Siege ripped off his gloves and stretched. He ordered the farmer to take over the twitch, while Siege removed the tubing. Siege and Andy walked out with the tubing and the vet bag before the farmer released the horse's lip and made a leap for the stall's gate.

The massive Belgian lunged once against the slats, swatted the air with a whip of his tail, and then stood shaking his head and pawing the ground. That done, he seemed to realize that he was no longer in pain. He lifted his head and whinnied. Finally, he turned around and stood calmly, as if nothing had happened.

The farmer smiled and nodded his head agreeably at Andy and Siege. "Danks!" he said in a kind of half-German, half-English accent.

Siege shook the farmer's hand and tipped his cap, and he and Andy walked to the truck.

"Wish I could hear you describe this afternoon to Abbey and your brother-in-law!" Siege laughed.

"Yeah!" Andy managed to say. But what he wanted to say was that he thought he'd stick to pastoring from now on.

CHAPTER FIFTEEN

BACK AT THE FARM

As Andy passed through the church office, the telephone rang and Opal answered. She said "one moment, please" and signaled for Andy to pick up at his desk.

"Hi, Pastor. This is Hal," the caller said, and Andy leaned back in surprise. Hal Morgan continued, "If you have a moment, I wonder if you could tell me where to find the Bible verse: 'God helps those who help themselves'?"

Andy smiled. "Sure, I've got a minute, and that's an easy one," he said. "The answer is that it's not in the Bible."

After silence on the other end of the line, Hal said, "Are you sure?"

"Yeah," said Andy, "I'm sure. God never tells us to help ourselves. He tells us to depend on Him. And He tells us to love and help others. But He never says that He helps those who help themselves."

Andy continued, "Proverbs 3:5-6 says *'Trust in the Lord with all your heart, and lean not on your own understanding; in all your ways acknowledge him, and he will make your paths straight.'* And Matthew 25:31-46 tells us that we are to help others as if they were Christ in need."

When there was no response, Andy asked, "Does that help?"

Again, there was silence. "Okay, then. Thanks, Pastor," Hal finally said, and he hung up.

Andy wondered what had prompted Hal's question. Perhaps Hal had an opportunity to help someone but was resisting. But then again, he may have simply run across the old adage and wondered where it had come from.

Either way, Andy hoped he had pointed Hal in the right direction. He was grateful that Hal still came to church and had felt free to call, in spite of Andy's outshooting him, many months ago. Hal never mentioned the shooting incident to Andy, and he was always respectful to him. But Andy did sometimes catch Hal in a group of men nodding in his direction. No doubt, the story was being shared again.

On March fifteenth, Molly and Paul spent their first night at the farm. Paul had taken a tour of the barn and a solo drive in the truck before supper, and now, before heading to bed, he sat on the front steps of the mobile home to look at the stars. Molly had settled Emily into her new crib in the nursery and had joined him.

Molly knew how much Paul loved the farm sky. They had both missed the deep blackness of the country night and the clouds of galaxies that stretched farther than the eye could see. When they had lived up north, Molly had had no idea that such splendor existed. The lights from the Chicago suburbs had shrouded this celestial beauty.

"The stars aren't the only things sparkling, tonight," Molly said. "I see happiness in your eyes."

Paul smiled and pulled her near for a kiss. His embrace warmed her.

"I'm really grateful to be back," he said. "Things could have been so much worse."

"But they weren't," Molly whispered. "And here we are."

They sat huddled together in the quiet for a long while, and Molly thought about how things would be getting back to normal in Cherish, too. She imagined Andy and Abbey wandering peacefully throughout the parsonage, with no competition for the bathroom.

"You know," Molly said, "we owe Andy and Abbey a great deal. As hard as it has been on us to be stuck in the parsonage, it must have been harder for them to give up their privacy and extra space for us."

"I know," Paul said. "And tonight, they get to dream undisturbed in their beds and sleep until noon if they want to."

Molly shook her head. "Have you forgotten about Winston?"

Paul chuckled. "Right. They have Winston, and we have Emily."

"And Phillip and Mac," Molly reminded him.

"Yeah," Paul said. And then he drawled, "But tonight, Emily's asleep, and those two old codgers are dog-tired, and they're wa-a-a-ay back there in the back, and we're wa-a-a-ay up here in the front." Paul pulled her closer and gave her a deep kiss. "You know what I mean?" he asked with a twinkle in his eye and a crooked smile.

Molly felt him softly brush a stray lock of hair from her forehead, and she felt his fingers linger on her cheek. She got the hint. The two of them helped each other up from the porch, and they quietly padded through the living room to their new bed.

When Molly awoke in the morning, Mac had already changed Emily, and he was curled with her in his lap in the recliner in front of the television set. The news was filled with disturbing references to El Salvador and the Nicaragua contras, and Mac was frowning. Molly was glad when he turned off the television. There was nothing encouraging to hear.

Molly improved everyone's disposition with a huge breakfast, and then Mac and Phillip helped Paul down the porch stairs and out to the barn.

The men's voices slowly faded as they walked away from the mobile. After a moment, it was quiet.

Molly realized that she hadn't been alone in the morning for over two months, and she savored the thought that today was hers.

Mid-morning, Sheryl Bennett dropped off a welcome-home gift: a pot of stew. Molly thanked her for the meal and for keeping Mac and Phillip fed, until now.

"It was my pleasure," said Sheryl. "It was good to see hungry men enjoying my cooking."

"Plus," added Sheryl, "your father has paid me handsomely, even though I told him this was my gift to you. You and Paul have helped us many times, and this was only a modest payback."

Molly was surprised to hear of her father's generosity. Her dad had certainly changed. He had always been very tight with a dime. Molly liked the new Mac better than the father she had grown up with.

As usual on Sunday, the Doakses attended their church in Harmony and Mac drove to Andy's church.

Mac had finally finished most of the Bible storybook, and the Sunday school lessons usually made sense to him now—especially if the lessons happened to draw from the stories he had read. He had also finished reading the book of John and was nearly finished with the other Gospels. Even the sermons were becoming more meaningful.

Andy was right, Mac thought. *The New Testament reading is feeding my soul.*

Mac's favorite Bible story, so far, was when Jesus called Peter to meet Him on the water. Mac could identify with the impetuous fisherman. Mac believed that he would have stepped out onto the waves, too. And he knew he would have sunk after only a few steps, just as Peter had. But Mac also clung to the fact that Jesus had been right there, ready to draw Peter back up. Jesus was a rescuer. Mac had been sinking, too, and Jesus had lifted him up.

CHAPTER SIXTEEN

ABUSE

On Wednesday, Mac came to Cherish for lunch, as well as dinner. He usually ate lunch at the farm and had Wednesday dinner with Abbey and Andy before the midweek service, but Molly and Paul had a luncheon meeting, today, at their church in Harmony, and Molly had suggested that Abbey and Andy invite Mac to Cherish for lunch, too. Abbey had taken the occasion to make Mac's favorite dessert: apple pie.

"I just hope the coffee holds out," she said as she cut the pie. "This is the last of it. If you two want more for supper, you need to go to the store."

Andy would go. Even though he seldom drank coffee with the evening meal, he'd need some for breakfast.

Mac rode along. And in the car, Andy was surprised at Mac's complaints about Phillip getting on his nerves.

"I thought you two got along well," Andy said.

"He's a cantankerous old fool," Mac muttered.

"Oh," Andy said quietly.

Mac elaborated: "According to Phillip, I didn't do anything right, yesterday. It didn't matter if I was collecting eggs or tossing feed; he had something to say about everything."

Andy waited before he suggested, "Maybe Phillip was having a bad day—or had something heavy on his mind that spilled over into the chores."

"It was a bad day, all right," growled Mac.

Andy hadn't heard that tone of voice from his father for a couple of weeks, and he was sorry to hear it again. He let Mac talk, and said nothing. Fortunately, their drive was a short one.

Andy always enjoyed a walk through Holcombe's Grocery. The store seemed to have at least one of everything. How they got so many goods on their limited shelves, Andy didn't know. He had once laughed to see imported Italian coffee. Mike Holcombe had explained, "Started stocking that for Connor Wilson, Jr. He asked if I could carry it. Whenever he's here to check out the progress of one of the new plays at his playhouse, he stops in to pick it up. Nobody else can afford it."

Andy wondered if the Italian brand really tasted that much better than the cheaper stuff he drank. But at the price Holcombe was asking for the fancy brand, Andy knew he would never find out.

"Reverend Garrett! Reverend Garrett!"

Andy wasn't sure where the voice was coming from. "Yes?"

"Phone call!" the invisible speaker said. "In the back."

Andy shrugged and handed Mac the usual brand of coffee. "It must be Abbey," he said. "She must have thought of something else she wants us to pick up."

Andy passed through a swinging door at the back of the store and followed an aproned man to a wall-mounted telephone. The receiver hung, twisting on a long cord, waiting for him.

"Hello?" Andy said, and he was surprised by Abbey's distressed reply.

"You need to get over to the Bartlett's, right away," she said rapidly. "Vera was screaming into the phone, and I couldn't tell what was going on. All I know is that she wanted you!"

"Thanks, Abbs. Dad and I are on our way." Andy jammed the phone onto the wall-mount and raced out to find Mac.

"We've gotta go! There's some kind of emergency."

Mac had already paid for the coffee. "Is it Abbey or…?"

"No. Nothing like that. It's a couple from town; the Bartlett's. Not sure what's up, but they called."

Mac barely got his car door shut before Andy pulled away from the curb.

The Bartlett place wasn't far, and when they arrived Andy pounded on the door. He and Mac could hear screaming, but no one answered. Andy hollered and tried to force the knob, but it was locked. Mac stood back and punched the door with his foot. The hinge broke, and the door fell away.

Andy and Mac raced inside and found Vera screaming on the floor of the kitchen. Her husband, who was straddling her, was swearing at the top of his lungs and bloodying her face with his fists. Before Andy could blink, Mac leaped at the man and knocked him off balance. The two men tumbled onto the floor, and Mac pinned Clay, a thin, wiry man, onto his stomach.

"Don't hurt him!" Vera yelled. "He's on dialysis! He's a sick man!"

Stunned at her intercession for the man who had just beaten her face in, Mac stared at Vera in disbelief, but he did not move from Clay's back.

Andy dialed the sheriff's office and reported the incident; he hoped he could be heard over Vera's screams in Mac's ear for him to let her husband up.

"You're crazy, lady, if you think I'm going to let him loose," Mac growled.

"But he's sick!" she insisted. And Mac spat back, "He's sick, all right! But he's not getting up until the police get here."

The cruiser must not have been far away—or perhaps a neighbor had already called before Andy had. The deputy stepped over the wreck of the front door and ran to the kitchen.

"Whoa! What's going on in here?" he demanded.

Andy hurried to introduce himself. "I'm Reverend Andy Garrett, Vera's pastor. I'm the one who telephoned. We got a call from Vera that she was in trouble, so we came right over. When we heard screaming and no one came to the door, we broke the door in and called you. And Clay, here, (that's her husband) had her pinned down on the floor and was beating her face in. We pulled him off, and then you came."

For the first time, Andy noticed a cooking pan on the floor and spaghetti splattered all over the kitchen. The dishes from the dinner table had been swept onto the linoleum, too. And a carton of milk lay on its side in a puddle. *What a mess!* Andy imagined Clay storming through the room, wreaking havoc in his wake.

And then, as Andy pulled a chair upright, he saw the toe of a timid tennis shoe withdraw into the shadow of the pantry. Andy crossed the kitchen and quietly peered around the corner to find the Bartlett's little boy, no more than five years old, huddled in the shadows.

Andy had seen the boy a couple of times, but he didn't know if Quinn remembered him. Andy eased down into a crouch and smiled.

"Hi," he said. The frightened eyes broke his heart, and Andy held out his arms. Quinn didn't hesitate; he reached for Andy, and Andy pulled him into all the comfort he could give.

Andy wanted to run out the door with him, to take him away, far from the violence. But he could not. Instead, he moved with the boy to the far side of the kitchen, away from the drama still playing out.

The deputy was frowning. "Okay, ma'am," he said, "I'm Deputy Harnish. I need you to tell me what happened."

Vera sobbed, "Please make that man let my husband up! He's a sick man. He's on dialysis, and that man shouldn't be sitting on him."

"All right, ma'am," Harnish said, and he motioned for Mac to let Clay up.

Mac released him, and Clay pushed himself off the floor with a balled fist, ready to punch Mac. The deputy was faster, however, and he slapped handcuffs on the aggressor and shoved him into one of the kitchen chairs.

"Look, mister," Harnish growled at him, "whether you're sick or not, if you don't stop fighting, I'm going to let that guy sit on you, again. Do you hear me?"

Clay glared and heaved his chest, but he did not move.

"Now," the deputy said to Vera, "let's hear what happened."

Vera continued to cry, and her tears mingled with the blood that smeared across her face. "It's my fault," she sobbed. "It's my fault!"

"Look, lady," Harnish said, "there's nothing you could do that deserves a beating. What started all of this?" He handed Vera one of the dish towels from the counter, so she could wipe her face and dry her tears.

With a quaver in her voice, Vera answered. "Clay likes his lunch right at Noon, and I was on the phone and didn't get things served right away. I know I should have hung up and called my sister back, but we were about done."

Harnish interrupted. "All of this was because dinner was a couple of minutes late?" He snorted in disbelief. "Lady, do you know how sick that is? This is not normal. Nobody deserves to have their face bashed in because dinner's a little late. I hope you're going to press charges."

Vera shook her head, "Oh, no. I don't want to press any charges." She looked at her husband for approval.

Clay returned a sullen glare and then rose up from his chair and shouted at the deputy, "I'm the one who wants to press charges! These two beat my door down, and this one laid his hands on me!"

Harnish stared at him.

That's when Andy said, "I'll press charges. I saw the whole thing. Where do I sign?"

Vera pleaded with Andy to let it go. "He didn't mean it," she insisted. "If I'd hung up when I should have, none of this would have happened. It's my fault!"

But Andy was adamant. "Vera, you called me, and I came. And I'm pressing charges."

Harnish sat at the table and wrote up the on-scene report. Andy, still holding the clinging child, read it and signed it.

"You'll get a call when this goes to court," Harnish said. "Thanks."

The deputy lifted Clay from his chair and led him out the door and into the squad car.

A neighbor woman, who was watching from the Bartlett porch, asked if Vera was okay. At sight of the child, the woman held out her arms. Quinn knew her and moved quickly from Andy's neck to hers. Andy felt confident that the neighbor would help Vera and the boy, and he nodded for Mac to go to the car. Before he left, however, Andy told Vera he was sorry he hadn't got here sooner. And Mac apologized for the broken door. He also pulled out a couple of large bills to pay for the damage. Wide-eyed, Vera took the money. (*She'll probably use it for bail money,* Andy thought. But he said nothing.)

"Call me at the office, tomorrow, Vera," Andy said. "I'll be glad to talk, then, okay?"

Vera didn't look at Andy, but she nodded. And the men left.

Back at the parsonage, Andy gave Abbey the bare details—just enough to quell her concern about Vera's hysterical call. But Andy didn't want to talk about it.

"Let's eat supper. I don't want my stomach upset again with that stuff," Andy said.

Mac broached the subject a couple of times during the meal and saw that Andy was serious about not wanting to talk.

But on the drive to Bible study, Mac could hold it in no longer.

"Can you believe that guy beat his wife for something so stupid?" Mac snorted. "And in front of her kid, too!"

Andy's muscles tightened, and he immediately prayed for help. Talk of the Bartlett's fight pulled acid into his stomach, and Andy wanted it to stop. But his dad went on.

Mac sounded self-righteous and condemning, and Andy clenched his jaw. He thought to himself, my dad saw the same thing I saw at the Bartlett's, but he saw it through an entirely different lens. Mac had seen—*but not felt*—the trembling child. Mac had seen only the bully that he had subdued.

In Andy's mind, the image of Clay's bloodied fists over Vera's face would not go away. Andy had always pictured blood and sickening punches in his youth, even though his father had never touched his mother during their fights. His parents' verbal violence had held the same power in his childhood imagination as the physical episode of this afternoon. As a small child, who had forced his fingers into his ears to block out the yells and the violent trashing of his own house, the scenes at the Bartlett home had been just as vivid.

Andy wanted to scream at his father, now, and only the mighty force of God and self-control held him in check. Andy knew that his father had no idea what the fight this afternoon had done to him. And now Mac wanted to talk about it with an air of arrogant detachment. Andy forced himself to take a deep breath and remain calm.

"Yes," Andy finally said, "it was awful."

Andy pulled the car into a spot near the church door. Choir director Marilyn Ingraham waved, and Abbey hurried out of the car to catch up with her. Andy didn't know if Abbey was hurrying out of the car to leave him alone to talk with his father, or not. And he wondered if they should talk. But there really wasn't time.

Even so, Andy didn't move. Mac was still berating the Bartletts, and Andy didn't want other church members to overhear. The Bartlett incident was not for general discussion.

"I hope they throw the book at that guy when you go to court," Mac said. He sounded proud that Andy would be upholding justice, like a soldier with a cause.

Andy simply said, "Yeah."

Mac looked puzzled by his son's tight-lipped response.

"So, what's wrong with that?" he demanded.

"Nothing, Dad," Andy said. "Nothing at all."

Now, Mac was frustrated. "I don't get it. What did I say?"

Andy massaged the tenseness in his neck and sighed. He knew he had to answer; he had to, somehow, make his dad understand. But he didn't know where to start, and he didn't have much time. They were supposed to be in the church.

Finally, Andy said, "Dad, that incident this afternoon is not for public discussion. Let's just keep it to ourselves."

Then Andy took a breath. "And Dad," he said, "what we saw this afternoon just about tore me to pieces. I wanted to shake that guy and yell in his face to stop."

Mac mouthed something akin to an amen, and Andy's breathing became uneven. He didn't trust himself, now, not to yell in his anger.

But he forged ahead, anyway. "Dad, you don't know how many times when I was a kid that I wanted to shake you, too, and yell *stop* in your face! But I was too little and too scared of you."

Mac fell back in his seat, and the righteous arrogance left his face. Andy could see that his father was stunned and rapidly taking stock of the past.

Andy continued, with chin quivering, "You and Mom used to scream at each other like those two did, today. And you might as well have hit Mom, for the impact it had on me and Molly. We were just little kids, Dad! We were just little kids who didn't know what to do."

Andy saw his dad stiffen. He could tell that Mac suddenly saw it all. For the first time, his father saw the fighting of the past through the eyes of a child who was just like little Quinn Bartlett—a poor, innocent child caught up in his parents' senseless hatred.

"No!" Mac cried out. "No! It wasn't supposed to be like that. It wasn't supposed to be that way. It was US, not you!"

And then Mac whispered, "I never saw you."

Andy gritted his teeth to keep from saying anything more.

"I'm sorry, son!" Mac cried. "I never knew! I always thought it was just your mom and me. We never knew!"

And then Mac's voice broke.

In that instant, Andy's replay of his anger and hurt paused—like the freeze-frame of a home movie. And the image on the screen of his mind panned wider—wide enough so Andy could see past his own hurt to the bigger hurt, the hurt of his dad. *So much pain,* Andy thought. *So much hurt.*

And in the same way that Mac had finally caught the image of his past fights through the lens of his children's eyes, Andy was suddenly able to see beyond his hurts through the lens of a healing God. Andy's built-up anger dissolved. And the child in the corner of his memory grew into a man who watched Mac and Rachel fight, with pity in his eyes. And Andy knew what he had to do.

As Mac held his face in his hands, Andy reached over and put his hand on his dad's arm. He whispered, "I forgive you, Dad." And Mac began to weep. Together, they cried.

A soft knock on the car window startled Andy, and he rubbed a sleeve over his eyes before rolling down the window.

"Are you two all right?" asked Danny Hart.

Andy realized that Danny and others from the church had passed the car as he and his father had been crying. Andy was supposed to be inside, now, starting the Bible study. He wiped his tears, again, and gathered his notes and Bible.

"We're fine, Danny," he said, with a little smile. "I'll be in, in a minute."

Danny nodded and moved on, and Andy opened his door. But Mac stayed in the car.

"I need more time, Son," Mac managed to say.

"It's okay, Dad," Andy said. And he left him.

CHAPTER SEVENTEEN

UNWELCOME ECHOES

Paul's leg was better, but he still couldn't crouch long enough to do the milking. Phillip continued with that chore for now. Paul could sleep in a bit longer in the mornings.

Phillip watched the milk squirt into the pail between his legs, and Mac spilled more feed into the trough. Mac had been quiet, but now he announced, "I've decided to keep the place up north, and I'll be heading back up there, soon."

Phillip raised his head in surprise. "Why the change of heart?" he asked. But Mac just shrugged.

"It's better this way," Mac said. "The kids don't need me around. They've got their own lives to live."

Phillip hoped Mac would change his mind, because he knew his kids would worry as they had before he'd come to the farm. They had enough on their plates, right now. But he could see that Mac didn't want to pursue the matter. Phillip didn't probe.

At Molly's lunch table, Mac remained subdued. He picked at his food, excused himself early, and disappeared into his bedroom.

Molly and Paul quizzed Phillip with their eyes. Did he know what was wrong with Mac? Phillip frowned, but shook his head. He didn't mention Mac's plan to leave. That was Mac's news, if he really meant it. Phillip was angry about it.

For the rest of the day, Mac remained aloof. Then Phillip winced when, at the evening meal, Mac brusquely announced his intention to go back to Herndon.

Phillip caught the concern in Molly's eyes, and he heard it in her measured response: "Sure, Dad, if that's what you want. But you need to know you're always welcome here."

"Yeah," said Mac tersely. "Thanks." And Phillip grit his teeth.

Phillip wondered what had changed Mac's mind and set this distance between him and his family. One minute Mac was planning to stay in the area permanently and, the next, he was announcing that he was going to leave. Phillip didn't get it.

"City guys!" he spat, under his breath.

That night, Mac's old nightmare returned. In the dream's grip, he relived the horror of the night Little Mac had died. But this time, Mac didn't scream out, like he had when he'd first come to the farm. No one awakened, except him. He sat dripping in sweat, with his heart pounding.

In the bathroom, Mac ran a cloth over his face, but the old sense of guilt would not leave him. He tried to will away the memory of Little Mac's death, but it wouldn't go. Nor would the echoes of his fights with Rachel. He was haunted by the eyes of his children, who he imagined cowering under the barrage of nightly verbal assaults.

Mac returned to the bedroom. The Bible on the edge of the nightstand lay open where he had left off reading. He saw it, there, and swept it to the floor. Then he threw himself prone on the mattress and jerked the covers over his face.

It was no use, Mac despaired. Nothing had really changed.

Something's wrong with Dad," Molly told Andy, over the phone. "He shuts us out and seems angry. I feel like the old Dad is back, and it scares me."

Then she added, "And Dad told us, last night, that he's moving back to Herndon. Did something happen, yesterday, while he was in Cherish?"

"That's a big yes," Andy replied. And he told her about the Bartletts.

"That little Bartlett boy was me," Andy said. "I wanted so badly to take Quinn home. I wanted him to never have to go through that again. But of course, I couldn't take him.

"And then afterward, Dad kept harping on how awful those people were to fight in front of their child. When I couldn't stand it, anymore, I vented. I told Dad that he and Mom hadn't been any different, and that you and I had been as hurt and helpless in the face of their fighting as that Bartlett boy had been in that food-splashed kitchen. And it stopped Dad in his tracks.

"I know it seems impossible, but I know that Mom and Dad never knew how their fighting hurt us. I doubt that Dad would have ever known if we hadn't gone to the Bartlett's."

Andy asked Molly, "Did Dad say anything to you about the Bartlett fight or our talk?"

Molly said, "No. I doubt that he knows what to say after all of that." Molly could only imagine what was going on inside of her father's head. The man had barely resolved his own hurt, and now he had his children's hurts to deal with, too—hurts he had never known existed. No wonder he was running away from them.

"Andy," she said, "we can't let him go home. We have to go through this with him. We all have stuff to resolve. I worry that he thinks it's all his fault. He doesn't see that we were all victims of the same hurt. We can't leave him alone, in this. We've already seen how badly he handled the guilt of Little Mac's death. He won't handle this any better. He'll just bottle it all up—and die."

"You're right," Andy sighed. "We can't let him go home. And we need to pray."

Opal asked if Mac was sick. "I noticed that he wasn't in church on Sunday. And other people have asked about him, too," she said.

Andy wasn't surprised that everyone had noticed. And he wasn't sure what to say. Finally, he told Opal, "My Dad's working out some things. I'm sure he'll be back soon. Thanks for asking and for saying a prayer or two."

Andy knew that Opal and other church members would continue to speculate. But he also knew that theirs was a loving concern, and he didn't begrudge it.

Opal gave a little nod, and sensing that it was a sensitive subject, she directed her focus back to work. "Since you're here," she said, "I want to cross-check the dates and times for Easter Week services for the April newsletter. Can you run through it with me?"

"It'll be like last year," Andy confirmed. "Wednesday Bible study will be canceled, and we'll meet Thursday for seven o'clock communion. There will be two services on Sunday: sunrise at seven and worship service at ten-thirty. Breakfast and the children's Easter egg hunt will be in between. No Sunday school."

Opal clicked the details into her typewriter. And she wrote in capital letters "HE IS RISEN" in the calendar square for April nineteenth.

She also had her poem ready, but Andy didn't seem to be in the mood. She left him alone. Besides, it wasn't her usual bit of humor. Today's poem was more serious. Opal reviewed the piece, herself, and typed it into the empty column she had reserved for it.

THE DAY THAT DEATH DID DIE
By Opal Reese

Dark like night, the sun grew black,
And all of nature mourned
To see the Son of God hang down
And suffer tree and thorn.

All the hope in the One who'd loved,
In the One who'd healed and fed,
Did die that day when the sky did cry
And love and sorrow bled.

But then, O joy!, the morning came
On the day that Death did die,
For the Lord flashed up into the dawn
And from the earth did fly!

Redeeming thunder shook the grave,
And all the soldiers fell
And trembled like the quaking stone
That thought to bottle hell.

And on His wings that Easter morn,
The day my Savior rose,
The fledgling spirits of the deep
Rode high as Heaven goes.

O praise the day that Death did die,
And praise the Lord above,
Who raised Forever in its place
With sacrifice of love.

CHAPTER EIGHTEEN

PRE-EASTER

Abbey had had no idea how much time Molly might spend with June Green before coming to the house. Molly had come to Cherish to take June some farm produce—including a big Easter ham—as a thank you for the use of her baby furnishings after the fire. Abbey hurried through her grocery shopping, even though she knew Molly had a key to the parsonage.

Sure enough, Molly's car was in the drive when Abbey pulled in and started pulling sacks of groceries from the trunk. Abbey elbowed her way into the kitchen and found Molly on the phone.

"I just don't know," Molly was saying. She entreated Abbey with her eyes, as if to say, "you need to get this."

Abbey set her bags on the table.

"Hang on," Molly said to the caller. "Abbey's just come in. I'll let you talk to her."

Molly put her hand over the receiver and whispered, "I answered because I thought it was you, since you were late. But instead, it's somebody named Georgia."

Abbey rolled her eyes. Some of a pastor's wife's responsibilities were obvious, like occasionally leading the ladies' prayer group or substituting for a sick Sunday school teacher. But some responsibilities were subtle, like fielding telephone calls from people like Georgia Wheeler. Unfortunately, Georgia refused to call the church office, since she had learned early on that Opal was an expert in handling her probing.

Unlike the first time Georgia had telephoned the parsonage during the day, this time Abbey was prepared. She took the receiver from Molly and untwisted some of the cord before answering.

"Yes, Georgia, how are you, today?" Abbey asked lightly. "We're all fine, thank you. How may I help you?"

Abbey tried not to let Georgia's whiney voice grate on her nerves.

"Well," said Georgia, "I hear that Grace Harper has a doctor's appointment in Harmony, next week. What kind of difficulties is she having, anyway?"

Georgia's first call to the parsonage, over a year ago, had come when Ernie Shiplett's prostate exam and scan had been scheduled. Ernie hadn't broadcast the reason for his trip to the doctor, but Georgia had thought it was her duty to pray for him—and she had demanded "to know the facts, first," so she could "pray intelligently and specifically." Abbey hadn't wanted to lie (she was tempted to say she didn't know why Ernie had an appointment, and she certainly didn't want Georgia telling others that "the pastor's wife told me…"), so Abbey had decided to tell Georgia that Ernie didn't want the details known at this time.

That had intrigued Georgia, no end, and had set in motion a vast whispering campaign of speculation. In the end, Ernie had been just as embarrassed to have to tell dozens of people that the test had shown nothing was wrong as he would have been to have had the prayer chain broadcasting and repeating the reason for his appointment prior to the exam.

This time, Abbey simply said, "Georgia, Grace has already shared that with several friends. I'm sure she'll share with you, too, if she feels it's necessary. Besides, God will know what you're praying about if you want to lift this up in prayer without knowing the specifics. God is pretty awesome that way, you know."

Then Abbey added, "Now tell me, Georgia, how's your daughter's acid-reflux treatment coming along?"

By redirecting the discussion to one of Georgia's favorite topics—either her own illnesses or those of her family—Abbey was able to turn the gossip back on the gossiper. When Abbey hung up, she was fairly proud of herself.

Molly giggled. "That was interesting!" she said. "I had no idea what to say when she started questioning me about somebody named Grace. And she wanted to know every detail about how Paul and I were doing and how you and Andy had been able to cope with such a difficult situation—'having everyone crowded into that woefully small parsonage.' And she was determined to find out all about dad's past, and how he had come to respond to the altar call, and why he had missed church last Sunday. She had heard something about Andy and Dad crying in the car on Wednesday night."

Abbey said, "If Georgia would spend half as much time in helping with the ladies' mission circle or in studying her Sunday school lesson as she puts into getting to know everybody's business, she would be a great help. Instead, she just takes up everybody's time by passing around bits of half-information and rumors that are best left alone."

Georgia was already part of the official church prayer chain, but she regularly persisted in pursuing other concerns that sometimes people didn't want to have shared. Legitimate prayer requests included those like the one Abbey had received earlier, today. Leo Ryan was heading to Harmony's doctors in hopes of curing two days of hiccups. Leo was an inveterate talker, and the hiccups had been sorely inhibiting the exercise of his overly-free expression. (In spite of his malady, Opal said Leo had taken twenty-five minutes to explain the problem to her and ask to be added to the prayer list.)

Grace Harper's request had been a private matter, however, and was not for the prayer chain. According to Grace's wishes, Abbey and Andy would lift up her "female problem" to the Lord in their personal prayers, and it was unlikely that Georgia would ever hear the reason.

Abbey hoped that Georgia would also never learn any more about Mac than she already knew.

Andy and Molly feared that one morning they would awaken to discover that Mac had left for Herndon in the middle of the night. Night flight would fit a pattern that Mac and Rachel had set on a previous visit. Their parents had left prematurely the first time they had come to see their children. They had announced that they were staying through the weekend, but instead, Mac and Rachel, with Grannie in tow, had unexpectedly left in the wee hours of Saturday morning. A note on the kitchen table had held an apology and a vague mention of an appointment with one of Dad's customers. Andy and Molly had never learned the truth of why they had left so early.

It would be just like Dad to pull something like that now, Molly thought.

She hoped he wouldn't. But just in case, Molly slept each night with an ear on alert, prepared to interrupt such a plan if Mac were to try it.

Andy was relieved when Mac showed up in church on Palm Sunday. Although his dad sat way in the back instead of in his usual middle-row seat near the front, Andy was glad he had come. Hopefully his coming, today, wasn't a goodbye, a last visit before he moved away.

Andy tried not to think about it as he rose to bring the morning's message.

The children's choir had already processed down the aisle with palm fronds and hosannas. And Andy now provided an overview of all the things the Jewish people of Jesus' day had expected the Messiah to be.

"We sometimes think we know everything God is planning and doing," Andy said, "until we discover that we have it all wrong. And yet God's plan goes forward, regardless of what we think."

Mac's eyes never looked up as Andy spoke.

"Are you coming for dinner?" Abbey called loudly to Mac before he could reach his car. He had not gone through the line to shake Andy's hand, and she had followed him.

Mac turned and sighed. "Sure," he said quietly. "I'll be there."

Andy wondered where his dad went after church. He didn't show up at the parsonage for nearly an hour, and Andy and Abbey had almost given up.

When they finally spied the Lincoln pulling into the drive, Abbey quickly pulled the roast from the oven, stirred the cornstarch into the pan juices, and made the gravy. By the time Mac washed his hands everything was on the table.

Andy offered prayer. And then the roast was passed in silence.

Oh, God, Andy prayed. *What are we supposed to be doing, here? What do You have in mind? Help me to know what to say and what not to say to my dad. We need to mend this hurt. We can't go on this way.*

Andy had barely finished his prayer when Mac cleared his throat and said, "This is good, Abbey. Thanks."

"You're welcome, Dad," Abbey returned, with a smile. "We've missed you."

Mac shrugged. A struggle played over his face, and he replied, "I've missed you, too."

It was another minute before Mac cleared his throat, again. "I just needed to think some stuff over," he said.

"That's fine, Dad," Andy offered. "It's okay."

Now Mac spoke quickly. "No. It isn't okay. I wasn't okay. And I'm not sure I'm okay, now. I-I just don't have it all straight in my head, yet."

"There's a lot of stuff to think about, Dad," Andy said quietly. "I understand. I've had a lot to think over, too. It's been a long few days."

Abbey passed the dinner rolls in silence.

"How's that kid from that house?" Mac suddenly asked, to change the subject. "Have you gone to court yet?"

"Not yet. It's set for this Tuesday."

Mac stared at his plate. "I just want you to know…" he began and then stopped.

Andy knew his dad was searching for the right words.

"I just want you and your sister to know that I wish I could turn back time." Mac's voice was tight. "I wish we could have—I wish I could have—been a better father to you kids. I never really thought about how our lives must have looked to you and Molly."

Mac's lips were dry. "I made a mess of everything!"

Mac pursed his lips firmly. "I don't know how you kids can ever forgive us for all the garbage your mother and I put you through. I keep seeing the little boy in that kitchen the other day and then seeing into the past with you and Molly. I imagine you hearing your mom and me fight, night after night. I can't understand how you turned out like you did."

He said evenly, "Every time you see me you must be reminded of all that horrible stuff. I don't want you to have to relive that all the time. So, I'm leaving tomorrow, to go back home. If I'm gone, you won't have to be reminded of it anymore."

Andy sat back in his chair and set his jaw.

"No, Dad. You're not going," Andy said. His tone was reminiscent of the one his father had used on Andy as a teenager. "Your going away won't make anything different. Our past together is still OUR past. It doesn't go away just because one of us leaves.

"What we need, instead, Dad, is to deal with this. We need to talk it out and face it. If we don't, it's going to be just like how you and Mom handled—or rather didn't handle—Little Mac's death. I can't let you bury this. It won't stay buried. It'll come out in ways that are even more harmful. If you go away we'll ALL be having nightmares we can't get rid of. We have to talk about this, Dad."

Mac gripped his table napkin.

"Dad," Andy said. "I know you feel guilty for all of this. And I know you wish you could turn back time. But it doesn't work that way. Time doesn't go in two directions, and we have to make our future, now. We have to leave the past in the past. It's still there to visit and learn from, but we can't let it rule us. If we do, we'll find we have no future. We won't be moving forward and making something new."

Then Andy said, "Dad, you need to know that I love you. It's not always been easy to love you, but I've never stopped loving you. And Dad, I need you! I need the father that God is shaping you to be."

Now Mac wept. "I don't know who I am, anymore!" he cried. "For a little bit, there, I thought I was free. But now all this mess has been dragged up from the past, and I feel like I'm right back where I was. I don't feel free, anymore. I just don't feel free."

Andy said, "Dad, it takes a lot of work to sort through this kind of stuff. It's-it's just like when you sorted through some of Mom's stuff and brought it to Molly's. You didn't want to look at it, anymore, because it hurt too much. You didn't want to be reminded. But there was stuff, there, that had to come out.

"In the same way, we need to sort through this stuff from the past. We need to clean out that closet and box it up. And then we need to bring it to Jesus. We HAVE to give it to Him. He's the only One who can handle it. And when Jesus takes it, He'll get rid of it. He'll get rid of it in a way we can't do for ourselves."

Andy then said, "I'll grant you, it may take us time to sort through this much stuff and pack it all up. It won't happen overnight. And there's no way we can get it all into one box. We need to pack it a little at a time, as we're able, and then bring it to Jesus—one box at a time."

Mac seemed to think about that. Finally, he said, "You're saying that you and I—you and I and Molly— can work on this together?"

"Yeah, Dad," Andy said. "We all need to work on it. We have to do this together."

Mac took a deep breath. When he let it out, he said, "Okay, son. I'll try."

CHAPTER NINETEEN

GENEVA AND GONDOLA

After his appearance at the courthouse, Andy described the experience for Abbey, including how nervous he had been and how he hadn't been prepared for Orville Taggert's role in the courtroom. Bailiff Taggert had sworn Andy in, complete with a Bible—and a floppy sleeve.

"I knew Orville had only one hand," Andy said. "I knew it. I've known for as long as we've lived here that he got caught up in that hay baler when he was a teenager. But I just wasn't prepared for the empty sleeve when he held out the Bible and raised his right arm and said 'repeat after me.' I guess it was nerves, but I had to beat back my impulse to laugh out loud. I'm still surprised I didn't!"

"I'm glad you didn't, Andy Garrett!" Abbey chided. "And you, a minister!"

"Well, I didn't!" Andy protested. "And I got through my statement, okay."

And then Andy said, "But it didn't matter. They let Clay go. I think it was a mistake. But Vera showed up, all sweet-faced and smiley, and she convinced the judge that it was all a misunderstanding and that her nosebleed had made it look worse than it was. She told the judge all about Clay's dialysis and how he was very sick. I just shook my head. There wasn't anything I could do."

Abbey shook her head, too. "It's hard to imagine that any woman would put up with that—sick husband or no sick husband. Sadly, I think abused women are as mentally ill as their abusers."

Andy agreed. He hoped he would never hear of Clay beating Vera, again. And he was pretty sure that Vera would never call him, again.

Children were running everywhere. Little Lizzie Potts stopped long enough to thrust her colorful basket of pink grass and plastic eggs up for Andy to see.

"Wow!" Andy exclaimed. "You must have found every egg in the churchyard!"

Lizzie grinned. Then her Easter curls bounced, and she dashed away to find more eggs before breakfast was served.

The boys were faster, and their parents had to snag them in so there would be enough eggs for the littler kids to find. Some of the children had been half-asleep during the sunrise service, but all were wide-awake now for the hunt.

The weather was perfect. Unlike last year when it had rained during the early service, this morning's sun had blazed over the horizon at just the right moment to herald, "*Up from the grave, He arose!*" The burst of daylight had made it easy to visualize the Resurrection and the discovery of the empty tomb. Easter sunrise was a crescendo of promise and hope.

When Andy preached at the ten-thirty service, he saw his father smile at the words of the angel: "*He is not here; He has risen!*" Andy thanked God that Mac was clinging to the work of the Cross and the triumph of the Tomb.

Three cars made up the convoy that headed for the farm after the service. Mac's Lincoln took the lead, followed by Andy and Abbey's car. Then Siege Logan's truck brought up the rear. Siege had been invited for Easter dinner, too.

"My, my!" Siege exclaimed after stuffing himself beyond his normal bachelor fare. "I haven't had a meal like that since I ate at Aunt Sooze's before I graduated from veterinary school! She could outcook anybody from the back hills of Kentucky!"

Siege sank into the sofa and patted his taut belly.

"I didn't know you were from Kentucky!" Andy exclaimed. "Our Grannie was from Kentucky, and she could make fried chicken that was fit to serve in heaven."

"Oh, yeah?" said Siege. "And did she make all-day beans and sweet corn bread?"

Mac bobbed a decided, "Oh, yeah!"

"And," said Siege, "did she ever give you the white-lightning cure?"

That brought laughter, even from Phillip, who had no relatives from Kentucky.

"That stuff could either cure or kill you," Molly said. "I'm surprised we aren't all blind!"

Siege laughed. "Yep, she was from Kentucky! I survived my share of that stuff, too." Then Siege asked, "Have you ever been there?"

"Only once," said Andy. "Our family drove there when my uncle Kermit died. Remember, Dad? We went to the funeral and had supper that night at Grannie's sisters' house."

Mac nodded with a smile. And so did Molly.

Andy continued, "I was young, but I remember it like it was yesterday. To begin with, my mom had put the fear of the switch in me before we got there. I was warned within an inch of my life not to laugh at my aunts' names."

"Oh, the names!" Siege chuckled. "How well I remember the names! My Aunt's sister's name was Beatitude."

And Molly replied, "And our twin aunts were Geneva and Gondola."

"Gondola!" Siege exclaimed. "No wonder your mom had to warn you. I would've had a switchin' for sure!"

When the laughter subsided, Andy elaborated: "Geneva and Gondola were spinsters. And one night they discovered a foundling on their doorstep. That's how we got our Cousin Ever'tt. He was probably five or six years older than I was, and my mom made me promise that when we got there, I would be nice and play with him. But when we got to the house and my grannie told me to go out back and say hi to Ever'tt, I couldn't find him. I finally caught him peeking out at me from behind a tree. He never did come out. I yelled 'Hi, Cousin Ever'tt!' and ended up going back inside. When I asked Grannie what was wrong with him, she said there was nothing to worry about. She crossed her forefingers—like this—and said, 'Ever'tt's okay. He's just got a mind like that.'"

Andy imitated her crossed fingers—the forefinger of one hand crossing the forefinger of the other hand to make an *X*.

Andy then said, "When I asked Grannie what that meant (Andy crossed his forefingers again), she said, 'Oh, Ever'tt's just got his wires crossed!'"

Siege laughed. "My Aunt Sooze had some of those same colorful expressions. I almost wonder if your family came from Moody Holler," he said. "I don't meet many people who 'get it' when I tell my stories. Most people think I'm making them all up."

It was Mac who spoke, next. "And nobody ever crossed Grannie. Not even me!"

"Nobody sassed Aunt Sooze, either," Siege said. "There would've been wrath to come!"

Mac slapped his knees at that and guffawed. Andy thought how good it was to see his father laugh again. There *were* some good memories from the past, after all.

CHAPTER TWENTY

THE BULL

Cherish farmers were divided about the timing of the spring rains. Many were unhappy because they delayed planting. For others, the crops were in, and the rain was a good excuse to discuss current events. The men swapped entrenched opinions at the hardware store while their wives gripped umbrellas and dashed between shops on the other side of the square. Hardware store owner Joe Seese didn't mind that the men argued inside the store entrance, but he did wish they'd buy something.

Showers threatened to last the whole week, but the sun finally peeked through on Thursday morning. The forecast predicted more rain, but the little bit of blue sky was welcome. Clifford Myers decided to take advantage of the break in the weather, and he telephoned the parsonage.

Out of habit, Andy asked Clifford what was wrong.

Everyone knew that disaster clung to the Myerses like old bubble gum on the sole of a Sunday shoe. Only Clifford Myers could shoot his own hound while hunting. (*At least it wasn't his own leg,* Stu Darrell had commented to Andy when he'd heard about that incident.) And only the Myerses could tangle with skunks, back into each other's cars, or install wall-to-wall carpeting before learning that their youngest son was highly allergic to the fiber. The Myerses always suffered more than their share of illnesses, and they broke an astonishing number of bones compared to the general populace.

"What's up?" Andy asked. "What's happened?"

"Nothing's happened, Pastor," Clifford declared in surprise. "Things are just fine. I was calling to see if you'd want to come with me, this morning, when I pick up my new bull."

Andy was so relieved that there was nothing wrong that he said, "Sure!" before he considered his reply. Now, he wondered if he had been rash. Would he be safe in the company of a Myers? In addition, Andy wondered what Clifford might be expecting from him.

Andy ventured, "I don't have to, uh, *do* anything, do I?"

After his experience with Siege Logan and the constipated horse, Andy had learned to be wary about volunteering. Andy envisioned himself and Clifford out in some field chasing a runaway cow for hours. He hoped he hadn't just agreed to do something he would later regret.

Clifford laughed. "I can't think of a thing. Just come and keep me company on the trip."

When Andy announced to Abbey that he was going on the road with Clifford, she wasn't happy.

"Andy! Do you think that's wise?" she asked with a stricken look.

"Just say an extra prayer," he told her with a grin.

When Clifford arrived, Abbey gave Andy an extra-long hug. She whispered a prayer in his ear at the screen door. Then she blew him a kiss as he and Clifford waved goodbye.

As much as he hated to admit it, Andy did worry a little about being on the road with Clifford. What kind of driver was Clifford, anyway? He'd never ridden with him, before.

After a few miles, however, Andy relaxed. It was silly to worry. Clifford was attentive at all crossroads, he didn't exceed the speed limit, the pavement was dry, and the clouds hadn't yet released any rain. Perhaps it would be an uneventful day. Andy asked for God's protection, even so.

"Our destination is near Highway 24," Clifford announced, and Andy calculated that the trip would take about forty-five minutes. *Surely not much can happen in forty-five minutes,* Andy reasoned.

Nothing did. After forty-five uneventful minutes, Clifford pulled his truck and livestock trailer into the drive of an impressive-looking cattle operation. He followed the path to the barn, swung around to the back, and slowed to park by the paddock. Clifford then jumped out. He lowered the trailer gate and pulled down the plank. A man on a dead run shot from the house to meet him.

Andy remained in the cab as Clifford and the farmer huddled over paperwork laid out on the fender. Andy tried not to listen, but it was impossible not to overhear their conversation. He was shocked to learn the price Clifford was paying for the bull. Andy had no idea that cows and pigs could be so expensive. He wondered how much money his brother-in-law, Paul, had invested in his livestock. Andy had never given it a thought, before.

Finally, Clifford and the bull's owner loaded the biggest bull Andy had ever seen into Clifford's trailer. Andy worried only once—when the bull tossed his head and shifted his weight on the ramp. But then the animal had come aboard with little prodding.

After the two men had shaken hands, Clifford climbed into the driver's seat, and soon the truck was back on the road.

Andy was curious about the bull. Clifford told him how much it weighed and gave the animal's breed and pedigree. Andy was impressed. He had known nothing about such things, before.

Finally, Andy asked, "I assume this bull is for breeding, right?"

Clifford confirmed his conclusion. "You bet," he said. "This animal's very valuable—too valuable to just slaughter and eat, if that's what you mean."

Andy asked, "With as much as the bull costs, do you get some kind of insurance?"

"Oh, yeah," said Clifford. "I'll be picking that up on Tuesday."

Andy pressed his concern. "Isn't that a long time to wait, Cliff? When you buy a car, you get insurance right away. Don't you need to do that for this bull?" The more he thought about it the more concerned Andy became. After all, this bull had just been sold to a Myers!

Andy pressed again. "This is only Thursday. Why wait until Tuesday? We could stop, now, on the way home. I'm in no rush to get back."

"Oh, it'll be all right," Clifford drawled. "I've got a field all set for him in the near twenty. We'll just drop him off, and I'll do the insurance later. Besides, I have to get back because I told Louise I'd be home in time to go to her mother's house for supper."

Andy couldn't help but feel apprehensive the rest of the way home. He hoped nothing bad would happen before the bull arrived at that special field Clifford had prepared. Andy whispered a prayer that they would get to the farm safely. He remained uncomfortable until they pulled into the Myerses' drive.

Louise waved as they passed the house on their way down to the field. Andy breathed in relief. There hadn't been a single close call. It hadn't even rained, although the clouds had hung low all afternoon. *Thank you, God,* he prayed.

Even the unloading now proved to be uneventful. Clifford opened the gate to the field he'd assigned to the bull, and the surprisingly docile beast lumbered peacefully down the truck ramp, through the gate, and into his private, lush pasture. Andy and Clifford leaned on the fence for a minute as the animal sought out the best part of the hillside for grazing. The bull seemed utterly indifferent to his new surroundings. If Andy hadn't known that it had just been delivered, he would have thought the bull had been there for years.

Finally, Clifford drove Andy back to the parsonage and returned home to get ready for dinner at his mother-in-law's.

Andy reported to Abbey, "You should have seen the size of that bull!" Then he added, "And yet, he was surprisingly easy to manage."

Abbey hugged him tightly, glad to know he was safe. Andy got the impression that she'd spent his entire absence praying, and he thought, again, how well the trip had gone.

Andy informed Abbey how much the animal had cost, and she was as impressed as he had been.

"All the more reason that I'm glad things went well, today," Abbey said.

"It does seem strange that nothing happened, doesn't it?" Andy laughed. "After all, it involved a Myers."

But then, Andy frowned.

He cocked his head at a niggling thought. "I sure hope that bull's not a disappointment on the breeding end of things."

That's stupid of me, he thought. *I'm being silly, now. I have no reason to suspect the bull is a dud.*

Andy swept the entire subject out of his mind—or thought he had. Unfortunately, the beast dominated his dreams, that night. It didn't help that the predicted rain and thunder finally rolled in with a bang and also punctuated his sleep.

"I spent the whole night replaying scenes of *Ferdinand, The Bull* and bull fights," Andy grumbled when he got up the next morning. "I kept imagining the Myerses' bull was like the cartoon character, Ferdinand, and that he didn't have the slightest interest in lady cows."

"*Lady cows* is redundant," Abbey corrected him.

"You know what I mean," he replied.

As Andy ate breakfast and finished dressing he pushed thoughts of the bull from his mind. But when he headed for the door the telephone rang. Abbey answered it and whispered, "It's Clifford Myers!"

Andy hurried to the phone.

When Abbey heard him cry, "Oh, no! Oh, NO!" she was certain someone was in the hospital, or worse.

"What is it?" she asked when Andy hung up the phone. "Who's hurt?"

"You won't believe it," Andy said. "It's the Myers' bull. It was hit by lightning, last night; they found him dead in the pasture this morning!"

"No!" Abbey exclaimed.

"I couldn't make this up," Andy insisted. "Why, oh why, didn't Clifford listen to me about getting that insurance, right away?"

Abbey sighed, too. She had prayed for Andy, and she had prayed for Clifford—but she'd never once thought to pray for the bull.

CHAPTER TWENTY-ONE

SIEGE MAKES HIS MOVE

The next Friday, Andy awoke and frowned. Abbey was away at the women's retreat in Ft. Marshall. She had spent the night, there, and Andy was on his own for breakfast. He didn't like his own cooking, and cold cereal didn't sound appealing. So, Andy decided he would dress early for the office and go to the Star Diner.

He brushed his teeth and pulled on his clothes, but the start of the day wasn't the same without Abbey's warmth and laughter. With only Winston for company, the house was too quiet.

By this time there should be bacon frying in the kitchen and buttered toast on the table. The coffee should be hot, and Winston should be begging for a handout—even though his dish held a generous amount of dogfood.

Abbey wasn't here to straighten Andy's collar and say a little prayer before he left for work. And he missed her soft goodbye kiss as he headed out the door.

Andy was glad that Abbey would be home for supper. Winston would be glad, too. The normally playful dog had glumly padded to his pillow when he had seen that Andy was leaving.

Downtown Cherish was bustling. What a surprise! Andy had had no idea the diner would be this crowded. Did everyone in Tobler County eat here for breakfast?

Everybody seemed to include Siege Logan. The vet sat alone in a booth, half-asleep. Andy walked over and slid in across from him.

"You aren't expecting anybody, are you?" he asked.

Siege yawned and shook his head. The vet looked like he'd either just awakened or hadn't yet been to bed.

He mumbled, "Sorry, if I'm not good company. I just got in from a call about three minutes ago. Been up all night. Since I missed supper, I decided to eat breakfast before hitting the hay. I've got to get in a little sleep before small-animal office hours, this afternoon."

Siege stretched and yawned again, and a tuft of hair that stuck out the back of his cap made him look like a little boy. Andy respected Siege's need for quiet and didn't start up any conversation.

In a couple of minutes, however, the waitress arrived to take their orders.

"Hi, Doc. What'll it be, today?" came the lilting voice of the server whose name badge read "Doreen." Doreen poured a steaming cup of coffee for both of them.

"You want the waffles, egg, and sausage, as usual?" she asked Siege with a cock of her head and a broad smile.

Siege nodded, and she murmured a sweet, "Sure 'nough, hon!"

Then she turned a dim eye on Andy. "What'll it be for you?" she asked. Her voice had lost its lilt, and she seemed distracted.

Andy gave his order and hoped she had heard him. Her attention had been on the veterinarian, who was now nearing unconsciousness. Andy doubted that Siege even knew Doreen was still there.

When she announced, "Got it," and picked up the coffee pot, Doreen flashed another smile in Siege's direction and called out, brightly, "Be right back!"

Andy couldn't resist. Siege roused, and Andy teased him.

"So," Andy said, "how long has Doreen been bobbing that ponytail in your direction?"

Siege reddened slightly and mumbled, "She does that every time I come in here. I think she likes me."

"Have you asked her out, yet?" Andy asked with a wink.

"Ask her out? Who said anything about asking her out?"

"What? Are you dating somebody else I don't know about?" Andy teased again.

Siege shook his head with a sleepy chuckle and said, "Who's got time to date?"

Andy had to admit that with farm calls at all hours and a small-animal practice to keep up, Siege didn't have a minute to himself, let alone time for a date. Andy felt sorry for the guy.

"Maybe someday you can take on a partner and grab a day off," Andy suggested.

Siege yawned and said, "Yeah, someday."

A few minutes later, Doreen swept in with waffles and sausage and a sunshine smile that she cast over only half of the diner booth.

"This should perk you up, hon," she said to the vet with a sympathetic smile.

Siege managed a half-smile, in return. And when Doreen moved on to the next table, he mumbled in mock sweetness, just loud enough for Andy to hear, "Thanks, hon!"

Andy laughed.

That night Andy beat Winston to the door to welcome Abbey home. Her hug felt good.

"Did you miss me?" she asked, and Andy's decided, "yes!" was followed by a passionate kiss.

Winston did his best to get in on the hug and was finally rewarded with a scruff of his ears and a rub of his belly.

"How about some spaghetti, salad, and garlic bread for supper?" Abbey asked. "I've been hungry for that, all day."

Andy sighed contently. "Perfect! I'll help with the salad."

Things were getting back to normal. In his mind, Andy said, "Thanks, Hon!"—and he meant it, with all his heart.

But even though things returned to normal at the parsonage, the network news reminded Andy that the world outside of Cherish was in turmoil. In the past weeks, an escaped criminal had shot the Pope during a public audience in Vatican Square, there were IRA attacks and hunger strikes in Northern Ireland, and there were shelling deaths at a beach in Beirut. And Horace Saunders never let a word of bad news go to waste.

The church-hopping farmer, with his obsession on The End Times, fed on all of the news reports and drew connecting lines to every prophecy in Scripture, no matter how remote. Then, in the hour before his standing barber appointment on the first Thursday of every month, Horace would pepper Andy with his conjectures, and he would challenge Andy to disagree that they were all living in the throes of the Tribulation period.

Andy made little headway during these discussions. Horace viewed the world from a balcony and believed that, somehow, as the End Times judgements unfolded, he would be untouched and could pontificate to his neighbors about the happenings, because he had read them in the book of Revelation.

Andy did his best, as always, to remind Horace that the goal of prophecy was not to speculate and view evil from afar, but to prompt those who read the warnings in Scripture to come to Christ's salvation while there was still time.

For all of Horace's study of the Bible, Andy observed with sorrow that the man knew less than Andy's father about the goal of faith in Christ. At least Mac knew that God was in the business of saving lives and changing hearts, even if Mac didn't yet feel he was making progress fast enough.

Usually Lizzie Potts was alone (except for Butter) on the front porch when Abbey came home from grocery shopping. But this afternoon it was later than usual, and since school was done for the day, Lizzie's brother Stevie sat waiting, too. Butter sat between them, with the tip of his plush tail swishing, every so often.

Abbey unloaded the groceries from the car and set them on the table in the kitchen. Then she opened the front door and invited her visitors in. Butter squeezed between Lizzie's legs and entered, first, doing his best to avoid Winston.

Everyone headed straight for the kitchen. The children knew you could only eat cookies, there, or outside; crumbs were not acceptable in the living room. Lizzie and Stevie settled into their chairs, and from the seat of another chair, Butter glared at Winston. Winston stared back--from a distance.

Abbey poured glasses of milk and was getting ready to hand a cookie to Stevie when she noticed that his hands were already full, with a spotted salamander.

"Now that's a handsome fellow!" she said in surprise.

"This is Spotty. I got him in your window well," Stevie announced proudly.

"I thought he looked familiar," Abbey replied as calmly as she could. "But I think you may want to put Spotty down and wash your hands before you eat a cookie."

Abbey provided a stainless-steel mixing bowl to house Spotty while Stevie ate.

"We're going to Grandma and Grandpa's tonight" Lizzie announced with her mouth full, "and we get to stay all day, tomorrow. And Stevie can't take his sala'nder."

"Yeah," Stevie acknowledged with a pout. "Dad says I have to let Spotty go before we leave, because we'll be gone a long time and he'll get homesick."

Abbey shook her head at his disappointment. "Maybe you could put him back in the window well, so he'll still be there when you get back," she suggested.

Stevie hadn't thought of that. He brightened. "Sure!" he said enthusiastically.

Now that he'd finished his cookies and drunk his milk, Stevie picked Spotty out of the mixing bowl and held him while Lizzie finished her treats.

Abbey wondered if Spotty would still be in the window well, when Stevie returned. She had no idea how the creatures got into the window wells, in the first place, so she had no clue if they stayed put once they were there. It would be interesting to find out.

Abbey also noticed that neither Butter nor Winston had any interest in the salamander. They were too fixated on each other, caught up in their mutual dislike.

In fact, the dog and cat were so absorbed in one another that Mac's early arrival for supper stirred an unexpected series of events. Abbey had known Mac was coming, but nothing could have prepared her for the spontaneous combustion his arrival initiated.

At the sound of Mac's voice in the living room, Winston jerked to his feet, barked in excitement, and flailed for purchase on the linoleum. Startled by the dog's abrupt behavior, Butter stiffened in an arched hiss and batted Winston's nose with open claws as the dog passed his chair. Winston howled, and the cat bounded into the middle of the kitchen table. Abbey, who hated cats on the table, swatted at Butter and shooed him, which caused Lizzie to spill her milk. Too late, Stevie grabbed for Lizzie's glass—and sent the salamander flying across the table and onto the kitchen counter. As Abbey yelled at the cat and Lizzie cried over her milk, Stevie shrieked, "Spotty's hurt! Spotty's hurt!"

Mac heard the yells and cries and ran to the kitchen, with a barking Winston at his heels.

The cat, now on the floor, yowled at sight of the dog and streaked for the front door. Winston took off, in loud pursuit. Lizzie cried and scrambled after Butter, and she knocked over her chair in her hurry. Stevie slid about on the spilled milk in an effort to retrieve the salamander—which seemed to have made his flight without harm and was scurrying lickety-split for the kitchen sink. Abbey was torn between reaching out one hand to help Lizzie right her chair and steadying Stevie with the other. And in the middle of it all, the now empty cookie platter clanged to the floor and rattled in a rapid, off-center clatter until it settled, flat.

The commotion made no sense to Mac, who stood in the doorway in shock. "What in the world happened?" he hollered, adding his own voice to the tumult.

Abbey grabbed her head and plopped down in her chair. How had this calm afternoon moment descended so quickly into chaos?

Dog, cat, salamander, boy, girl, and father-in-law. *Never again,* Abbey thought!

Mac never did quite understand the commotion he had unexpectedly stirred.

"You should've seen the place!" he exclaimed to Andy, during supper. Abbey just shook her head.

"Kids and animals, everywhere!" Mac said again. "It was like a zoo!"

Finally, Abbey laughed. She tried to picture it all from Mac's viewpoint, and she decided it was rather hilarious.

"Mac," she asked, "didn't you ever have goofy things happen when Andy and Molly were kids?"

Mac thought for a moment, with a look on his face that seemed to say, "not on your life." But then, Abbey could tell that something had popped into his mind.

"Well," Mac said, "there was this time when the kids were small and Muff stirred things up with a door-to-door salesman."

Andy immediately recalled the incident Mac. "I remember that day!" he exclaimed.

Mac continued. "Rachel answered the door to find a salesman on the porch that she didn't have time to talk to. So, she said 'no thank you' and started to shut the door. The guy, however, made the mistake of putting his foot in the way, to keep the door open so he could say something else. Rachel cried out in surprise, and that's when Muff appeared out of nowhere and attacked the guy's shoe. The salesman screamed. He knew something had attacked him, but from outside the door, he didn't know what. And the worst part was that he couldn't get his foot out of the door because Muff wouldn't let go of it.

"Rachel frantically tried to get Muff's jaws loose, but it was impossible. (That's a bulldog for you!) Rachel ended up calling me, and I came home to find the guy in hysterics on my living room floor and hitting Muff, who was snarling and shaking the man's foot. The salesman kept sobbing, 'Get that thing off me. It's killing me! It's killing me!' And Rachel and the kids were crying because the man was hitting Muff.

"I spent several minutes working on Muff's jaws. When they finally unlatched, I never saw a guy with a sore foot scramble as fast as he did! He was out the door and down the street, in no time. And I'll bet he never tried sticking his foot in anybody's door, after that."

Wide-eyed, Abbey exclaimed, "You're lucky the guy didn't sue you!"

Andy said, "I don't know that he could have won. After all, he's the one who 'entered the home' without permission."

Abbey wondered. She said, "People win all kinds of crazy lawsuits, these days. I'm glad you didn't have trouble like that."

"Nope," said Mac. "No more trouble. Rachel said she never saw that guy, again. And I liked Muff from that day forward. I knew she could protect my home!"

"She was a good dog," Andy agreed. "And so is Winston."

Abbey laughed at that. She wasn't sure Winston had that kind of fight in him. He couldn't even face down a cat!

At the mention of his name, Winston wagged his stubby tail and looked up. Did someone have a treat?

For the second time on Tuesday, Andy tried to reach Chelsea; he had hoped to catch her this morning. He needed to mark off the dates on his calendar for state church camp. He usually planned a fireside devotional for one of the nights with the campers, and he wanted to make sure he kept that week free of conflicts. But Chelsea wasn't home. He'd have to try again, later, after his lunch date with Abbey.

Abbey was right on time. Andy had requested that they walk to the Star Diner early, to make sure they got a seat for lunch.

"See you later!" Andy called to Opal as they headed out.

Their only delay was a quick stop at the boutique on the Square. A little cotton dress in the window had caught Abbey's eye. Butter-yellow was her color, and she wondered if the shop had her size. In minutes (she didn't even take time to try it on), the sample in the window disappeared into Abbey's shopping bag. She would try it on at home. Andy had "Ooooohed!" when she had held it up in front of her, and that had solidified her decision. He now carried the dress bag.

Although it was only eleven twenty, the diner was nearly full. Andy and Abbey took the last empty booth. Doreen slid coffee in front of them and smiled absently.

"What'll it be, today?" the indifferent waitress asked.

Andy placed his order, and Abbey hesitated, torn between the baked steak and the broasted chicken.

Suddenly, Doreen's attention snapped from Abbey's decision-making to the doorway, and Doreen's mouth gaped. Abbey followed her stare, and when Andy looked, his mouth gaped, too.

Siege Logan had just ushered in Chelsea Mitchell, and the two of them stood waiting for an empty spot to sit.

Chelsea waved when she saw Abbey, and Abbey excitedly pointed to their booth, to invite them to join her and Andy. With Siege in tow, Chelsea made her way past another couple that was waiting for a seat, and she slid into the booth next to Abbey. Siege took his place next to Andy.

Once everyone was seated, Doreen coldly asked Abbey, "Well, are you going to order?" Abbey shot her a glance that said, "I'll let you know in a moment." (*What's up with her,* Abbey wondered?)

Abbey finally settled on the broasted chicken. Doreen jabbed the order onto her pad, and Abbey heard the same cold tone when she took orders from Chelsea and Siege. Then Doreen abruptly wheeled about and set off for the kitchen.

"Well," said Abbey, "she sure has a bee in her bonnet, today! I've never known her to be so short."

Andy laughed. "Yeah," he said, as if he knew something she didn't. And Siege offered the slightest shrug and a grin.

Their reactions put Abbey's antenna on alert. And then it came to her. She knew! She would confirm it, later, with Andy. But she was sure she had it figured out, and she smiled.

Chelsea had missed the hidden exchange and was sharing her news. "I got to help deliver twin calves this morning!"

Andy asked Siege, "You mean you didn't call me? I thought I was your favorite unpaid partner!"

Siege laughed. "Not this time. I called Chelsea because the other day she mentioned she had seen a calf born in her grandparents' barn when she was a kid, and it had been a special moment in her life. So, when Junior Harris called to say he wanted me on hand for a first-year calving that he felt sure was twins, I immediately thought of Chelsea."

"And I loved it!" Chelsea said. "I love calves. They're all wobbly and cute."

"And she helped rub 'em down, like you did with the piglets the night you went with me," Siege said to Andy.

"It's just a shame it wasn't midnight like it was for me," Andy replied with a grin.

Siege knew he was being teased. He admitted, "It is kind of unusual for calves to be born early in the day."

"Uh-huh," said Andy.

After a brief interlude, Abbey asked Chelsea if Howie Thompson was still taking guitar lessons from her. Before Chelsea could answer, however, Siege interrupted.

"I didn't know you played guitar!" he exclaimed. "I play banjo. We ought to do a duet for church, sometime!"

Chelsea nodded enthusiastically. "Sure! That would fun. Do you know *Will There Be Any Stars in My Crown*?"

Siege suggested, "How about *I'll Fly Away*?"

On they went, through the list of possible songs.

Doreen arrived and wordlessly plopped platters of food in front of everyone, turned on her heel, and started to stalk away. She clenched her jaw and blew out a frustrated breath when Abbey stopped her and asked for more butter for the rolls. On her next pass, Doreen didn't even face the booth when she flipped the butter packets onto the table in front of Abbey.

Abbey covered her smile and looked at Andy. He winked.

I was right! Abbey thought. Andy's wink had confirmed what her woman's intuition had suspected: Doreen had never had a chance.

CHAPTER TWENTY-TWO

JUNE WEDDING

Abbey saw the notice in the paper and ran with it to the television room. Andy followed her finger down the page to an obituary headline that read: *Clayton W. Bartlett.* The article provided only Clay's age (52) and Vera's and Quinn's names, and it stated that Clay had died of complications from a long-time illness. The article also listed the visitation and funeral hours—and that Rev. Grassley would be officiating on Saturday at the Ball and Ferris funeral home. There was nothing more.

Andy sighed in relief that he had not been called to do the service. He wasn't sure he could have been objective.

Even though Clay's behavior had not indicated it, Andy did hope he had known the Lord. And Andy thanked God that Vera and Quinn were free.

Mac still caught himself swearing, even though he had learned to confess it. And Mac had been memorizing Scripture verses and trying to fill his mind with praiseworthy words. The lapses into swearing didn't happen as often as before, but Mac was, nevertheless, still frustrated at his inability to conquer it.

"I just wish I could catch myself BEFORE the words come out!" he insisted to Phillip, one day. "I hardly know the words are there. And then the next thing I know, they're sizzling through the air, and I can't take them back."

Phillip asked, "What kinds of things make you so angry that you end up swearing? Can you avoid those things?"

Mac thought for a moment. "I guess it's mostly when somebody crosses me, or when I think they have. I hear them say something, and I take offense and defend myself."

"Hmmm," thought Phillip out loud.

"Shouldn't I defend myself?" demanded Mac. "I know when I'm right!" He heaved his chest and stared in challenge.

Phillip did not respond.

"You do know that Wendy was a miracle baby, right?" Amanda Smith asked Abbey after Bible study. Amanda, a former pastor's wife at Cherish (now widowed for eleven years), told Andy and Abbey that Wendy Caplinger had weighed just two-and-a-half pounds on delivery and had spent many months in a special neo-natal care unit in a Decatur hospital. For a long time, Mitchi and Erroll Caplinger hadn't been able to touch their little one, except through the gloves built into her incubator. But Wendy had survived. And the day Wendy had come home had been a tearful one for the whole church. Everyone had followed her daily progress and prayed for her development. Amazingly, by kindergarten Wendy had caught up; no one would have guessed that she had been a critical-care preemie.

Like the average farm girl, Wendy had helped with chores, become active in 4-H, and learned to be self-sufficient. It was no surprise that, when planning her wedding at age nineteen, she and her mother made nearly everything.

The day of the rehearsal, Abbey admired the cake—a work of art—and the arrangement of beautiful flowers from the Caplinger garden. And she praised the dress Wendy's mother had made. (Abbey had caught a sneak peek on a visit to their farm.) As requested by Wendy, the dress was a replica of Cinderella's first ball gown—the one made by her mice friends—but all in white. Since she had been a little girl, Wendy had dreamed of being married in that dress.

Abbey might also have admired the soft-yellow bridesmaid dresses—except that there were so many of them! Nine bridesmaids meant that there would be twenty-two people in the wedding party, plus Andy. Abbey wondered if Andy knew. Andy was not a fan of complicated weddings.

"Yes, I know," he said when she mentioned it to him. And he growled, "I suggested that Wendy have some of the party stand on the floor, but she's insisted that they'll all fit on the platform. I try not to think about it. There's not enough room!"

That night, at the rehearsal, however, Wendy had everyone stand chest-to-shoulder. It was tight, but it worked. There was just enough room for Andy to stand between, and a step behind, the couple on the platform. And the rehearsal proceeded, and concluded, without a hitch. Abbey sighed in relief.

Then, however, the groom pulled Andy aside. Abbey overheard the young man whisper, "At the wedding tomorrow, I'm going to surprise Wendy and sing to her." Abbey saw Andy smile helplessly and nod his head. Only after the groom had walked away did she hear Andy whisper to himself, "I hope he's not playing a guitar—there's no room!"

Andy seemed distracted the rest of the evening, and as he slipped under the covers, Abbey heard him breathe, "Please help us, tomorrow, Lord. Don't let anybody fall off that stage!"

The church looked beautiful, and Abbey took her seat on the bride's side of the sanctuary. She watched as the mothers of the bride and groom were seated, and the music changed to the strains of *Trumpet Voluntaire*. Andy and Joe emerged and waited. As scripted, the wedding party entered and took their temporary places on the floor in front of the platform. Then Joe and the congregation turned their attention to watch Wendy radiantly approach on her father's arm. The music soared.

Like a princess at a ball in her Cinderella dress, Wendy majestically advanced, and her train unfurled in elegant folds behind her. Her Prince waited in awe.

But when Wendy stopped at the front of the sanctuary, Abbey's eyes grew wide. She saw that, even though Wendy had reached the front of the room, her long train hadn't yet completely unfurled. It was the longest train Abbey had ever seen! And Abbey knew that it spelled trouble.

Andy inquired, "who gives this woman?" and Wendy's father gave her away with a kiss. Erroll side-stepped the bothersome train and slipped into his seat. Mitchi covered her mouth with a tear-stained handkerchief.

Andy now took his place on the platform to face the congregation. As rehearsed, the wedding party then climbed the stairs, and Wendy and Joe followed. The beaming couple stopped in front of and facing Andy. And the ubiquitous train covered the aisle and the stairs in white tulle.

An uncomfortable twenty-three persons now crowded the platform. Eighteen of them stood scrunched, chest-to-shoulder, with no room to spare and with lots of "schmushed" (a Lizzie word that Abbey found appropriately descriptive) yellow taffeta and smartly tailored tuxedos. Abbey tried not to think about the train, but it was hard to ignore it.

Andy intoned, "Dearly Beloved," and Wendy and Joe completed their vows in sweet repetition. Andy smiled, and then he paused for the surprise musical moment.

Abbey saw Andy step back as Joe turned to face Wendy. The introductory strains of *There is Love* wafted from an off-stage guitar, and Joe smiled and took Wendy's hands. Wendy's eyes filled with tears, and when Joe finished singing, the betrothed hugged, tearfully.

Abbey could no longer see Andy between the couple; Joe and Wendy stood too tightly, side by side. And so it was, that from somewhere behind the crowd on the platform, and completely unseen, Andy announced, "Now by the power invested in me by the State of Illinois, I do hereby pronounce you man and wife. You may now kiss the bride." The still invisible Andy introduced the newlyweds as "Mr. and Mrs. Joe Folden," and the organ recessional swelled.

Now Abbey grimaced. This was the moment that she had foreseen. How was the recession going to work? What could possibly be done about the exceptionally long bridal train? It was everywhere!

In other weddings, the bridal train draped only a portion of the stairs and was easily swept aside by the Maid of Honor, so the newlyweds, the bridesmaids, and the groomsmen could descend. But today, there was no prospect for a simple *sweeping aside.* And of course, no one could walk on the train.

Abbey's mind raced through various scenarios. Should she jump up and try to help? But what could she do that wouldn't embarrass Wendy? Abbey remained rooted in her seat, and she helplessly watched the Maid of Honor struggle with what to do. The young woman appeared to be frozen with indecision. And the organ kept playing.

Abbey finally decided she had to help. But before she could get to her feet, she saw the Maid take a deep breath and lift her chin. In a dramatic gesture, the young lady handed off her bouquet to the first bridesmaid. Then, with exaggerated dignity, she stooped over the train on the stairs and did what she had to do: she began to "gracefully" sling folds of the train over her shoulder to clear a path for the rest of the wedding party.

Several members of the congregation gasped as the train piled higher and higher above her. But the festooned Maid stood with stately poise behind Wendy, as the bride and groom started down the stairs. The Best Man met the Maid when it was their turn to descend, and the chivalrous young man off-loaded half of the train onto his arms, took the Maid's elbow, and regally escorted her down the aisle and through the doors at the back of the sanctuary. The rest of the wedding party followed, close behind, without delay.

Someone at the back of the congregation applauded.

Now, Abbey sprang into action. Ignoring the ordered dismissal of the crowd, Abbey bolted through the back doors and into the assembly room, where the receiving line was forming. The minute Mitchi Caplinger saw her, the Mother-of-the-Bride broke out of place. The two women raced toward each other, and when Mitchi reached Abbey, she pleaded loudly: "Scissors!"

Abbey didn't stop to reply. She raced away, and in one of the classroom cupboards, she found a suitable pair of shears. In mere seconds, Abbey was assisting Mitchi.

Behind Wendy's back, the two women worked quickly.

Still caught up in the celebration of her big moment, Wendy never noticed that thirty feet of train did not follow her from the church. The massive ball of white tulle disappeared into the church's janitorial closet, where it could be collected, later. The luxurious excess was never missed.

CHAPTER TWENTY-THREE

THUNDER

Andy expected Paul and Mac to be out in the field when he pulled into the farm drive. He had seen other farmers out working, hurrying to finish whatever farmers did before the clouds on the horizon swept in.

If his dad and brother-in-law weren't in the field, Andy hoped they were busy elsewhere with chores. He had come to talk with Molly, alone.

As he made his way up the steps, Andy could smell something delicious, and he hoped the baking was out of the oven and ready to eat, while they talked. But when he opened the door, Andy saw his father seated at the kitchen table.

Mac did not look up from his apple bread and coffee. He just said "'morning," in a slightly defensive tone.

"Hi!" Molly said brightly. "What a pleasant surprise! I wasn't expecting you." She quickly sliced another piece of apple bread and poured another cup of coffee.

"Had a minute, and thought I'd stop by," Andy said with a nod, but he avoided his dad's eye.

Emily welcomed her favorite—and only—uncle with a squeal and a grin. Andy picked her out of her high chair and rubbed noses with her. She giggled and grabbed at his hair. He kissed her cheeks and settled her back in her seat.

"She's got sticky, from juice, all over her," Molly warned. But it was too late. Andy could feel it, now. Molly wiped Emily's nose and hands with a damp cloth and handed the cloth to him.

"And," Molly said, "she's got a wet diaper." Accordingly, Molly hauled the baby into her arms. "We'll be back in a minute," she called over her shoulder.

Alone, now, with his father, Andy focused on mashing the remaining crumbs on his plate with this fork. Then he washed them down with a prolonged draft of his coffee. With nothing more to eat, he sat back in his chair and stared out the window.

Mac broke the silence with, "I know why you're here; I didn't show up for church, yesterday." Then he grumbled, "And I had my reasons." Mac's tone implied it was nobody's business but his own.

Andy nodded and stared at his hands, laced around the coffee mug. He said nothing.

Mac blurted, "I don't want to talk about it," as if Andy had chided him for his absence. But Andy had said nothing, and Mac fidgeted and stared at his cup.

Although they could hear Molly baby-talking in the other room, the only other sound was a fly buzzing in frustration against the window pane.

"Okay!" Mac finally exclaimed. "I-I felt like a hypocrite. I don't belong in church. I can't live like that. It's just not me." He shoved his palms down on the table as if defying Andy to object.

Again, Andy said nothing; he simply stirred a little more sugar into his coffee and tested it. He never looked up.

"You don't understand," Mac insisted. "I'm right back where I was! I can't change."

Now Andy spoke.

"So, what happened, Dad? Did something happen?"

Mac sighed. "I blew it," he said. "I just blew it, that's all."

Andy waited, and his father squirmed.

Finally, Mac said, "I yelled at Phillip." Then he said, "Actually, I swore at him. He's all high and mighty about how stuff has to be done. And I told him I wasn't stupid. And…"

"I see," interrupted Andy. "You let your pride come between you two."

Mac threw himself back in his chair and folded his arms across his chest. "Well, who does he think he is? I've been around the block a few times, and I know a thing or two."

"So where is Phillip, now?" asked Andy.

Mac answered quietly, "He left."

"He left?" Andy asked in surprise.

"Yeah, he left. After we argued, he just packed up his stuff and left," Mac said.

"Ah," said Andy. "He went back home."

"I guess so," said Mac. "I think he called Paul and told him he didn't think Paul needed him here, anymore; Phillip said he had other stuff to do back in town."

"So, Paul and Molly don't know that you two argued?" Andy asked.

"I don't believe so," came the terse reply.

"Ah," said Andy, again.

Now Mac became defensive. "So, what do you expect me to do about it? If he wants to leave, that's his business, not mine!"

"I'd say it's everybody's business," Andy countered. "You two had a job to do, and now you're squabbling like a couple of little kids. And you: a retired boss of a big company! How would you have handled this if it was a couple of your employees?"

Mac exhaled in exasperation and shook his head at the ceiling. "What's that got to do with anything?"

"Really, Dad? You don't know?" Andy asked.

Now Mac was angry. "Who made you the arbiter, anyway?" he growled, and he tossed his chair back and stalked toward his room at the end of the mobile unit.

He didn't go to his room, however. Instead, Andy heard the backdoor slam, and he heard Mac stomp down the stairs. A car started, and Andy saw the Lincoln make a quick loop in front of the barn and disappear down the lane.

When Molly returned with Emily, Andy sat alone at the table.

"I heard some of that," she said. "These walls are thin. It's too bad, isn't it? They were getting along so well. But knowing those two, I suppose it was bound to happen at some point. I'm just glad it happened now and not when Paul needed them more."

Then she added, "I didn't even know Mac didn't go to church, yesterday. He left for somewhere in his car, and we assumed he was going to Cherish. He probably drove around so we wouldn't know he wasn't with you guys. Just like a little kid who somehow thinks his parents aren't going to find out if he skips school."

Andy said, "I figured you and Paul didn't know about it, because you didn't call and say anything. I did try to call once, right after church, but there was no answer. I knew that if Dad was sick or there was some other family problem you would have let me know."

Then he said, "I know it's hard to be a new Christian when things don't seem to change like you think they should."

Molly nodded. "I just hope he hasn't completely given up."

"I know," said Andy. "I don't want to push. I need to pray and let God work on Dad's heart."

He and Molly sat, looking at their cups.

Outside, a storm thundered in and rumbled. Clouds that Andy had seen approaching as he had driven to Harmony now spread across the full expanse of the sky, and lightning discharged in rapid flashes. Molly turned on the overhead lights against the storm's darkness, and she looked out the window. Andy knew she was worried about Paul getting caught in the field.

Then, just as the rain swept in, in loudly thundered sheets, Paul yanked open the door and stomped his way inside. Water dripped from the bill of his cap and his wet shirt. He set the cap on the washing machine and grabbed a towel from a pile of dirty laundry to wipe the wettest parts of his face and arms.

"I almost beat it," he said, as he removed his muddy boots. "I saw the lightning in the distance, and I didn't want to be out on the tractor when it reached the field."

Molly ran to fetch a dry shirt, and then she cut another slice of apple bread and poured him a cup of coffee.

"I'm glad you're safe," she said. "And now that you're here, you need to hear this."

When Mac left the farm, he drove with determination and without a destination. He didn't care where he went; he just had to get away.

Justification of his anger toward Phillip roared through his mind in a self-righteous blast, and he ratified it with a smash of his fist on the steering wheel.

Mac loudly condemned everyone but himself. "That stuffed mule! Who does Phillip think he is, anyway? And what do those church people know?" he shouted. "They all sit in judgment of me. And Andy! Oh, Andy! That kid thinks he knows everything. I certainly know better than that! He's not been a saint all his life!"

Mac's neck muscles bulged as he jutted his chin, stiffened his body, and balled his fists in rage. He shouted at the windshield for a few minutes more.

But then all of a sudden Mac felt drained. Afraid he would run off the road, he pulled to the side and stopped. His breathing became irregular, and tears threatened to spill down his cheeks. Now, he was mad at himself for crying. "This is stupid!" he shouted to no one in particular.

But even as he said it he realized he had been shouting at God. He struck the steering wheel, again. But his shame overwhelmed him, and he crumpled over the wheel.

He rocked for a few minutes and then yelled out a wordless cry. He threw himself back in his seat. A couple of drops of rain splattered on the windshield and surprised him.

Mac had not paid attention, until now, at how dark the sky had become—and how alone he was. Flat, featureless fields and miles of brooding sky extended as far as his eye could see. His car was a mere dot on an uninterrupted plain, beneath a breast of churning, angry clouds.

A mighty crash of thunder and an immediate bolt of lightning startled him. It shook the car and jarred his bones.

Mac thought about leaving, but where would he go? There was no escape from the omnipresent sky. And so, he remained in park on the side of the road and let the forces of nature do battle over the Lincoln and the landscape. The power of the wind as it drove the rain over the fields stirred him. And lightning seemed to flash between every column of clouds. The rain beat against the car's roof and the hood, and he could feel the impact of the multiple vibrations throughout his body. It was the only thing he felt. It seemed odd to be untouched and cocooned in the car against the violence of it all.

He knew it would end soon, but it seemed to go on and on. The lashing of the Lincoln continued for several minutes, and Mac could only wait.

Finally, the rain began to let up, little by little, and the deafening rumbles of thunder echoed and re-echoed, first mighty and then progressively softer, as their cloud source began to recede.

Mac thought about how, at any other time, he would have been unnerved to be caught in the storm's center, unprotected, in the middle of nowhere. But even before the ebbing of the thunder's crashes Mac had felt strangely comforted—even protected. Somehow, the powerful rumble seemed to envelop and shelter him from some other unseen fury.

Mac's mind flew to a scene from a nature film of an angry sow bear protecting her cub from a mountain lion. Mac had cheered when the mother had risen on her hind legs and roared at the lion. The hungry cat had tucked his tail and slunk away.

In this moment, Mac had felt as if the thunder had been protecting him—that it had been roaring away some danger he'd not even been aware of.

As the storm abated, Mac whispered humbly, "Is that you, God?" And then he quietly said, "I'm sorry. I'm so sorry!" A tumble of words poured from his lips about his foolish pride and his sin against Phillip. And the cleansing tears of repentance fell.

One final rumble, off in the distance, eventually whispered that all was well, that the danger was past.

Mac wiped his tears on his sleeve and put the car back in gear.

When he pulled onto the road, Mac did not return to the farm. Instead, he headed for Cherish.

Mac knew that Mondays were Andy's days off, but he stopped in front of the church, anyway. He reasoned that if Andy hadn't already returned home, he would have to pass the church to get there—and Mac wanted him to see the car. He wanted Andy to stop.

Recovering from the downpour in a dry shirt, with a cup of hot coffee and a slice of fresh apple bread, Paul listened to the story of the tiff between Mac and Phillip.

"Well, that explains a lot," Paul said. "All I could get from my dad was that he left because I didn't really need him anymore—and because I still had that (quote) 'pigheaded idiot' for help if I still needed something."

Andy rolled his eyes. "What a stupid mess!" he said. "Unfortunately, we can't spank 'em. You got any other ideas?"

"Oh, give them time, and they'll come around, I suppose," suggested Paul. "I just hate to see it end this way."

"I agree," said Andy.

As they talked, the rain began to let up, and Andy decided to take advantage of it. He hugged Molly and nodded a goodbye to Paul.

Andy prayed as he turned down the lane on his way back to Cherish. And he wondered: would his dad and Phillip ever make up? He knew they were both stubborn and pigheaded. It would take some doing for God to smooth over two sets of strong feelings.

God, Andy prayed, *please don't let this turn my dad back from his newfound faith. And remind my dad, again, that this all takes time. I pray that Satan isn't able to discourage him or sink his claws into him, again! Guard and protect him. I know he's my dad, but he's just a child in the faith. Protect him, Father, from the storms that would drive him from Your arms.*

Andy was surprised. Was that the Lincoln in front of the church? He pulled in quickly behind his dad's car and honked. Mac waved from the big car's window and opened the door.

"Can we talk?" Mac asked, when Andy caught up to him.

Andy greeted a startled Opal when he led his dad into the pastor's study.

Then, Andy started a pot of coffee (usually Opal had one hot by the time he rolled in on workdays, but this was a Monday), and he invited his dad to have a seat. Andy bypassed the desk chair and came to sit beside his father.

"Son," Mac began, "I'm sorry this has happened. I didn't mean to be a smart-a…" He stopped, unsure if he could say that word in church.

"I know, Dad," Andy said. "These things happen, sometimes. The devil knows exactly how to get at us, and it's usually some petty thing that strikes a spark. Then before we know it, it's in a full blaze. But"—Andy paused— "the important thing is what we do next."

Mac sighed. "That's just the point. I don't know what to do next. I've told God I'm sorry, and I've apologized to you. Now, do I go over and tell Phillip I'm sorry? What if he doesn't accept it? What then?"

And then Mac asked, "And how do I keep this from happening, again? I'm still me, and I'm still a *pigheaded idiot.* That's what Phillip called me, and I guess I am."

Andy thought for a minute, and he prayed silently before answering.

"It's not easy, is it?" Andy said. "Even for Christians."

Then Andy said, "Old habits are hard to break, even when you realize how hurtful they are."

Mac nodded and said, "I just keep doing the same things. And now I've lost Phillip as a friend."

"And Phillip has lost you as a friend," Andy suggested.

Mac expelled a snort. "Some friend I am!"

"You two were good for each other," Andy insisted. "And, together, you saved the farm. That's not something to sniff at."

"I guess not," Mac admitted, although his eyes never left the floor. "But I can't keep from lashing out when Phillip, or anyone else, crosses me. What am I going to do? I'm not much of a Christian."

"*Not much of a Christian*, huh?" Andy countered. "Well, what did you expect? Who said you were suddenly going to be perfect the minute you turned your life over to Christ? I don't recall ever preaching that, and I doubt that you've found those words in your Bible. It just isn't so."

"Well, maybe not *perfect*," Mac said, "but I had hoped that at least I'd be a little better than I am. Instead, I don't think I've changed, at all."

"Ah," said Andy. "But that's where you're wrong. You've changed dramatically, I think. And you're still changing. God wouldn't have it any other way. Dad, do you remember when we talked, a little while back, about how you're a newborn who is being raised by your new Heavenly Father? And we talked about how the Holy Spirit is starting to open your eyes to see the person your Father God is molding you to be?

"Well, Dad, Satan is working, too. And his purpose is to make you feel defeated—to feel like you're not growing and that God has abandoned you because *'you're not much of a Christian if you still mess up so often.'* That's the devil's way of operating. He's an accuser and a discourager. He whispers defeat in your ear, at every opportunity."

"Yeah," Mac admitted with a frown. "That sounds about right. But what do I do about it? I can't just turn it off."

Andy objected. "Oh, but you can! You can turn it off. Don't fool yourself. And don't underestimate your strength and God's power! You just need a reminder, Dad. And I have just the thing to help you to remember. You should memorize this Bible verse from James 4:7: *'Submit yourselves, then, to God. Resist the devil, and he will flee from you. Come to God and He will come to you.'*

Andy asked, "Do you see how it says that you can *resist the devil, and he WILL flee from you?"*

"But I DO resist," Mac insisted. "I do resist, and nothing happens."

Andy softened his tone when he answered. "I don't want to counter your statement, Dad, but I have to ask if you're sure you're really resisting. When the anger rises, are you consciously, at that moment, pushing against it? Or are you stoking your anger and justifying your defense? Do you realize only afterward that you should have curbed your feelings?"

Mac looked down. He had to admit that he had not *resisted.*

"It's hard to resist, at first," Andy allowed, and he added as a side note: "It's even hard to resist after you've been a Christian for years.

"But in any event, we have to train ourselves to watch for the sin and head it off. And to do that we need the help of the Holy Spirit. In your case, you should ask the Holy Spirit to help you recognize your situation BEFORE you unleash your tongue. The devil is hard at work blinding you to the danger. Only the Spirit can be counted on to project the truth. You have to learn to listen to the Spirit's prompting. And you need to hide God's Word in your heart so the Spirit can recall it to you in that split second when the temptation rises. You might want to learn Scriptures like James 1:19: *'be quick to listen, slow to speak, and slow to become angry'* or Ephesians 4:26-27: *'In your anger do not sin. Do not let the sun go down while you are still angry, and do not give the devil a foothold.'*"

Mac nodded. "Good advice," he said.

Andy now ventured, "Training yourself to recognize the signs that you're heading into a potential anger situation is just as important as trying to put a lid on it after the anger has boiled up."

"I can see that," Mac said. "But even if I recognize it, I'm not sure I can stop it."

"Ah, but you can," assured Andy. "You can—if you ask God for help. That's the key. The verse in James 4:7 that I suggested you memorize doesn't just say *'resist the devil and he will flee from you.'* It also says TWICE to *'come near to God.'* When your mind and focus are on God and you are walking closely with Him, you will not be alone when temptation strikes. Instead, the first words on the tip of your tongue will be a prayer to God for help. And He will be there."

"Satan is a bully," Andy continued. "And bullies like to attack when we are all alone—either by sneaking up on us, or with a full out attack. But Satan's gang isn't as keen to get into a scrap when we have some good backup. When you have God's army behind you, you can shout *'No!'* to the bullies. You can shout *'Leave me, in the Name of Jesus! Take your deceitful and lying ways with you!'* and the bullies will leave. They are no match for Christ's power!

"And then, immediately, you need to turn your mind away from your anger. Don't focus on the situation, anymore. Instead, pull up something good and positive about the object of your anger, and thank God for it."

Mac murmured. "I wish I had done that. I wish I would have thought about how much Phillip has taught me about the farm. And I wish I would have remembered how he was always there to listen when I had questions about you kids. That's the stuff I miss, now."

"I'm sorry, Dad," Andy said quietly. "Phillip was a good friend."

Mac sighed.

Then Andy said, "Dad, I've just had another thought that might help you put your anger into perspective. Do you want to hear it?"

"Sure," Mac said. "I'm in no hurry."

"Okay," said Andy. "Let's imagine that you knew you were going to inherit $900 billion in less than two weeks, and this afternoon someone steals $50 from your pocket. Would you really care the same about the $50 theft as you might if you weren't inheriting the $900 billion?"

Mac said, "That's a lot of inheritance!"

"Exactly," Andy said. "Your attention would be so focused on the $900-billion inheritance that you would scarcely notice the $50 theft. Well, that's what our reaction to hurts and attacks should be like. Why should we care if someone presumes on the pittance we cling to, here, when it's like nothing compared to our final reward? When we focus on Jesus and the promise of eternity with Him, we can shrug our shoulders and say, *'I don't care about the things that used to seem so important. I have more in my account than I will ever need.'*"

Mac's eyes grew wide. "That's true!" he said. "As a Christian, I don't have to defend myself or try to be something I'm not; I already have it all. Everything I could ever dream of is mine to claim, one day. And as you said, it's guaranteed and can never be taken away. I really like that! Hopefully, I can remember that!" he said. "Thank you!"

But then Mac sobered. "But what do I do about Phillip? I've already messed up. He's the only friend, here, I've had! It tears at my insides that I hurt him. I want to be friends, again."

Andy's heart ached for his father. He suggested, "If you want, we could pray about it, right now, Dad. We could ask Jesus to help soften Phillip's heart and to give you the right words to say to get things back on track."

Mac spoke quietly. "I'd like it if you would pray with me."

Andy nodded, but he also gently counseled, "And Dad, if it doesn't work out the first time that you talk with Phillip, don't get discouraged. He might need a little time. Remember, he's a lot like you."

Mac hung his head and laughed meekly. "Yeah, I get it," he said.

PART THREE
CLEANSE ME

CHAPTER TWENTY-FOUR

FATHER'S DAY

"Opal! What's wrong?" Andy asked. He had never seen his quirky, perky secretary cry. What could, possibly, have brought Opal to tears?

Andy bent down to comfort her, and Opal leaned over to sob on his shoulder.

"I'm sorry," she said. "It's my friend, Clara—the one who moved to North Dakota. Her daughter's doctors discovered an inoperable heart defect, and Sheila has died. Clara called to tell me about it, and I felt terrible that I couldn't have been there with her. But as Clara was sharing, I felt like I was there in the hospital room with her and her granddaughter, Anna."

Opal said, "Clara told me a beautiful story about Anna and the day Sheila died, and this morning I tried to write it down. That's why I was crying. Writing it down made me live it with her."

Opal wiped her eyes and gave Andy a wan smile. "I won't be putting this one in the church newsletter," she said, and she handed Andy a piece of paper that he realized was a poem.

To treat the moment with the weight it deserved, Andy pulled up a chair and read the page.

Across the top, Opal had typed, *"For my friend, Clara. In remembrance of Sheila."* Andy slowly read the rest.

ANNA'S PRAYER
by Opal Reese

The hum of the machines had grown silent,
And loved ones were gathered all 'round.
And the pastor ministered one last time
Over one who was heaven bound.

She was a saint who would be sorely missed,
And her fight had been so long.
Her husband stooped for one last kiss,
Before that chance was gone.

And then the voice of his little girl
Surprised them all with her prayer.
In the simple words of uncluttered faith,
She breached heaven to lift up her care.

"Hush, Lord Jesus," little Anna commanded,
In the whispered tones she'd so often heard.
"Hush, when you come into Mama's room."
(And in her sleep, her mother stirred.)

"You see," Anna said, lifting up her small hand
As if directing the Master's gaze,
"My Mama's been so awful sick,
And heaven is so far away.

"So, let your angels carry her, okay?
Just tell them to hush and come down lower,
Not to make noise, and don't wake her up—
And then softly pull closed the door."

And the angels came, everyone knew,
When Anna's prayer was ended.
And her mother was gently carried away,
And the winged hosts of heaven attended.

It was such a quiet passing,
And the room was hushed and calm.
Then Anna smiled and simply said.
"Now, when Mama wakes up she'll be home!"

And that day, Mama woke in paradise,
Free from all hurts and pain.
All had been healed, and all sin was removed
By the blood of the Lamb that was slain.

O, Lord, when I die may the angels haste
And gently bear me o'er.
And as I wake to see Your face,
May You quietly close the door.

O bid the angels come,
And bid the chariots fly!
Open the gates of heaven wide,
As our flight transcends the sky.

Andy wiped a tear on his sleeve.

"This will be a treasure for your friend," he said. "It's beautiful."

Opal flew to North Dakota for Sheila's funeral. Andy knew his secretary wished that Clara lived closer to Cherish. Death was familiar, now, to both of them.

Opal's husband had died, years ago, and Opal had raised *her Brenda* (Opal always referred to her daughter as *my Brenda*) by herself. It had been hard to be alone, but it had grown even harder after her Brenda had married and moved to Ft. Marshall—just far enough away that Opal couldn't see her, every day.

Andy assured Opal that he would be all right while she was gone. He would bravely do battle with the office equipment and the telephone until she returned. And he prayed for a safe journey for her and comfort for her friend.

The mimeograph took pity on Andy in Opal's absence. He breathed a sigh of relief when his Father's Day handouts rolled off the machine without a glitch.

Andy reflected that, over the years, Father's Day had been difficult for him. Andy envied the uncomplicated relationship Abbey had always had with her father. Herb Preston was a prince of a man, with a consistent temperament and a gentle sense of humor. Andy tried to imagine a childhood with a father like that.

Andy also thought about how his love for his father had changed when God had become his Heavenly Father. God's unconditional love had shown Andy what a relationship between a son and a father should be. Andy had been able to look up to his Heavenly Father, and he had come to trust God to shelter him.

Andy decided this was the reason why he especially enjoyed Opal's June poem: *My Daddy Can Do Anything*. Opal's poem spoke of monsters under the bed, and Andy recalled the powerful "monster voices" that had once shouted outside of his childhood hiding place in the bedroom closet. It had taken God's intervention to banish the hurt of those memories and all the secrets of the dark past.

MY DADDY CAN DO ANYTHING!
By Opal Reese

My Daddy's blink gave the twinkle to the stars,
And He colored the smile on the sun.
His fingers piled up a mud-pie heart,
And He blew bubbles into mud-pie lungs.

And little Mud-pie Adam, who was Daddy's first boy,
Let go of my Daddy's hand.
He'd broken my Daddy's special-made world;
He was afraid, and he took off and ran.

But my Daddy saw him behind the door,
And He made him come out and see.
And the spanking hurt Daddy as much as him,
And things weren't the same as they used to be.

And all the things Mud-pie Adam had broke'
Stayed broke' for a long, long time.
But one day, my Daddy sent Jesus down
With some nails, a tree, and some vine.

And my Daddy pulled a big hammer out,
And He pounded Himself on the tree.
And it hurt, and He cried, and His blood came out—
But He didn't stay dead; He got free!

And my Daddy and Jesus are just the same,

And Adam is just like me.
And when Daddy died and came back to life,
He did it because He loved me.

When monsters are hiding under my bed,
And I am afraid and I cry,
My Daddy shows up and turns on the Light,
And the monsters all wither and die.

And my bedroom is safe because Daddy is there,
And He covers me up with His wings.
My Daddy is the most awesome Dad—
God, who's my Daddy, can do anything!

As Andy moved to step into the pulpit, *amens* filled the sanctuary. Leo led the chorus. Now free of his hiccups, Leo's yell could be heard above all other voices. "Amen!" he bellowed with abandon.

The *amens* had nothing to do with Andy and everything to do with the special music that still hung in the air. Everyone, including Andy, had been thrilled and amazed. Who knew that Clifford Myers could play the harmonica?

Andy had been looking forward to hearing Siege on the banjo and Chelsea on the guitar. But when the music had begun (and wonderful music it was!), Clifford had leaped from his pew and whipped out a harmonica that Andy had never seen. Instantly *I'll Fly Away* was transformed from a rousing duet hand-clapper into a glorious trio pew-bouncer! The entire congregation had flown out of their seats and stood clapping and singing along. If anyone had bothered to look they would have seen the prisms of the giant sanctuary chandelier dancing.

Surely God must love bluegrass! Andy thought. And then he wondered, *And how do I follow this?*

Andy knew that even his most enthusiastic sermon delivery was no match for the music they had just heard. But he tried, anyway, and the Spirit blessed his attempt—especially when he got to the part about our hope of Heaven. In an inspired moment, Andy asked the trio to come, again, and reprise their song. He knew that everyone was still stomping their feet and flying away, anyway, so they might as well go out from the service with *"Hallelujah, by and by"* on their lips.

The reprise stirred even the normally sedate Luther Sharp, who jumped up and shouted, "play it again!" the minute the benediction faded. And the musicians did.

I'll Fly Away continued to ring in Andy's ears, long after church, because Abbey sang and bounced it all the way to Harmony.

Molly served her ham to the fathers, first, in honor of their day. And Paul said, "We love you and appreciate all that you've done to keep the farm going until we could get back, here."

Fortunately, Mac and Phillip had reconciled—just in time for this occasion. Phillip still refused to return to his bedroom in the double-wide, but he did promise to come, occasionally, to help Paul with major chores. Phillip insisted that he was truly ready to retire, this time.

Mac stayed on. But even he would soon be out of the mobile home and away from the farm. The sale of Mac's house in Herndon closed last week, and Mac told Andy that his new place, just outside of Cherish, was now move-in ready. "I'll be settling in, after one final trip to Herndon," he said.

It was time, thought Andy. Paul was back to one-hundred percent of his energy and strength and could handle most things on the farm, alone, now.

Other things had settled, too. Mac seemed to have fewer questions about church and his faith, and Andy worried less about him. Mac had made progress in reading the New Testament, and he was more engaged in Sunday school and in Wednesday night Bible study. When Mac quoted, "We are to *'live in harmony with one another. Do not be proud,'*" from Romans 12:16, one Wednesday evening, Andy had beamed, and Mac had returned a sheepish smile.

Then, as if Mac had thought the concept might be new to Andy, Mac had told his son, "I've been trying to pray for the people who make me mad. It's hard to stay mad at someone when you're praying for them, you know?"

Andy had curbed his urge to cry out, "I'm proud of you, Dad." (The words had been on the tip of his tongue but would have sounded superior). Instead, he had enthusiastically replied, "What a great idea, Dad!" Mac had seemed pleased to be able to impart this newfound wisdom with his preacher-son, and Andy had praised the Holy Spirit.

Andy's pride and praise had swelled, again, when Luther Sharp had asked Mac to be an alternate usher, and Mac had accepted. It was another sign that the people of First Baptist saw Mac as a brother in Christ and that Mac now felt he belonged.

CHAPTER TWENTY-FIVE

BOTCHED OPERATION

Without so much as a glance in Andy's direction, Doreen scribbled his breakfast order and sashayed away. On his own, again, until Abbey returned from the state women's conference, Andy had hoped to find Siege at the diner, and he hadn't been disappointed. Siege had beckoned him to his booth, and the two now sat waiting for their breakfast.

Siege wasn't sleepy, today. Instead, this morning, the veterinarian was livid. He seemed glad of the company and the opportunity to spew out the reason for his wrath. Andy had never seen Siege angry.

Doreen had barely left the booth when Siege growled, "Do you remember when I took you to that pig farrowing, several weeks ago? Well, I took Chelsea with me, last night, on another farrowing, and I wish I hadn't!"

Uh-oh! thought Andy. *Has something happened between the two of them?*

But Siege's next words banished that thought.

"I would never have put her through that if I'd known this guy was that stupid!" Siege said. He spat the words, and Andy leaned in.

Andy couldn't resist saying, "I thought pigs didn't usually have too much trouble with births."

Siege instantly replied, "Yeah. Well, sometimes they do. And this call didn't sound that different from when you and I went out, except that this farmer was an idiot!"

"So, what did he do?" Andy asked.

Siege needed little prompting. "Forrest Tranor called for me to come out, and Chelsea and I took off pretty fast," he said. "It was my first time to his farm, and from Doc Gilman's records, it looked like Gilman had only been called out there once. Anyway, when we got there I pulled my bag from the truck, and Chelsea and I headed for the barn. But before we'd gone two steps, we heard a call from behind us and saw a guy waving us to the house.

"'Not there!' yelled Tranor. 'In here! Come here!'

"I wasn't sure what was up," Siege said. "Wasn't the sow in the barn? I even muttered to Chelsea that maybe the sow had died and the guy had the piglets in the house.

"When we reached the front door, I could see that Tranor was in a panic. He shoved us past him and pushed us down the hall to a large linoleum-floored kitchen. And there it was! I couldn't believe my eyes! All splayed out ON TOP of his huge dining room table was a massive muddy sow, twitching and heaving. It was bizarre! Tranor's wife and two kids were staring at us, and all around the edges of the table were the Tranor family's half-eaten chicken dinner. An ugly swipe of mud and blood trailed across the kitchen floor and ended where the table began. And the minute I saw that sow I knew what had happened.

"'What have you done?!' I yelled over that nearly dead animal. And then I yelled 'You idiot!' right in front of his kids. (I was sorry for that, but he *was* an idiot!)"

Siege's voice rose over the chatter of the diner, and Andy saw people looking in their direction. Andy hoped no one thought Siege was calling *him* an idiot.

Andy quietly ventured, "So, what had the man done?"

Siege thrust himself back in his seat and spat, "That stupid farmer had cut that sow! He'd thought he could do a Caesarean. I'm sure I could have got those piglets out, but he didn't give me a chance. He didn't call me until he'd already messed her up, good!"

Then, in spite of the pancakes and eggs that Doreen had plopped in front of Andy, Siege colorfully described the condition of the animal, including the ugly gash through which her intestines bulged.

"The sow was lying in a dark pool of blood that was about to spill over the lip of the table top," Siege said. "And I yelled, 'Well, mister, you've killed a nice-looking animal that probably could have been saved, along with these piglets that I have little hope are salvageable, now, either.' I stared him down and said in his face, 'So you haven't saved a dime by not calling me in the first place, have you?'"

"I probed the birth canal," Siege said, "and it was just like when you and I went out. I separated the piglets and pulled one out so the others could follow. And then, because the sow had finally died, I went ahead and opened the uterus and pulled out the rest of them. But even as I was removing the membrane sacks and rubbing those little bodies, I could tell it was hopeless. Seven dead piglets! For nothing!"

Siege finally threw his hands in the air and admitted, "I apologized to Tranor's wife, but she never said a word. There was nothing more to be done, so I gathered up my things, tossed my instruments into my bag, clenched my jaw, and said through my teeth, 'You'll get my bill in the mail.' I grabbed Chelsea by the arm, and we stalked out of that house without looking back.

"As I threw the pickup into gear and churned the ground to get out of there and down the lane, I gripped the steering wheel as if I were strangling Tranor. That's when I remembered Chelsea, and I looked over expecting her to be shocked.

"But she wasn't!" Siege exclaimed. "I think she was madder than I was! Chelsea's arms were folded tight across her chest, and she was redder than fire.

"'Just what in the world was that stupid farmer thinking?' she snarled.

"And do you know, Andy? Right then and there, I knew I loved that woman, more than words can tell!"

Siege's face reflected an amalgam of anger and wonder and bliss.

Then Siege said, "And Chelsea snorted, 'Can you tell me how in the world that man got that pig on that table?'

"I told her I wondered the same thing. I said, 'It's a cinch she didn't walk up there on her own!'

"And then we both started laughing. It was all so unbelievable.

"'And all of those dinner dishes!' Chelsea said. 'His wife has every right to clobber that man!'

Siege told Andy again, "I just love that woman!"

And Andy grinned.

CHAPTER TWENTY-SIX

THE SHOW MUST GO ON

On the Fourth of July, revelers gathered in the town park around the pond. Andy and Abbey spread their blanket to watch the sky turn pink and gold and to fill with stars and spirals. Every burst was duplicated in the pond's dark mirror, doubling the night's delight.

"Did you see that one?"

"Wow! That one is green."

"Look at all of the star trails on those two!"

Earlier, a set of rousing patriotic melodies had poured from the bandstand. But at the close of the evening children put fingers in their ears against the *bombs bursting in air.*

With hearts still pounding from the spectacle and eyes readjusting to the blackness of the night, the townspeople relived the highlights on the walk to their cars.

"I think it was better than last year's."

"I liked the one that looked like a flag."

"I like the ones that whistle!"

It had been a perfect night. And Andy was amazed that all of Cherish had become as one in the celebration in the park. How different it was from Herndon and Chicago (except maybe at a ball game): different and wonderful. He loved this small town.

And he loved his beautiful wife. He pulled Abbey close when they got to the car, and he gave her a kiss, in the dark.

"Happy Fourth of July!" he whispered.

July meant picnics. And now Mac had seen it all: cows and bingo. Who would have thought there could be a connection?

Mac leaned against the fence behind Junior Harris's barn and wiped the perspiration from the back of his neck. Although it was hot, it was a perfect day for the church outing—and the most unusual game Mac had ever played.

He and Bob Parks scratched squares on their bingo cards to catch up from earlier in the morning. It was an all-day game, and so far, no one had won. Bob Parks hooted with glee when a cooperative cow left a deposit in one of the chalked grass squares that corresponded to the number of a square on his printed bingo card. In confirmation, the bingo caller (Clifford Myers) yelled out "O-53!"

"Only one left," Bob declared. He circled the hopeful spot on his card.

Mac chuckled. He had mucked enough stalls at Paul's farm to have little regard for cow dung. But here, the cow-pies redeemed themselves, if only to entertain the First Baptist picnic goers.

Bob excused himself. "Ann's motioning for me to come, so I'll see you around. Good luck on the bingo!"

Mac left the fence, too, and wandered back to the potluck tables. Now that lunch was over, most of the main dishes had been removed, but the dessert tables still brimmed with baked goods and an assortment of sugary delights. Mac selected a three-inch slice of coconut cake with half-an-inch of gooey icing and waited while Brooke By-the-Way poured him a cup of coffee. He then guided his paper plate to where his family had gathered for the next event.

"It's time for the watermelon-seed spitting contest," Walter Fisher's voice announced over a portable loudspeaker. "Kids, first, and adults to follow. Children, hurry and take a seat if you're participating!"

Mac watched as a score of kids scrambled onto the benches at one end of a cleared dirt patch. Slices of watermelon rose like a mountain behind the benches, within easy reach of the contestants.

"We'll go one at a time, down the line," said Walter over the speaker. "You each get three tries. Wait for us to announce and record your best distance before the next contestant takes a shot. Miss Leah By-the-Way will go first."

Benjamin and Brooke By-the-Way loudly cheered for their daughter—and the spitting began.

"Pfffssst! Pfffssst! Pfffssst!"

One by one, after Leah's three spits, other youngsters projected seeds into the dirt. Each employed their best technique with great enthusiasm. The last on the bench, Luke Hart, gave it his all—and garnered the most laughs. Luke's missing front teeth were a liability.

"I think he projected the most spit!" Mac guffawed. He didn't know all of the church children, but he had cheered them, just the same.

The children collected their awards and danced about in the praise of their parents. Mac doubted that many adults would now compete—*probably just a couple of old farmers,* he guessed. He knew he wouldn't be one of them. He certainly had no intention of humiliating himself with spitting, even though Andy tried to tease him into it.

"I don't see you lining up, either!" Mac retorted.

But when the adults took their places on the bench, Mac saw that there were six men—and Fannie Weller. Mac recognized the woman but couldn't remember her name. Surely, she was too sophisticated and a little advanced in years for this competition.

"Who's the old gal?" Mac whispered in Abbey's ear.

Abbey smiled and explained that Fannie Weller had won the adult competition for the past two years, and she was set to keep her title.

Mac looked doubtful.

Then Abbey added, "Fannie runs the boarding house for many of the Cherish Playhouse underlings during each theater season. She's an amazing woman and keeps up communication with all of her girls as they move from Cherish to Broadway. But as you can see, for all of her fancy theater connections, Fannie isn't above a good seed-spitting competition!"

"You don't say!" Mac shook his head in disbelief and viewed the action with renewed interest. Could a woman, especially a slightly older woman, really compete in something like this? Fannie intrigued him.

With the ninety-degree sun beating down unmercifully, Mac—and everyone else—noticed that Fannie's second-best wig had curled at the edges, and a stream of perspiration trickled down her neck. But Fannie seemed focused, and she set her spitting stance while the men took their turns before her.

After five men's efforts fell short, it was church-board chairman Luther Sharp's turn. He managed to put in an impressive spurt of ten feet, seven inches—three inches beyond Fannie's best win over the last two years. Fannie, however, appeared unconcerned. The crowd watched as Fannie set her sights on another three to six inches beyond Luther's mark. Her chin said she could do it, and she rolled the first seed between her tongue and the roof of her mouth until just the right moment for release.

Because she knew that, this time, she had stiff competition, Fannie reared back farther than she ever had. And (she told everyone, later) she envisioned a kind of snap to her neck that would project the seed with extra force. Mac saw her close her eyes, position the seed in the roll at the tip of her tongue, grab a mighty intake of air, and then thrust the seed with her tongue, a huff of breath, and the snap of her neck as far as she could make it go.

And it did go! Fannie's seed shot past Luther's by at least two inches. But her effort cost her. Her second-best wig had also taken flight. The hairpiece landed, squarely, in Lou Webb's lap, and in his surprise, Lou hollered out, "Bingo!"

Mac didn't know that Fannie had never been seen in public since her early forties without her wig, but it was evident that she was mortified. More worried about her bare scalp than her modesty, Fannie pulled her skirt up over her face and head. Mac drew back his head, in surprise, and Abbey and several others rushed forward to shelter Fannie from the astonished stares of men, women, and children. Amanda Smith reacted, too. With no thought for the food she sent flying, Amanda tore the tablecloth from under the desserts and rushed to wrap it around Fannie's head so she could retreat with her dignity.

Fannie had taken only a few steps in her turban, however, when she stopped. She turned to look at the crowd—and she burst into laughter.

"I won, didn't I?" she declared. And she couldn't stop laughing. Her giggles caught up the rest of the crowd in the hilarity of the situation.

"By a hair!" shouted Stu Darrell, and the crowd roared again.

Ivey Webb plucked Fannie's wig from Lou's lap and presented it to Fannie with a curtsey.

Mac could hardly talk. He doubled over and gasped for breath.

Then, instead of retreating in embarrassment, Fannie stood tall. With her chin held high, she snatched the tablecloth from her head and planted her second-best wig where it belonged. She, then, put her hands on her hips and laughed.

"I've always said," she chortled, "the show must go on!"

Walter presented Fannie with the annual contestant trophy, and the crowd whistled and cheered, wildly.

Andy learned from Amanda Smith that Fannie's boarders this summer were all members of the stage crew and would never be seen by the play's audiences. It was unusual, but this season's performance had no supporting cast of underlings. All of this year's actors and actresses were headliners, and they all had fine rooms in the top Harmony hotels. It didn't matter to Fannie; she would mother the stage crew as if they were on-stage somebodies.

"I love them all!" she always said. "These are my kids."

Fannie's "family" had grown over the last twenty years since Cherish favorite-son Connor Wilson, Jr.'s illness had forced him to cut short a promising Broadway acting career and return home. Connor's father had started the Cherish Playhouse for his son; and Connor, Jr. had convinced Broadway actors to add Cherish to their tour schedules. The playhouse had operated nonstop ever since.

When the *Cherish Observer* announced the beginning of ticket sales for the fall theater season, Mac made a special trip to town to reserve seats near the front for opening night. He had been impressed with the production that he and Rachel had seen on their first visit to Cherish, and he now wanted to treat the whole family. Two years ago, neither he nor Rachel had had any idea that tiny, out-of-the-way Cherish had such a theater.

Mac had been impressed that headliners he had seen at the Arie Crown in Chicago had also played here: Mickey Rooney, Robert Conrad, Forrest Tucker, and Eve Arden. But Rachel had been more impressed to garner an autograph from one of her favorite soap-opera stars, who also gave her a kiss on the cheek at the Cherish Playhouse stage door. It was one of the few times that Mac had seen Rachel happy. He had teased her about her autograph and her kiss from Rory Duke, and she had relished sharing her brush with fame with the ladies back at her hair salon.

Rachel's signed playbill had been her most treasured possession.

Andy and the rest of the family had never sat so close to the front of any professional theater. But then, there were no bad seats at the Cherish Playhouse.

On opening night, the cast received a standing ovation, and Betsy Palmer accepted an armful of roses from a local admirer. Miss Palmer had thrilled them all with her portrayal of Suzie Hendrix, a blind Greenwich Village housewife who managed to thwart a couple of deadly drug thieves.

Andy could still feel his heart pounding from Roat's unexpected leap across the stage (after the thief had been thought to be dead). Even Mac had yelled out, and several in the audience had screamed. It was thrilling to be scared once in a while, Andy decided, as long as it was vicariously. And who knew that a refrigerator light could mean the difference between life and death?

Mac was the first in line at the alley door to get Miss Palmer's autograph. Betsy flashed Mac a smile and added his name with hers to his *Wait Until Dark* program.

Mac admired the piece of paper and her picture, and he smoothed away all of the wrinkles. "I'm going to frame this," he announced, and he saw Andy grin. He knew Andy thought he looked every bit as star-struck as Rachel had been to meet her favorite television actor. Mac didn't care. This had been a great night.

Now, Mac wanted everyone to see his new house. "There's dessert waiting at my place," he said. "I'll lead the way."

CHAPTER TWENTY-SEVEN

NEW HOUSE

Mac's home surprised them all. Andy, for one, had expected an overly decorated monstrosity like the ostentatious showplace his mom and dad had established on the bluffs in Herndon. But instead, Andy found every room to be tastefully appointed.

"Do you like it?" Mac asked. Then he admitted, "I had help."

Andy whistled his approval. "Very nice, Dad," he said. And Molly whispered, "Wow! You had a good helper."

Mac explained, "A lady from the church helped. She heard I had bought this place, and she said she used to be an interior designer. So, I hired her."

Andy tried to think who that might be, and he finally asked, "Who was it?"

Mac said, "Her name is Emma."

"Emma Peters?" Andy asked in amazement.

"Yeah. Emma Peters. Very nice lady," Mac said.

Andy saw the surprise on Abbey's face too. Emma Peters had a lovely home, but neither Andy nor Abbey had suspected she was an interior decorator. Perhaps she had been in that business before her husband, Jethro, had become ill. Jethro had contracted ALS, and Emma had been his devoted caregiver until he had died about a year ago. Andy and Abbey had not known them prior to Jethro's illness.

Mac proudly guided everyone from room to room, and Andy observed that everything was a pleasant mixture of old and new. Mac had kept the Herndon dining-room set but had replaced the master bedroom suite. He had kept Grannie's rocker but had replaced all other chairs. He had kept the Wedgewood dinner dishes but had replaced the cabinet that held them.

Andy also saw some of Lizzie's crayon drawings on Mac's refrigerator door.

One of the extra bedrooms in the house had become a den, with a massive leather recliner, a large television, and richly paneled walls. Andy pictured his father reclining there with a remote in his hand. Another bedroom had been furnished as a guest room, and there Andy spied his mother's autographed theater program over the dresser.

"That was a good memory," Mac said. "I can still see your mother fingering her cheek after Rory Duke's kiss." Then Mac said, "Your mom used to watch that stupid soap opera every day. I used to get really jealous of that guy."

Andy rolled his eyes and elbowed his dad. "Right! I'm sure you did," he said.

Mac laughed, and Andy realized that he and his dad had just shared a joke. Andy was certain that it was their first.

In her hurry to get everything done before her Labor Day weekend with her granddaughter, Opal had finished and copied off the September newsletter without Andy's review. When Andy saw it, folded and stapled on his desk, he hoped she had remembered to include the hayride. He peeked at the calendar (he shouldn't have doubted her), and he peeked at her poem.

WHILE THE ARK'S IN PARK...
by Opal Reese

WHEN God said He'd send the rain,
It came. It came.
WHEN God said He'd make it rain,
He meant what He said,
And down it came.
Don't stand in the dark while the Ark's in park;
Be smart and run! Get in that Ark!

WHEN the floods come pouring down;
Too late. Too late.
GET on board, don't fiddle around,
God meant what He said:
"Outside you'll drown!"
Don't stand in the dark while the Ark's in park;
Be smart and run! Get in that Ark!

WHEN He pushes shut the door,
Stand back. Stand back.
IF YOU'RE not in, it's way too late.
God meant what He said,
"No time to wait!"
Don't stand in the dark while the Ark's in park;
Be smart and run! Get in that Ark!

For WHEN those floods begin to rise,
You'll drown. You'll drown.
DON'T THINK "there's time to hesitate,"
God meant what He said,
And the floods won't wait.
Don't stand in the dark while the Ark's in park;
Be smart and run! Get in that Ark!

For WHEN those floods begin to rise,
You'll drown. You'll drown.
DON'T THINK "there's time to hesitate,"
God meant what He said,
And the floods won't wait.
Don't stand in the dark while the Ark's in park;
Be smart and run! Get in that Ark!

For ONLY those who listen up
Will float. Will float.
Don't THINK that He will be ignored,
God meant what He said,
Now GET ON BOARD!
Don't stand in the dark while the Ark's in park;
It's sprinkling out! Get in that Ark!

Andy imagined Opal watching him as he read. He grinned. The refrain of *Don't stand in the dark while the Ark's in park* was stuck in his brain, now, and he knew he would be repeating it all day.

Catchy poem, he thought. *It might make a fun song, if somebody could come up with a catchy tune for it.*

CHAPTER TWENTY-EIGHT

RUMORS

"Stop by, any time you're out our way," Molly had always insisted. "We keep a pot of coffee on."

Today, Siege had accepted her offer. A Harmony farm call had resolved more quickly than he had expected, and he realized that he was done for the day. Molly asked him to stay for dinner.

Siege chatted, now, over Paul's shoulder, while Paul finished the milking. Siege commented on how well Annabelle's wound had healed, and Paul quipped, "She had a good vet." Paul started to ask Siege to check on a minor wound on another cow, but he stopped. He realized that it would be presuming on their friendship. Molly had cautioned Paul about picking Siege's brain whenever he was here on a social visit. Molly called it "getting free advice."

Siege saw the cow's wound, however, before Paul could finish his aborted comment. And Siege went out to his truck to pull out his bag.

Uh-oh, Paul thought. *I'm in trouble. If Molly sees Siege with his vet bag, she'll think I've conned him into some free doctoring. Maybe she won't see him out at his truck.*

But Molly had seen Siege from the kitchen window, and she pointedly stared at Paul at dinner and said to Siege, "I hope Paul didn't pump you for free veterinary advice while you were talking out in the barn."

Siege saw Paul deflate, and he realized the difficulty. Siege winked at Paul as if to say, "I've got this."

Then he disarmed Molly with, "You forget! I'm getting a free meal out of the deal—and an invitation to the family's Labor Day picnic."

Molly hadn't expected that. "Oh! Labor Day. Right!" she confirmed.

Paul could see that Molly assumed her husband had already offered Siege the invitation in exchange for his services. Paul was out of the doghouse.

How can Siege think that quickly? Paul wondered. But he was glad that he did!

Labor Day meant leisure, even on the farm—once chores were done, of course.

"Aren't those steaks done, yet?" Paul cried. (Mac had just started grilling the meat, now that Paul had pulled the potatoes and vegetables out of the fire-pit.)

A couple of hot fruit pies cooled on the counter. And Molly's end-of-the-garden salad with homemade dressing filled her largest bowl. Andy and Abbey stuck their homemade ice cream in the freezer until someone called for *ala mode.* And Phillip and Siege brought themselves.

Over dinner, Phillip dominated much of the conversation. Paul whispered to Molly, "I think Dad's been spending too much time at home, alone, and hasn't had a chance to take his words for a walk."

Phillip's topic began to turn contrary, however, and Paul cringed to hear, "Labor Day never took into account all of us farmers; it's just a big city-guy holiday." Before Mac could get his blood up, Paul shot a quick question to Siege.

"Siege, did your Aunt Sooze grow up on a farm?"

Siege had caught the need to change the subject, too, and he fielded the hand-off.

Siege said, "Not a farm, per se. When Aunt Sooze was young, the families in Moody Holler had little plots of sweet potatoes and green beans and the like, but they had little else. The men, like Uncle Defiance, worked in the coal mines instead of at farming. And most of them contracted black lung and left their families with virtually nothing to fall back on. Moody Holler was a poor little huddle of people. Because *nobody* had anything, the families would share whatever they had (or could get, by hook or by crook). One time, a neighbor stole a pig from somewhere and butchered it. Then he held a lottery for the parts. Sooze hoped her family might get some bacon or a jowl. But instead, they got what was left over: the head, minus the brain."

"Soup?" Paul asked.

Siege laughed. "That's probably what you or I would have done with it. But no. Sooze said her mom made head cheese, of a sort. Sooze said she cut off every bit of flesh from that thing and sliced it, thin as paper—ears and snout and all. Then she stirred lard into it and spread the top with a cornmeal mixture and more lard. The whole thing was set out in the sun so the lard could melt through it. Then she lowered it, down, to sit on top of the water in the well, to cool and congeal. When she pulled it up, she sliced it, pan-fried it, and served it with sorghum."

Paul made a face. "I can't imagine," he shuddered. "We have so much here on the farm, it's hard to think of people struggling like that and having to make the most of virtually nothing."

Siege nodded. "Sooze said that she and her siblings grew up on sorghum and whatever they could scavenge. The kids usually didn't have but a bite of cornbread for breakfast, and they'd pick wild berries along the way to school, until things froze."

"At least they went to school," Paul noted. "Some people in the backwoods didn't believe in schools."

"Not for girls, anyway," said Siege. "Sooze didn't learn to read until she left the holler."

Then Siege added, "Very few people could read, and some folks couldn't give you the date they were born. Births didn't happen in hospitals. Birth records were by word of mouth—whatever the family remembered. To prove to the teachers that a boy was old enough to go to school, they'd have him reach over his head and grab his ear. If he was ear-grabbin' age, he could go to school. If he wasn't, he stayed home."

"Huh!" Paul said. He looked at Emily in her high chair and observed that her little arms couldn't reach over her head in the way Siege had demonstrated. Paul wondered how accurate arm growth was in determining age. He might do an informal experiment with some of the kids at the church on Sunday.

"And after all that sad talk," interrupted Molly, "I think it's time for ice cream and pie, don't you?"

Then she added, "I almost feel like we should pray again—we have so much. And maybe pray for those in the world who still have little opportunity and little to eat."

Paul agreed. The family bowed their heads and thanked God a second time for their many blessings. Then Paul asked God to bless all those who were less fortunate.

"And help us to be generous in our charity," he said. And everyone said, "Amen!"

When Opal returned from her Labor Day week with her family, Andy caught her daydreaming at her desk.

"Earth to Opal. Earth to Opal," Andy teased.

Opal apologized and sighed happily. She declared, "That little Zephyr is the sweetest baby ever born!"

Andy didn't want to argue; but everybody knew that his niece, Emily, was the sweetest.

"And she loves music," Opal said. "Her momma says she patty-cakes to *Twinkle, Twinkle Star,* and she wakes up clapping. Such a happy child."

"And," sighed Opal, "She can almost say 'Gramma.'"

Andy indulged Opal's daydreaming, and in the back of his mind he wondered how long it would be before Emily could call him "Uncle."

A few days later, Opal stood her ground. She was adamant about what she'd seen. Andy suggested she had been daydreaming, again.

"I know what I saw," she said.

Andy didn't think so. He couldn't imagine that it was true.

He asked again, "You say you saw my dad with a woman, having dinner?"

"That's right," said Opal. "And you know her."

"Okay," Andy finally said. "Spill!"

Opal could hardly get the words out fast enough. "My sisters and I were in Ft. Marshall, and we went to the Italian Olive, where they serve unlimited salad with your meal. And that's where we saw them. I don't think your dad recognized me. But Emma did."

"Emma Peters?" Andy exclaimed. "My dad was eating out with Emma Peters?"

Opal folded her hands and nodded decisively. "That's right!"

Andy marveled. "Well, what do you know!"

For the last couple of weeks, Mac hadn't come to dinner before midweek Bible study. Andy had assumed it was because he now had his own place in town and could easily swing by a drive-through for some take-out items that he could eat while watching the evening news. Andy wondered, now, if his dad and Emma had been going out all this time. Or was Emma Peters feeding him at her house?

Emma was a free woman, of course, and so was his dad. But Andy hadn't given it a thought that his dad might start to date. He had not imagined his dad with someone. But he realized, now, how unreasonable that was.

Emma Peters! Andy tried to imagine his dad with Emma. And unconsciously, he compared Emma to his mother.

Emma's a woman who can hold her own, he thought. *After all, she took care of Jethro and the needs of their house for many years. And she's a good cook. Her dishes at church potlucks always disappear first. She's an immaculate housekeeper. And Emma's attractive—not the beauty that Mom was, but attractive. And a relationship with Emma would start clean. No baggage. No ghosts from the past.*

Andy decided that he approved. Not that his dad needed his approval to start dating. But Andy felt that Emma and Mac might be good for each other.

He laughed. He couldn't wait to tell Abbey. But he decided not to tell Molly. Mac should be the one to tell her, in his own time. *After all,* Andy thought, *I'm not supposed to know, yet, either.*

CHAPTER TWENTY-NINE

HEAVEN?

Andy observed that Mac and Emma always arrived separately for Sunday service and mid-week Bible study. And they didn't always sit together. He guessed that they weren't ready to have people link them as a couple. Or maybe they had already broken up. Andy wondered if and when his dad might share about it.

When Mac remained in the sanctuary one Wednesday night after everyone had left, Andy wondered if the time had come. But instead, Mac had a question.

"What can you tell me about what Heaven is like?" he asked.

Andy reined in his thoughts about his dad's dating. Instead, Andy's mind raced through all of the ways Heaven is portrayed in the Bible—and all of the ways that people interpret those clues. He decided the best answer was, "Heaven is where we'll be with God, and we never have to leave."

"And we'll see other people there, too, won't we?" Mac prompted.

Andy thought of all the times he had imagined Heaven as a place of reunion for people who had died. Christians not only came face-to-face with their Lord, in Heaven, but they were also reunited with friends and loved ones. When Grannie had died, Andy had pictured her in her favorite hat and with her lips rouged, laughing with Jesus and old friends over the same stories she had told while on earth. Then, when his mother had died, Andy had imagined her joining that group and sharing in their laughter.

Of course, these were speculations, but the Bible did say that we will recognize others in Heaven, and we would definitely be in the presence of Jesus.

"Yes, we'll see people like Grannie and Mom," said Andy.

"And Little Mac?" Mac asked quietly.

"Yes," said Andy. "Little Mac will be there, too."

Andy saw questions in his father's eyes, and he waited for his dad to put them into words. Mac shifted his weight and finally said, "Does Rachel worry about me?"

Now Andy knew what was bothering his dad. "I don't think so," Andy said, "for two reasons. One, the Bible says that Heaven is paradise and that, when we see God, we will be happy and free of the worries and concerns of this earth. And two, the Bible says of us Christians on earth, that we are on a journey God has set out for us. So, since He is in charge of our lives, down here, no one in Heaven needs to worry about us."

Mac nodded, but his brow remained furrowed with more questions. He asked, "I imagine that when I die and Rachel and I meet in Heaven, things will be different between us, right? I mean, will we still remember all the bad stuff that messed us up?"

Andy opened his Bible, so he could quote accurately. He said, "The book of Revelation (21:4) tells us that God *'will wipe away every tear from their eyes. There will be no more death or mourning or crying or pain, for the old order of things has passed away.'"*

Andy then said, "I'm not sure if this means that all of our hurtful memories will be done away with, or if we will keep those memories but that God will touch them in such a way that they no longer hurt us. Either way, those memories won't affect our relationship to Him or others while we're with Him. It wouldn't be Heaven if we were still mourning our sins and hurts from earth."

Mac nodded. "That's what I think, too."

Then he asked, "Will Rachel know me when I get there?"

"Oh, yes," Andy said. "That's pretty clear in Scripture. In Matthew 22:32 Jesus repeats God's words from Exodus 3:6, *'Have you not read what God said to you, "I am the God of Abraham, the God of Isaac, and the God of Jacob"? He is not the God of the dead but of the living.'* In quoting this, Jesus is saying that we are still who we are and we don't lose our identity, even after we die."

Mac nodded again. But then he asked, "So, if Rachel and I are still who we are, are we still married in Heaven?"

Andy couldn't help but smile. He understood his father's dilemma. Could a Christian marry again, or would that mess up some eternal plan? Andy didn't want to reveal that he knew about Emma, so he answered without alluding to anything personal.

"Ah!" said Andy, and he turned back to Matthew 22. He read from verses 23 to 30:

"'That same day the Sadducees...came to [Jesus] with a question. 'Teacher,' they said, 'Moses told us that if a man dies without having children, his brother must marry the widow and have children for him. Now, there were seven brothers among us. The first one married and died, and since he had no children, he left his wife to his brother. The same thing happened to the second and third brother, right on down to the seventh. Finally, the woman died. Now then, at the resurrection, whose wife will she be of the seven, since all of them were married to her?' Jesus replied, 'You are in error because you do not know the Scriptures or the power of God. At the resurrection people will neither marry nor be given in marriage; they will be like the angels in heaven.'"

Mac leaned back in his chair. "Huh!" he said. "I don't necessarily get the part about marrying your brother's wife, but I guess it's pretty clear that marriage is just for us on earth."

"Right," said Andy. "And the part about the brothers marrying is something from an earlier culture, which we don't do any longer."

"It could get messy," Mac said, and he smiled.

Andy smiled, too.

CHAPTER THIRTY

WINSTON

Nothing Abbey did would make the car start. She sat at the intersection, helpless, while cars behind her honked angrily. Drivers in Harmony were not as patient as those in Cherish. Finally, she threw up her hands and opened the car door. When she got out, so did a young man from a couple of cars back.

"If I push, can you steer the car through the intersection and over to the shoulder?" he asked.

Abbey breathed a sigh of relief. "Oh, yes! Thank you, so much!"

She climbed back behind the wheel, and the young man got the vehicle rolling. A woman directed traffic until the car had cleared the intersection and was out of the way.

"I'd be happy to take you to a repair station," the woman offered, and Abbey gratefully accepted.

Why did this have to happen, today? I just wanted to do a little shopping. And it's so late, now. I need to get home and let Winston out.

Andy was at an evangelism training session in Decatur with Luther Sharp and wouldn't be home until after supper. *Poor Winston!*

Abbey called and asked Molly if she could pick her up and take her to Cherish. Molly promised to be there, shortly. The repair shop collected the car but said they couldn't work on it until morning, and Abbey sighed. *Great! I'll have to presume on someone else for a favor when the car's done. I just keep messing up everyone's day.*

Molly told Paul where she was headed, and she and Emily started out.

Poor Abbey! Molly thought. *There's nothing worse than being stuck away from home with car trouble—except maybe if it's winter and it's freezing cold and there are no other cars around or places to call from or you've gone off the road and are hurt…*

The more Molly thought about all of the worse scenarios, the more she was glad that Abbey was safe.

"I can take you to the farm for supper," Molly suggested.

But Abbey told her she had to let Winston out. "It would be best if you just drop me off in Cherish, and I can eat dinner at home," Abbey said.

"Or," said Molly, "I have a better idea! Why don't we let Winston out and then go to the Star Diner for dinner? I'm hungry for some baked steak. We can make a girl's evening of it."

"But won't Paul need supper?" Abbey protested.

"Leftovers," said Molly. "Paul can make a sandwich from last night's roast beef, and I'll reward him with fried chicken tomorrow."

It was settled.

Winston wagged his body, glad that someone had finally come home. He dutifully did his business and hurried back inside. He put his feet up on Molly's legs and sniffed Emilie's feet.

Molly decided that Winston missed Emily. Whenever they came to Cherish, he would snort his welcome and station himself beside her. His eyes never left the baby during their visit.

She wondered what would happen if she put Emily on the floor. She'd always been a little afraid of that, in case Winston would get too rambunctious. And Emily had never been so close to the dog. The new farm dog, the one that had replaced Skipper, was a puppy and had too much energy to be trusted. Plus, he had no house manners. Winston was more settled and obedient. So, today, with no other distractions, Molly decided to try it.

Winston immediately licked the baby's cheeks. Instead of crying, Emily laughed, and with Winston's face between her little hands, she kissed his nose. Her tiny fingers explored his wrinkles and jowls, and Winston sat transfixed.

Molly knew the friendship was solid when Winston brought Emily his favorite stuffed toy.

"Now, I'm going to have to wash that slobbery thing a little more often!" Abbey laughed.

Winston's eyes grew sad when everyone left for the diner.

"Winston is really Andy's dog," Abbey said, between bites of salad and baked steak. "Winston always wants to be right next to Andy on the sofa in the television room. I might as well as be on the moon, for all the attention I get when the two of them are together."

"I'm not surprised," said Molly. "Andy and Muff used to be best friends when we were kids. I can imagine how Andy carries on with Winston."

Abbey laughed. "The other night, when I was helping Betty Darrell finish decorating for a Sunday school party at her house, Andy brought some work home. He laid out his books on the television room sofa to work, and Winston wasn't a bit happy. Andy said that he pawed the edge of the sofa and snorted to let Andy know that the books were in his spot. But Andy ignored him.

"Finally, Winston slumped on the carpet and just stared while Andy worked.

"But after a while, Winston heaved himself to his feet, padded past Andy, and went to the back door. Andy said he stood there whining urgently. Andy muttered under his breath and had to mark his place in three different books before he got up. He said he finally trudged through the living room and kitchen, and Winston looked up at him by the door as if to say 'what took you so long?' Then, Andy turned the knob and held the door open. But Winston wasn't there. Winston had disappeared.

"Andy called for him, but Winston didn't respond, so Andy backtracked through the kitchen and living room. And when he got to the television room he realized what that square-headed pooch had done.

"That dog had pushed away those books and made a spot for himself! He had been smart enough to pretend he had to go out, so Andy would leave the room. Can you believe it?"

Molly laughed. "They are smart! Muff was no dummy, either."

Abbey said, "I just had no idea that dogs could be so conniving. I don't remember any of the pets I grew up with being that smart."

"And determined," said Molly. "They aren't called 'BULLdogs' for no reason. I think it's because they're so bullheaded!"

Andy borrowed June Green's car to take Abbey back to Harmony in the morning to pick up the car. And they stopped for a minute to visit at the farm. The new puppy greeted them, already doing his job of announcing their arrival with a series of high-pitched yelps.

Andy, of course, got out and tussled with him, and Moose followed them to the house.

"Why 'Moose?'" Andy asked. "He's not that big."

Paul pointed to his feet. "See those paws? He'll be growing into those, soon. His papa is a big bear of a thing. He's going to be a 'Moose,' all right!"

"Well," said Andy, "I suppose, the bigger, the better for a farm dog."

"Yeah," said Paul. "Not like that spoiled rotten, low-to-the-ground thing you've got!"

"Oh!" Andy exclaimed. "I'm wounded to the core!"

They laughed and headed inside for coffee.

Back at the parsonage, Andy chuckled that Winston had no idea what people really thought of him.

CHAPTER THIRTY-ONE

SEARCHING FOR LIZZIE

The cool, starry autumn night was perfect for the church hayride. Bundled in jackets, scarves, and hats, church families and friends settled into the bed of straw on the wooden wagon and drew woolen blankets over their laps. Clouds of misty breath swirled around the heads of the two massive draft horses as they patiently waited for everyone to finish boarding the wagon.

"Chk! Chka! Giddap."

Finally, at the low sound of the farmer's voice, the horses' ears flicked back. At the driver's urging and a slight jiggle of the reins, they lowered their heads and put their shoulders into the initial pull. The wagon lurched, and with a creak of harness leather and the sluggish jog-thud of wheels over muddy ruts and potholes, the horses drew the wagonload of hushed passengers away from the bustle of everyday life. They were gently borne into the heart of a peaceful darkness presided over by the timeless stars and a benevolent moon.

Occasionally someone would call out or laugh, but for the most part, the confidences on the wagon were muted and lazy. Even the teens, gathered in the back with their feet hung over the end, giggled and gossiped quietly.

The only complaint was that the ride had to end.

"It seems like we just started," murmured Abbey. Andy held her arm as she slipped off the wagon edge and onto the little platform. A second round of passengers prepared to board.

The campfire they now gathered around exuded a welcoming warmth. With a cup of hot chocolate in one hand and a charred hot dog in the other, Abbey and Andy settled onto bales of hay and watched the sparks fly upward.

"Isn't this the greatest taste?" Andy asked no one in particular.

Once the last wagonload had returned and consumed their meal, and after the flaming logs had burned low, the bundled assembly toasted marshmallows to slap between graham crackers and squares of chocolate. Pleasantly full and starry-eyed, the huddle of families stared at the fire and into the sky, ready to listen to Andy and his devotional thought.

"Isn't it beautiful to be out here, tonight," Andy began, "where we can look at the world in a different light? Our perspective changes when we're surrounded by nature and are away from our usual routine. We see the same sky every night from our backyards, but for some wonderful reason, out here it seems more vast and profound. At home, we feel the same chill from the wind, and we rush inside to avoid it; but here we rush to the campfire and gladly huddle together with backsides to the cold and front sides to the warmth. At home, a supper of hot dogs never tastes the same as the wieners roasted over an open fire. And s'mores just aren't the same over an electric burner on the stove."

Andy let that image flicker in the minds of his listeners, and they smiled. Then he continued.

"Just as the everyday things we enjoy take on an enhanced pleasure when we draw apart into nature, the same is true of our time with God. When we draw apart and focus on Him, He helps us see our blessings in a new light: His light. Jesus made it possible for us to walk in two worlds: one we see with our physical eyes, and one we see with our spiritual eyes. It's our choice whether or not we lift up our spiritual eyes to see heavenly things. Each time we say, 'Hello, Father, help me to draw apart with You for a while,' He opens our spiritual eyes to see the earthly things around us from His heavenly perspective. Tonight, the stars and the moon are simply reminders that there is more. The skies point us to Him. Let's take a moment, now, to lift our hearts and to thank our Creator for the wonderful promise of heavenly things that are ours in Christ."

Andy guided everyone's prayers beyond the darkness. No doubt, God added them to His treasured collection, gathered into the great golden bowls of incense before His throne.

At Andy's amen, Abbey started to softly sing the first verse of *How Great Thou Art*, and everyone joined in with worship on their lips. The music left their hearts full with praise, and no one moved for several minutes. It seemed the moment should last forever, but it could not. The outing had come to an end.

Moms and dads gently roused their slumbering toddlers and rounded up their older children. With gentle good-byes and with their blankets and food baskets in hand, families made their way to the cars.

As Abbey rose to twist the closure on the last package of marshmallows, she heard Sylvia Potts call out, "Has anyone seen Lizzie?"

When no one answered, Sylvia repeated her cry. "I'm looking for Lizzie. Has anyone seen her?"

Again, no one responded.

Sylvia passed among the departing families and asked if they'd seen her little girl. Parents shook their heads, and Sylvia quizzed their children. But no one seemed to have seen Lizzie.

Abbey thought it strange. *Where is Lizzie?* she wondered.

"I can't find Lizzie!" Sylvia insisted when she returned to the fire ring. "I thought she was eating s'mores, back at the serving table with the other children. I went to get her and she wasn't there. I've checked with families who are leaving, and they haven't seen her. And I don't know where else to look."

Abbey tried to remember when she had last seen her little friend. She had helped Lizzie with a hot marshmallow, but Abbey realized she hadn't seen her after that.

Betty Darrell corralled her boys and leaned in to say, "I remember seeing Lizzie petting one of the farm cats after we melted the first round of marshmallows, but I don't recall seeing her later. Are you sure she isn't with Stevie?"

Sylvia mumbled that no, she wasn't with Stevie. As if to verify it, Stevie ran up to say he hadn't found Lizzie, yet. Sylvia clung to him as if her son would disappear, too.

Abbey worried. *What's happened to Lizzie? We need to find her.*

She helped Sylvia check with the few people who were still hanging about. Some of the families with older children helped to question others, too. They were all sure Lizzie had to be somewhere, with somebody's children.

Stu Darrell, Danny Hart, and Bob Parks caught a huddle of teens playing with a glowing ember from the fire. The men put out the smoldering remains and sent the boys to find their parents. The boys hadn't seen Lizzie. And neither had the farmer who had driven the hay wagon; a careful check through the hay confirmed that the little girl was not there. The farmer finally drove the horses away, to get them settled into the barn for the night.

A couple of men passed among the cars that remained, but no one reported having seen Lizzie after they'd started the s'mores. A couple of women recalled the little farm cat that Betty had mentioned, but they hadn't seen the cat again, either.

With every negative report, Abbey worried more, and Sylvia's alarm grew. Family after family left for home, and in the quiet that remained, Sylvia shivered. She wanted to go home, too—with her two children. But where, dear God, was Lizzie?

Stu, Danny, and Bob finally sent their families home in the Darrell's car, but the men remained; they assured Sylvia they would stay until Lizzie was found.

The men began to call in various directions into the night. Deep baritone and clarion tenor voices shouted at the top of their lungs and then strained their ears in hopes that a little voice would answer. But no matter how loudly they cried out, Lizzie did not respond.

"She's here, somewhere," Danny assured Sylvia. "We'll keep looking."

Stevie's eyes grew large when his mother suddenly screamed, "She can't have just vanished!" and she yelled, "Lizzie! LIZZIE, WHERE ARE YOU?"

Abbey's heart constricted; she shared Sylvia's fear.

After combing the clearing for the sixth time with the men, Danny shook his head. "This doesn't make sense," he said.

Larry voiced the fear he'd pushed from his mind, until now. "I think she's in there, Andy," he dared to say, and he pointed to the cornfields. Then Larry whispered so his wife couldn't hear: "Lizzie would be answering if she was close or wasn't hurt. We've got to find her!"

More than a half-mile of corn flanked the clearing on all sides. Where should they start?

As the four men approached the edge of the field nearest the campfire, Andy realized for the first time the corn's height and how thickly it had been planted. He had always pictured it in wide rows with easy paths to walk down, but he could see now that the mature and drying corn had filled in what he had imagined as paths. The corn ridges rippled the ground and made it difficult to walk. Searching the field at night was going to be a challenge. Would a little girl have walked into a field like this? Andy had a hard time imagining it. Venturing even a few feet into the field in the dark was daunting, and once you got in a short distance, it would be easy to get turned around.

Evidently worried about the same thing, Bob Parks pulled his car around and aimed its headlights at the field. Now, if someone didn't search in too far, the lights would give a direction to return to. The searchers spread out about twenty feet apart, and gripping their flashlights, they began to trample their way into the field and call out Lizzie's name.

Abbey and Sylvia remained by the fire, to wait helplessly.

At least we're warm, thought Abbey. But then she imagined Lizzie, cold and alone. Abbey whispered a prayer: *Lord, send Your angels to warm her and to help us find her!*

Sylvia sheltered Stevie from the cold, and Abbey poured the last of the hot chocolate to warm the cups in their hands. The women listened, tuned acutely to every sound.

Stevie absorbed his mother's fear, as he leaned against her, and when he whimpered, Abbey assured him, "They'll find her."

Finally, Abbey tore her mind away from the search and cast about for something to take Stevie's mind off the fear that hung in the air.

"Have you caught any salamanders, lately?" Abbey asked, although she was aware that it was too cold, now, to find them. She had been unable to think of anything else to say. "I remember the one you caught a few months ago in our window well."

(Abbey didn't mention the commotion that had sent the salamander flying through her kitchen.)

"That was Spotty," Stevie recalled, brightening. "I put him back into the window well before we went to Grandma and Grandpa's house, but he must have moved while we were away. When I got home, he was gone."

Then he added, "I found a garter snake, though."

Sylvia frowned. The snake had not been her favorite.

"What did you do with the snake, once you caught him?" Abbey asked.

"I had a cage my dad made, with dirt in the bottom and some branches and screen stuff on the sides so he could breathe and so you could see 'im."

"What did you feed him?"

"Worms and bugs and…"

Sylvia interrupted. "We kept the cage outdoors."

"I can only keep my snakes and salamanders for three days," Stevie continued. "My dad says I have to let 'em go after that because they get homesick. I think that's why Spotty moved. He must have had family somewhere else."

Abbey smiled. "Well, that sounds like a good plan. It would be really sad if the things you caught got too homesick."

"I had a hamster, once," Stevie offered. "I didn't have to let him go after three days. I don't think he had any mommy or daddy, so I got to be his family."

As they talked, Sylvia closed her eyes. Abbey knew she was praying, begging God to let them find her little girl.

"What's your favorite animal?" Abbey asked the boy.

They chattered on, about animals, Stevie's friends, and what he was learning at school. The time passed slowly, and the search continued.

Stevie grew less and less talkative, and his eyelids began to droop. Abbey could see that he would be asleep in a few minutes, and she was relieved. She had run out of questions to ask, and she wanted to listen and pray.

God, she prayed, *please help us find Lizzie, soon.*

Shortly after eleven, Walter Fisher's pickup returned. Walter called out, "I've brought backups!"

Sylvia turned, ready to thank whoever had come to join in the search.

But instead of a truckload of men prepared to wander the fields with flashlights, out bounded Walter's two old dogs. The animals jumped playfully around their master.

Sylvia smiled wanly. Abbey knew she had been hoping for an army instead of two skinny old dogs.

"Sylvia, do you have any of Lizzie's things I can have the dogs sniff?" Walter asked. His exceptional blue eyes twinkled pleasantly in the flicker of the fire.

Sylvia looked doubtful. "Those don't look like hound dogs. Are they search-trained?" she asked.

"Oh, not really," Walter answered. "But I figure every dog has some ability to do that."

I don't think so, Abbey thought to herself. She doubted that Winston would qualify in any way as a search dog. But Abbey tried to believe that Walter's dogs were different. It couldn't hurt to let his animals add to the effort.

"I also called the State Patrol," Walter said, "and they said they'd send some help."

Now Sylvia's eyes displayed gratefulness.

Then, because Stevie still slept on Sylvia's lap, Abbey brought Lizzie's stuffed bunny from the car. Walter let the dogs lick and smell the worn, furry toy.

"Okay, boys," he said. "Let's go find the bunny girl!"

Walter switched on a large industrial flashlight, and he led the dogs into the cornfield in the west section, across from where the other men were looking.

"Please be careful," called Abbey. "Don't YOU get lost."

Unaware that Walter had come, the other men continued their search in the east section. Abbey had just commented on how quiet it had become, when Andy and the others stepped out of the field. Their sagging shoulders registered defeat.

Abbey explained that someone from the State Patrol was coming, and that news drew grateful nods. Then she said that Walter had just begun searching the west section with his dogs.

At that, Larry and Andy immediately jumped up to join Walter. Danny Hart stayed by the fire, and Bob Parks turned off his car lights, checked his battery, and hurried to catch up with Larry and Andy. It was easy to follow the trail the others had smashed as they'd made their way forward.

Danny suggested the women go home. He would stay by the fire and meet the State Patrol when they came. Sylvia refused to leave, at first. But she finally relented because of Stevie.

Abbey went with her, not wanting Sylvia to worry at home, alone. Neither of the women would sleep until Lizzie was found.

After she had let Winston out, Abbey sat at Sylvia's kitchen table and drank coffee and prayed with her. Butter waited by the door for his friend to come home.

"They'll find her, soon," Abbey said, to assure Sylvia and herself. "I'm sure they will."

Back at the campsite, the wind picked up, and Andy felt the cold. His jacket had been adequate for the hayride, but it wasn't warm enough for the middle of a cornfield after midnight. Walking helped, and he prayed that God would, somehow, keep Lizzie protected from hypothermia.

The dogs were disappointingly silent, so unlike the dogs in the movies that bayed in the distance, hard on the scent of their prey.

These scrawny animals are virtually useless, Andy thought. *Walter hasn't even put them on leashes— probably can't find the leads,* he thought uncharitably, as he recalled how cluttered the Fisher home was.

Larry growled, too, that the dogs were worthless.

The dogs ran free as if playing a game. They scampered ahead and then circled back for a pat on the head.

Andy tipped his flashlight to look at his watch and saw that the hands were close to midnight. He wondered if the State Patrol had come. They had heard only one another.

Please, Lord, keep Lizzie safe and help us to find her, soon, Andy prayed over and over. *Open our eyes and ears, and point us in the right direction.*

The dimming flashlights would be useless, before long.

"I can't imagine Lizzie could have walked this far," Larry said. "She's just a little girl!" He choked back a sob.

The men knew he was right, but no one wanted to turn back.

Walter called for the dogs. They had been gone for several minutes, now. "Come on Hank! Come on Bandit!" Walter shouted. But unlike before, the dogs didn't emerge from the corn.

Andy wondered if the animals had grown tired of their game and had wandered off.

"Now, where could those fool dogs have gone?" Walter grumbled. "It's not like them."

Andy shook his head. Now they were missing a little girl and two dogs. He couldn't get excited about the dogs, right now.

Bandit suddenly bounded out of the corn and whipped his tail around Walter's legs. Begging for a pat on the head, he pushed his muzzle into Walter's palm.

"Well, there you are!" Walter laughed. "Okay, now where's Hank? Come on, Hank!" he called.

But Hank did not come.

"Where do you suppose that crazy dog is?" Walter muttered. He had bragged earlier that the two dogs were virtually inseparable. It was unusual for one to return without the other.

They waited, but Hank did not appear.

Walter looked puzzled, and then he suddenly whispered, "What if Hank found Lizzie?"

Energized by his own suggestion, Walter bellowed for Hank at the top of his lungs. And because Walter was so insistent, Larry and Andy did the same. With no other hope in sight, they all tried to think this might be the answer. It was unlikely, but they had nothing else to hold onto.

Then Bandit barked. When he did, Andy thought he heard Hank bark back. It was very faint, but the others said they had heard him, too.

It had grown quiet again as they had strained to hear the dog's bark. The only sound was the light breeze rustling in the stalks and teasing their ears.

Then Bandit barked, again, and whined next to Walter—and Hank barked a reply.

Hank's bark was not nearby, and Andy tried to gauge where the sound was coming from. It seemed to come from more directions than one—a trick of the ear.

Walter willed Bandit to bark. When he did, they all agreed that Hank's reply came from behind them, which seemed odd. It meant that Hank had gone into the field across the road. No one had imagined that Lizzie would have crossed the road.

Bandit barked, again. At Hank's reply, this time, Larry bounded off toward the road and left the rest of them to catch up as best they could.

Bandit did not leave Walter's side as they stumbled their way forward. The dog with them continued to bark, and Hank replied, every time.

On the other side of the road, Hank's barks grew louder. The men panted and crashed through the field, hearts pounding with hope.

In the lead, Larry and Andy crashed together through a wall of stalks and into a little hole in the field. There sat Lizzie with a big golden dog wrapped around her to keep her warm.

Walter and Bandit crashed through, last, and Bandit wiggled his way over to lick Lizzie's face. Then he pranced around Hank and sat down beside him. The dogs jostled one another in greeting.

"Good dog, Hank! Good dog, Bandit! Good boys!" Walter exclaimed, over and over, and he patted their heads.

Larry ran his hand gratefully over Hank's muzzle, as he stooped to gather up his little girl.

Lizzie sighed a quiet, "Hi, Daddy," and Larry pressed her into his shoulder. She was cold. Larry opened his jacket to fold her closer to his warmth, and then he laid his head on his child with a sob.

"I know'd you'd come," Lizzie said. "I called when you hollered, but you couldn't hear me."

It also looked as if Lizzie had been sleeping in the little clearing. Perhaps she had been asleep when Hank and Bandit had found her. Now, as Larry held her close, Hank licked her shoes and hands.

Then the two dogs bounded ahead of the group, back to the road and across to the campfire.

Walter kept shouting for the benefit of the those at the fire, "We've got her! We've got Lizzie! She's okay!"

Andy heard echoed shouts of "Hooray!" from two voices: two men and no women.

At the campfire, Danny raised his hands to praise the Lord, and then he explained that the women had gone home. Deputy Engle shook Larry's hand and said how glad he was that the little girl had been found. Then Engle radioed from his squad car for the helicopter to turn back.

"I'm so sorry for the bother," Larry told him when he heard about the helicopter. But the trooper answered, "No problem.

We're glad you found her. It's mighty cold out here tonight for a little girl to be lost."

"And now," Engle said, "I can be going. We can ALL go home and get a good night's rest!" He tipped his hat and strode away to the patrol car.

As he departed, Lizzie rubbed her eyes and said sleepily, "I lost the kitty. She went in there, and I almost had her, but then I couldn't find her. And then I couldn't get out. I called, but nobody answered, 'cept Jesus."

Larry smiled and hugged her fiercely. "I'm so glad you're okay, honey," he said.

But Andy asked, "What did Jesus say, Lizzie?"

The little girl yawned, and Andy thought she was too sleepy to answer. But then she said, "He didn't use words, but I heard Him. He just said, 'don't cry. You just settle down, Lizzie. It's okay.' And then I wasn't afraid. And then the big dogs came, and the yellow one slept with me."

She rested her head on Larry's shoulder, and her eyes closed.

"Thank you, God!" whispered Larry.

Andy silently prayed, too. *Thank you, God, for speaking to a lost little girl, just like you talked to me, years ago, when I was lost and didn't even know it.*

Andy was grateful that Deputy Engle had asked the dispatcher to telephone Sylvia to let her know that Lizzie was on her way home. He knew it would stop their worry, and they would be ready for the men to get home.

Andy and Danny smothered the remains of the fire, and Larry wrapped Lizzie in the blankets his family had covered themselves with on the hayride—a hayride that had faded into yesterday.

Without the fire, the night grew utterly black. Andy flipped on a flashlight that Deputy Engle had loaned them, and they all walked to the cars.

On the way, Larry stopped Walter. "Walter," Larry said, "I have to tell you I'm sorry. I didn't believe those dogs were going to be any good. I wasn't nice in my thoughts about you—even though you had come back to help. I'm sorry. I want to thank you for helping find my little girl. I thank God for you, and I love that big yellow dog!"

Danny and Andy had had similar thoughts, but they said nothing. Larry had said it all.

Walter seemed humbled. Next to him, the dogs sat, unaware of the heroes they'd become. Their only concern was if they were going home, now. Walter opened the truck gate, and they jumped in.

Then Walter said, "You know, I have to admit that I didn't think they'd be much good, either. But it was the only thing I had to offer for the search. If that had been my little girl, I wouldn't have been able to rest until I found her. Thank God, we did!"

Even in the dark Andy knew that Walter's blue, blue eyes were glistening with tears. Andy reflected that although Walter and Charlene had a cluttered home, there was no clutter in their hearts.

Andy slept until nearly noon the next day, after he had roused at eight to telephone Opal with news of the happy ending. He knew she would be inundated with calls from families hoping to hear that Lizzie had been found safe. While everyone (except perhaps Georgia Wheeler) would avoid calling the Potts or the parsonage for fear of waking them, they would all check with Opal at the church office to get the news.

Opal even received a call from the *Cherish Observer.* A reporter had learned of the State Patrol's request for a helicopter. By mid-afternoon, the reporter had taken pictures of Lizzie and her family, and he'd visited Walter's home for photographs of Hank and Bandit. The story appeared in the evening paper— but was heard on the local radio broadcast, first. Luther Sharp said it was also picked up by the *Decatur Dispatch,* and he had seen it on Decatur television.

Luther said the Decatur anchor on the Lizzie story had led off with, "Now, for the dramatic canine rescue of a little four-year-old girl, lost at night in a Tobler County cornfield…"

That's where Mac heard the story, too, and he called Andy to make sure his little friend, Lizzie, was okay.

CHAPTER THIRTY-TWO

JUNIOR'S DENTURES AND OTHER LOCAL LORE

Small town stories live on. Lizzie's rescue rose to the level of legend-supported-by-truth, and it fit nicely into the annals of Cherish First Baptist's favorite tales: Andy's shooting prowess, the bat in the sanctuary, the boiling baptistry, and the homeless Catholic man who had passed himself off as Baptist when he was discovered asleep in a First Baptist pew.

Andy marveled that unlike what one might suspect, the stories remained fairly accurate in their telling and retelling. What Andy heard about Lizzie's rescue at the grocery store matched well with what he overheard at the barbershop and at the hardware store. But the telling of one tale always led to the telling of another. That's how Andy learned three things about his church members that he had not known before Lizzie's rescue.

First, he learned from Ivey Webb that the Webb name held a genetic secret: Deacon Lou Webb and his family all carried a gene that resulted in at least two webbed toes. In the middle of the hardware store, Ivey had ordered Lou to take off his shoes and socks to show Andy and to verify her story. "Yessiree," Joe Seese had commented, along with several others who had now seen it for themselves. "That's quite a useful genetic trait, if you happen to be a swimmer." The crowd at the hardware store had laughed, including the good-natured Lou Webb.

Second, Andy learned the reason for Church Moderator Luther Sharp's limp. It seems that the wind had blown Luther's shirttail into the spinning power take-off stub of his idling tractor, one day. One minute he was transferring silage, and the next he was being whipped about and virtually stripped naked. Luther's shoulder and left arm were bloodied and torn up, and his left leg was severely broken. Fortunately, the driver of a passing school bus had seen it all, and he had rushed to the farmhouse to call the emergency squad. The incident had left its mark on the children in the bus, however, and had spurred extra caution in every farmer in the county. Everyone said that Luther was lucky to be alive.

Third, Andy learned why usher Junior Harris refused to wear his false teeth. Evidently Junior had come across a buckshot dog in the middle of one of his fields, one spring, and he had jumped off the tractor to pick up the injured animal. But Junior had neglected to make sure the tractor gear was disengaged, and as he bent over to collect the dog, the tractor rolled. The front wheel caught Junior's foot before he could get out of the way, and the tire didn't stop. It continued to roll relentlessly up his body. Junior had struggled to angle himself away from its path but had been largely unsuccessful. Then just before the tire rolled over his head, Junior had thought to spit out his false teeth. Junior's head had ballooned to the size of a watermelon from the blood that had been pressed upward, but he'd had no broken bones. The freshly tilled soil had saved him, and spitting out his dentures had saved his jaw. Junior, who had always hated the fit of his dentures, anyway, now complained that they fit even worse. The dentist confirmed that his loosened, more fluid jaw, was affecting the fit, and Junior had vowed from that day forward to never wear his false teeth, again.

Each week, Lizzie Potts shared her Sunday school papers with Mac. Andy knew that whenever he visited his dad's place he would find a Lizzie crayon drawing on Mac's refrigerator door.

Andy teased Lizzie one Sunday that he was jealous of Mac because she never shared any of her pictures with Andy. Of course, the next Sunday Lizzie came prepared.

"This one's for you," Lizzie said, and she handed Andy one of two drawings she had made. "And this one is for Misto Mac," she added, keeping one in her little fist.

At Lizzie's insistence, Andy examined both pictures. Mac's masterpiece was a lovely rainbow of red, green, and black, and Lizzie explained that the purple stick figure on the orange cube was Noah on the ark.

"Noah looks really happy to see the rainbow," Andy offered, and Lizzie agreed.

"He didn't like the rain, at all," she said solemnly.

Then she asked, "How do you like your picture?"

Andy appreciated that seven-year-old Rachel By-the-Way had helped Lizzie label her drawing. The words across the top read: "to Pastr andy FROM LizziE," and the bottom was labeled: "adaM and the Snak."

Andy deciphered that the tall, brown-and-green mass on the left was a tree with one very large red apple. And the purple squiggle hanging down from a branch had to be the "snak." The two stick figures were, no doubt, Adam and Eve.

Andy praised Lizzie's artwork and posted it on the parsonage refrigerator door. Whenever Lizzie and Butter came for cookies, Lizzie always checked to make sure it was still there.

CHAPTER THIRTY-THREE

THANKSGIVING AND ECHOES

Mac arrived at the farm on the Tuesday before Thanksgiving with the largest turkey Molly had ever seen.

"It's a fresh one, not frozen," Mac proudly announced. "I got it from the Bennetts."

Molly could barely lift it, and she knew it would never fit into her largest roaster. Mac had come prepared, however. He next presented her with a huge, new, electric roaster.

"Sheryl Bennett said you'd probably need this. She couldn't loan me hers, so I bought you one," Mac said, looking satisfied that he had thought of everything.

Molly gave him a hug and a kiss. "This is perfect, Dad! Thanks," she said.

Then she added, "We could feed half the county with this bird!"

Mac fidgeted for a moment, and Molly could tell he had a question. Mac finally asked, "I wonder if I could bring a guest? Before I invited them, I wanted to make sure we had enough food."

Molly couldn't hide her surprise.

"Sure, Dad," she said. "Who are you thinking of inviting?"

Mac blushed. Molly had never seen her father embarrassed.

"It's a friend," he finally said. "A lady friend."

Molly's mouth flew open. "A lady friend?" she managed to say.

"Yeah," Mac said sheepishly. "Her name is Emma. She goes to Andy's church."

Molly recalled that Emma was her dad's interior decorator. "Sure," Molly said. "Emma is definitely welcome!"

"Andy, Dad's bringing a woman to our Thanksgiving dinner!" Molly exclaimed over the phone.

Andy smiled and replied, "Is it Emma Peters?"

Molly shouted, "You KNEW? When did this happen?"

Andy told her about Opal's report of seeing Mac with Emma, a few weeks ago.

"Wow!" Molly said. "Do you think it could turn serious? I'm going to have to think about this. I just never expected…"

"I know," Andy said. "I had to think about it, too. But you know, we shouldn't be surprised. It's probably the best thing that could happen to Dad."

Molly said nothing for a moment and then said quietly, "It would be nice for him to have a relationship with someone who isn't tied to all that stuff from the past."

"That's what I decided, too," Andy said. "I feel like God's giving him a new start. I can't begrudge him that."

"And," Andy added, "I don't think Mom would, either."

Molly couldn't get over how many things had changed since last Thanksgiving.

Phillip stared. No one had thought to tell him that Mac was bringing Emma to Thanksgiving dinner. Paul realized that his dad was the only one without a partner. To make sure his dad didn't feel left out, Paul made it a point to sit next to him while they waited for the meal to be ready.

"You're awfully quiet," Paul told him. "Are you feeling all right, Dad?"

"Oh, yeah," Phillip answered quickly. But then he added more confidentially, "It's just the anniversary of everything. It's hard to be celebrating, here, and not at the farmhouse. Everything, today, makes me miss the old place and Olivia."

Paul felt ashamed. He and Molly had been so caught up in their own loss, that they hadn't stopped to think how deeply the loss of the farmhouse had also affected Phillip. The farmhouse had been Phillip's home, too, long before it was theirs. He had grown up in that house; brought his bride, there; raised Paul, there; and then retired from there. It had been an anchor for his life and a guardian of his memories, and now it was gone.

Paul thought about what holidays had been like when his mother had been living. Olivia Doaks had been a sweetheart of a woman, sweet in face and personality. Everyone who met her for the first time went away feeling like Olivia had adopted them. She bore a distinct twinkle in her eye, and she cocked her head slightly whenever she listened to you.

The farmhouse had kept her memory alive. Even after he and Molly had moved in, Paul had sometimes imagined his mother's voice calling him down to breakfast. And sometimes at night he had recalled the muffled sounds of his mother and father talking in the rooms, below,when he was supposed to be asleep.

Holidays had been his mom's favorite days. And Dad was right; Thanksgiving wasn't the same, this year, without the old house. All of the cherished memories felt farther away. The double-wide held no history of his mother or the family's past.

Paul felt homesick. And he understood how much more his father must be feeling it.

"Why don't we take a walk, Dad?" Paul suggested. "It'll be a little while, before dinner is served. We have time."

Phillip didn't object. Paul announced their pre-dinner intention to the women in the kitchen.

"No problem," Molly assured them. "We'll yell if you're not back by the time the food is ready."

Everyone else was engaged in discussion. Mac and Emma hardly noticed them leave.

At the foot of the outdoor steps, instead of heading for the barn—as he usually did whenever he went outside—Paul headed for the grove. He knew that was where his dad wanted to go.

About a quarter of a mile from the house, set on a little rise, a fenced-in area with three trees and nine stones awaited them. Names like Ebenezer, Beulah, Obadiah, and Jessie called out to them when they entered the gate. Doakses and Turners. With dates that spanned a century, and more.

It was the pink granite, highly polished stone that drew them, today. Olivia rested there.

Paul saw that his flowers had been replaced, probably yesterday, so he knew his father had been here. He suspected that his dad came every day, secretly. Paul hadn't seen him at the farm; his dad had probably come down the path from the other end of the pasture. Unless you were looking, you wouldn't notice anyone, there.

Paul settled with his father on the stone bench, and the men scanned the skies in silence for several minutes. The shadows from sunlit clouds checkered the fields and moved on. The gnomon from the sundial, set in the ground before them, cast its shadow on one o'clock. Dinner was always a little late on a holiday. A killdeer trilled as it wove and bobbed across the path the men had just left. One lone butterfly that had somehow survived the cold days, flitted its kisses on the last of the roses along the fence.

"I know she's not here," Phillip said, "but I feel closer to your mom when I visit here. I can talk to God here, easier, too. It's quiet and peaceful, and the sky is like His smile."

His dad's words tugged at Paul's heart. Paul missed his mother, and he missed what his father had been with her. She had tempered Phillip's rough edges. His dad had been strong and proud and invincible. Mom's death had sucked something out of him that had never returned.

Paul said quietly, "I miss her, too, Dad."

Tears coursed down his father's cheeks, and Paul noticed that he didn't bother to blot them.

"I'm getting old, Son," Phillip said. "I don't know how many years I have left, but I want you to know that I'm proud of you and what you've been doing with the farm. I know you left Harmony, years ago, because we couldn't work together—too many differences of opinion. But I'm glad you and Molly are here. I hated it that the old place burned down, but I'm glad you're all safe, and I'm glad you're all still here. It feels like life goes on. It's a reminder that things don't die forever. It reminds me that we're made for life, we're made for each other, we're made for Him."

Paul sighed. He didn't like to think about the changes. Even though he loved his life and his family, he sometimes missed the past. And he hated the thought of his father going away one day. Of course, he would be in Heaven, then, and reunited with his Olivia. But Paul coveted more time with him, and he thanked God for the time they still had.

"I love you, Dad," Paul said.

It seemed right to say it, today.

"I know, Son," said Phillip. "And I love you too."

They sat for several minutes before a faint call sounded from down the hill. "Dinner's ready," it said.

The hungry party barely made a dent in the turkey.

"There's enough meat here for the rest of the month!" exclaimed Molly. "The kitchen freezer will be filled with turkey for a long time."

"At least we didn't run out," insisted Mac. "I had no idea how much Emma might eat!"

Emma laughed. Molly thought it was a nice laugh. And she liked the way her father behaved around Emma. Dad was relaxed and seemed gentler. Molly couldn't help but wonder if this was how he had been with Mom before the tragedy had struck. But then she recalled that they had started out poor, and Dad had always been stressed with making ends meet. Perhaps he and Mom had never had any perfectly relaxed moments. There was no way of knowing.

The baby liked Emma, too. Mac and Emma took turns entertaining Emily after dinner, while Molly and Abbey picked the turkey carcass and stored the meat and other leftovers. At the old house, Mac and Emma would have been on the porch, in the swing. Here, they were confined to the living room, with everyone else.

While she worked, Molly gazed through the kitchen window at the little patch of ruins she could see. She let herself think of the fire and her escape with Emily from the upstairs window. She had trusted Dad with her baby and then with her own life. Before that dreadful moment, Molly had feared more than trusted her father. His voice of command had always made her cringe. But that night, just a few months ago, she had heard his voice of command ring with a reassuring tone of "I'm in charge." They had needed him and his authority at that moment. Molly could not have imagined, then, the change that would come over him—the way God would redeem him.

Today, her father didn't even look the same. The worry lines were gone. The anger that had burned behind his eyes for as long as she could remember was gone. His voice was lighter, and he seemed to have found a sense of humor that Molly had never known him to have.

And Molly wondered, would he marry again? Her dad still had vitality and drive; the work at the farm had proven that. And he definitely had the means. Dad could nicely support another wife.

If he married Emma, Molly reasoned, someone who was from here, it might mean that Dad would stay here and be here to watch Emily grow up. Molly had never had a grandpa, but Emily had one. It would be nice for her to continue to grow up with him.

Molly wondered about Emma. Would she become a friend? Would Molly be able to confide in her in ways she had never been able to confide in her mother?

Emma would have no expectations of her, no desire to live life vicariously through Molly, so Molly could be herself—a self that Molly was happy with.

Molly recalled that her mother had almost managed to affirm her, once—on her last visit. When Rachel had admitted how sick she feared she was, she had helped make everything ready for Emily's arrival. And Rachel had not questioned any of Molly's decisions. Molly remembered how her mother's sickness had changed her, made her see the things that were truly important.

And Molly was glad that her mother had come to know the Lord and had found the peace that had eluded her for so many years. Molly often pictured her mother as happy, now, in Heaven, with no regrets, no tortured memories, no bitterness toward Dad, and no striving for something she could never achieve.

Molly thanked God for taking care of her mother and for the way He was now transforming her father.

PART FOUR
WHITER THAN SNOW

CHAPTER THIRTY-FOUR

DISPLACED ABOMASUM

"Pastor?"

After all the time they had spent together as friends, it was odd for Siege to call him *Pastor*, and Andy instantly went on the alert. It sounded like a call for Andy's pastoral capacity, instead of his friendship.

"Sure, Siege. What's up?" Andy replied, ready for whatever might be coming.

"I was just wondering," said Siege with what sounded like a forced casualness, "if you might want to come with me on a call in a few minutes. I have a cow that might have a displaced abomasum, and I may need an extra hand."

Andy laughed lightly. "I have no idea what you just said you needed help with. But sure, I'll go home and put on my farm clothes and wait for you to pick me up at the parsonage."

After he hung up, Andy frowned. Something in Siege's voice had sounded *off*. Was something wrong?

He wondered why Chelsea wasn't going with Siege on this call. Were the two of them having problems, or was Chelsea just busy?

Andy hoped the couple wasn't having issues. He had seldom felt so sure of two people in his life as he had about Siege and Chelsea. They seemed so compatible and well-suited to one another. Andy hated to think that they might not make it to the altar.

Andy laughed, now, at himself. *Altar.* He had gone there in his mind, and Siege hadn't even proposed, yet.

Andy shot up a prayer for God to help work out any problems they might be having. At the parsonage, Andy told Abbey he was going with Siege on a vet call.

"Really?" she said. Andy could tell by the tone of her voice that she was asking the same questions he had just asked himself. It had been a long time since Siege had asked Andy to go on a farm call. Chelsea was the vet's usual partner, now.

When Abbey seemed surprised, too, Andy didn't feel too badly about having second-guessed his friend. He knew that Abbey felt something might be wrong and would be praying while they were gone.

Andy tried to think of all the advice he might give, if this turned into a counseling trip.

After Andy climbed into the truck, he learned they were on their way to Junior Harris's farm. It wasn't far, and Siege didn't talk much on the drive.

When they arrived, Junior was surprised to see Andy. "Didn't expect to see you, here, Pastor!" he exclaimed. "Did the vet bring you in case the cow died?"

Junior giggled and pointed out the cow he had called about.

The animal seemed normal to Andy, but what did he know? He and Junior watched as Siege checked the cow over and listened intently under her massive left side with a stethoscope. Evidently, whatever was wrong with the animal had happened once before, because Siege told Junior that, this time, he would try to fix the problem, once and for all.

Junior nodded his approval. "She jest can't seem to keep things in place, can she?" he said. "Other than that, she's a fine cow." Junior nodded that fact to Andy, and Andy nodded back, even though he had no idea what he was agreeing about.

As Andy watched, Siege drew out a very large half-circle needle (with a six-inch-curve diameter) and deftly threaded it with a heavy ("a #8 Braunamid," per Siege) suture thread. Siege carefully stuffed the threaded needle into an apron pocket, where he could grab it quickly when the time came.

Now, as Siege whipped out some rope and started to rig it between and around the cow's feet in a particular pattern, he cocked his head in Andy's direction. "As I suspected," he said, "she's got a displaced abomasum." Andy nodded dumbly. "The abomasum is one of her stomachs," Siege explained in plain English, and Andy mouthed an "Oh," as if now he understood it all. But Siege continued. "It belongs on the right bottom of her belly, but it's fallen to the left. We're going to try to get it back in place and stitch it, to keep it secure."

Now Siege stood up, and Junior pulled Andy over to stand beside the cow. Junior had anticipated Siege's next words, as if he and Siege had done this before. For Andy's benefit, Siege said, "This is a 'roll and tack' job, so we've got to get her down and roll her."

Andy had no idea what that meant, but he followed Siege and Junior's lead. They all surrounded the cow, but not too close, and Siege pulled on the ropes he had laid out. To Andy's astonishment, the cow immediately, and gently, sank to her knees.

"Now," called Siege, "get her onto her side!" All three men bent over and began to push and roll the cow onto her side. Once they had succeeded, Siege grunted, "Now, onto her back!"

After a couple more rocks, back and forth, the cow rolled completely upside down. Andy had never seen a cow on its back, and he burst out laughing. Junior grinned but kept his attention on the task.

Siege was glued to the cow's belly, now, with his stethoscope. "The loose stomach should float up," he said, and he listened intently as he and Junior rolled the feet-up animal slightly from side to side.

In mid-rock, Siege suddenly signaled a stop. He whipped out the needle from his pocket and thrust it into the animal's belly. Junior held the cow in position as the tip of the curved needle came out about five inches from where it had gone in. Apparently satisfied, Siege hurried to apply something to the puncture, and then he pulled the needle to draw the thread through, as if sewing. Once the length of it had been drawn, Siege deftly knotted the entry thread to the exit thread and snipped the ends. It left a neat stitch on the right side of the cow's belly. With all of the other unusual activity, the cow hardly seemed to have noticed.

Siege stuck the needle back into his pocket.

"All done," he said. "Let's get her back on her feet."

This time, Andy had a better idea of how to do that, and with Junior and Siege he rolled the cow once more to help her gain momentum and get onto her knees. The cow gave a final heave and worked her legs to rise. Standing, now, she eyed them all warily and shied away as if she thought they might try to bring her down, again. But she seemed none the worse for the experience. The only consequence was the neat little knot on her belly.

"That ought to keep her," Siege told Junior. "But if she has any trouble at all, call me immediately."

"You know I will," said Junior. "I don't wait around on stuff when I think there's somethin' wrong. I don't want my animals to suffer when they don't have to."

Siege shook Junior's hand and said, "I wish all of my customers were as conscientious as you, Junior." Andy knew Siege was thinking about the Tranor farm and the dead sow on the dinner table.

Junior shook Andy's hand and teased: "I've heard you've just about got your vet license, Pastor!"

"I'm still in the early learning stages," Andy grinned. "But I think I'll stick to preaching."

"It doesn't hurt to get your hands dirty, a bit!" Junior said. He pointed at some cow dung that had gotten onto Andy's gloves and pants. "Good clean farm dirt!" Junior declared with a giggle.

Andy smiled. "You're right about that. You don't get much of this stuff in town."

Junior continued giggling. He loved being able to tease his pastor over something that was second nature to him on the farm. This was his element, just like the church was Andy's.

As they latched the paddock gate behind them, Junior flashed his toothless grin. *What a happy, gentle man,* thought Andy. *Gentle with people and gentle with animals.* Andy liked that.

Andy observed how meticulously Siege put everything away in the truck. Andy imagined it was important to have supplies and equipment disinfected, and clean, and in their places, ready to grab when needed on the next farm call.

They waved good-bye to Junior, and the truck stirred dust down the lane on its way back to the hard road. Siege held to a slower pace than before, and Andy heard him clear his throat several times. *Here it comes,* thought Andy. *He's getting ready to talk.*

Sure enough, after more painful throat-clearing, Siege began: "Pastor, I-uh, I wanted to talk for a minute about some things."

Andy held his breath. How he hoped things weren't going sour between Siege and Chelsea.

Then Siege said, "It's about me and Chelsea," and Andy's stomach tightened. It didn't sound good.

"I really like her a lot," Siege continued in a strained voice. His manner left Andy waiting for the "but."

Siege pressed forward and said, "I think she really likes me, too." Andy began to be hopeful. But he waited.

"And, well"—Siege gulped—"Well, I'm thinking of asking her to marry me."

Andy's heart soared!

Siege nervously kept his eyes on the road, as if he was afraid of Andy's response.

"GOOD!" Andy exclaimed so forcefully that Siege jumped. Siege's nerves had been stretched so taut that Andy's exuberant exclamation had sent him off his eat.

"Thank goodness!" Siege exhaled. "I was so worried you might have reservations. I wanted to make sure it was okay with you before I proposed. I mean, she's one of your staff members, and..."

"And I heartily approve!" said Andy, finishing the sentence for him.

Siege accelerated, probably without even realizing it. His eyes danced, and he couldn't stop smiling.

"I love her," he told Andy. "I've never been so at ease with anyone in my life. And she 'gets it' about my job. I'd never have to worry that she couldn't handle my hours and all the interruptions."

"And?" Andy prompted.

Siege reddened. "Yeah," he said. "She's pretty, too."

Andy grinned.

Siege gripped the steering wheel as if the truck were going to fly. "I'm going to ask her tonight," he said.

Then Siege nearly sent Andy off his seat and onto the floor when he wheeled quickly to the side of the road and slammed on the brakes.

"Here's the ring!" he said excitedly, and he drew out a small velvet case from the glove box.

"Whoa!" Andy cried. "She's going to need weight training to hold that thing up!"

Siege laughed. "It's not THAT big. But it is one of the bigger stones I could find. Nothing's too good for her!"

"Where are you going to pop the question?" Andy asked.

Siege had it all planned and couldn't wait to tell. "I'm going to take her to an early movie in Harmony. Then we're going to Drawbridge Steakhouse for supper. And then we're going to drive back to Cherish and swing around the pond at the park. There's a bench, there, that I've had my eye on. That's where I want to ask her. Then that can be our bench whenever we visit the park."

Andy teased, "And it should be nice and dark by the time you get there, so you can cuddle a little, too." Siege reddened.

Andy could picture the scene in the park. It reminded him of when he had proposed to Abbey. It had been a full-moon night, and the stars had twinkled above them, but they had barely noticed.

Suddenly Siege asked, "You don't think she'll say no, do you?"

"Not on your life!" Andy said. "I've seen how she looks at you. That gal is crazy, head-over-heels about you! And you'd better snatch her up, right now!"

"I will," said Siege. "I will!" And he pulled back onto the road with a glowing grin that nearly lit up the road before them.

The remaining miles dissolved quickly, and Andy could hardly wait to tell Abbey the news.

Abbey could hardly stand it.

"I wonder where they are now," she kept asking, with one eye on the clock and one on the movie she and Andy pretended to be watching.

"I'm so happy for them!" she said. And then she said it, again, "I'm so happy for them!"

Winston could tell that his owners were excited about something, and he pranced in front of them with his favorite toy. Perhaps they wanted to play?

Finally, at 11:45 the telephone rang.

"It's them! I know it is!" Abbey cried, and she raced Andy to the phone. She got there, first, and her squeal told Andy all he needed to know.

"Oh, Chelsea!" Abbey cried. "I'm so happy for you! Have you set a date, yet?" Then Abbey said, "Oh, of course, you have time to decide that. But I'm just so happy for you!"

Andy hollered, "Congratulations!" into the mouthpiece next to Abbey's chin, and they heard Siege call out, "Thanks!"

"You two have a wonderful evening," Abbey told Chelsea, "and we'll talk more, tomorrow."

Then Abbey said again, "I'm just so happy for you!"

CHAPTER THIRTY-FIVE

PEANUT BRITTLE

Georgia Wheeler had never had so much to gossip about. The preacher's father was stepping out with Emma Peters (the woman's been bereaved for barely a year!), and the youth director was engaged to the veterinarian (he's never going to be home; poor marriage that's going to be!), and on top of it all, the young Folden couple was expecting (must have conceived on their wedding night! Tsk! Tsk!).

Since few people shared anything with the loose-lipped gossiper, Andy could not imagine where Georgia got her information. He muttered, "I wonder if the CIA needs another agent."

Then on second thought, he said, "I take that back. With her lack of restraint, Georgia could be a danger to our national security!"

Molly was pleased to get an invitation. "Of course," she said. "I'd love to come."

Emma had invited Molly to make peanut brittle. It would give Molly a chance to get to know Emma better. And Molly had never made peanut brittle, before.

"I've asked Abbey to come, too," Emma said. "I hope that's all right."

"Of course," Molly replied. "In fact, I can pick her up when I get to town, and she can show me where you live."

"Perfect!" said Emma. "It will be wonderful to have you, both, here."

Molly looked forward to Saturday.

Abbey and Molly knocked on the door of the neat, little, two-story home, and Emma Peters ushered them inside. Emma's eyes glowed, and she smothered them with hugs.

"Welcome," she said. "It's going to be fun to cook together. And I love making peanut brittle."

Emma took their coats. "Let's go to the kitchen, first," she suggested, and they followed her there, through the living room and dining room.

Molly evaluated the décor. Tastefully done, she thought. Molly realized she had been expecting something over-the-top, because Emma was an interior decorator, but although the marks of an interior designer were here, nothing was "in your face." The rooms were welcoming and comfortable.

Molly noticed two recliners in the living room, and she couldn't help but imagine her father in one of them. She smiled.

In the spotless kitchen, Emma handed each an apron, but Molly saw no ingredients or utensils. She wondered where everything was. The counter held only two recipe cards, and when Emma collected those, the counter was completely bare.

"Here's a copy of the recipe we're going to make," Emma said. "You can take this card home with you."

How thoughtful, Molly reflected. The cards were neatly printed and titled: "Pulled Peanut Brittle."

"*Pulled* peanut brittle," mused Molly, out loud. "I always thought you *poured* peanut brittle."

"That's what most people do," agreed Emma, "but *pulling* makes it so much better. I think you'll like it."

Emma put on her apron, now, and said, "Shall we go down and get started?"

By "down," Emma meant downstairs. They were evidently going to be working in the basement.

So, that explains the bare kitchen, thought Molly.

On the bottom step, Abbey stopped and remarked in surprise, "I've never been down here. Look at this setup!"

Molly murmured, "It's wonderful!"

And it was. The basement had been finished so that one half was a huge kitchen, and the other half was a recreation room with a television set, sofa and chairs, and a ping-pong table.

Molly loved the kitchen. It was like stepping back into the 1950s. Molly remembered appliances like these from her childhood, when she and Andy had sat around a similar Formica-topped table on plastic-covered chrome-legged chairs. Even the linoleum pattern on the floor stirred memories.

Raw peanuts, sugar, and other candy-making supplies lined the Formica counters, along with pots and pans from the era. The nested mixing bowls were exactly like those Rachel had used. And so were the Pyrex pitchers and the copper-clad measuring spoons.

But there were too many supplies. Molly saw dozens of bags of raw peanuts, a stack of five-pound sugar bags, bottle after bottle of corn syrup, and a surprising collection of vanilla extract, baking soda, and salt. Surely, they didn't need all of this!

But then, Molly noticed the scores of colorful tins stacked around the walls of the recreation room. If every one of those tins was to be filled with peanut brittle, they were going to be here for a long time— certainly a lot longer than the couple of hours

Molly had thought this enterprise would take. She'd have to call and tell Paul not to expect her for lunch or supper.

"Are we going to make all of this into peanut brittle?" Molly asked.

Emma laughed. "That's right! I used to do it every year with my sister, before she passed away. And then Jethro got sick," she said. "It feels good to be doing it, again. Those tins are for all of my family and friends. And there are enough for your family, too!"

"Wow!" Abbey exclaimed. "I don't think we're going to be going home anytime soon!"

Emma reassured her. "Don't worry. Mac's advised your husbands to fix a sandwich or to pick up a drive-through meal for lunch (I have sandwiches for us, by the way), and when we're done making candy, Mac is going to take all of us out for supper. Mac's over in Harmony, now, to help Paul with Emily. He'll bring Paul and Emily to Cherish, after chores are done."

Molly grinned. *Well, what do you know?* she thought. She loved the idea.

"Are you ready to get started?" Emma asked. She rubbed her hands together, excitedly.

"Let's do it!" said Abbey. And Molly echoed her.

"Okay!" chirped Emma. Then, she reached into the refrigerator and brought out a stick of oleo for each of the women. "First," she said, "we prepare the tabletop."

At the question in their eyes, Emma demonstrated her technique: she unwrapped the oleo half-way and began to "crayon" it over the entire surface of the Formica table. Molly and Abbey giggled and copied her, like a couple of first-graders. It was every child's dream—permission to make a mess!

When they finished, Molly and Abbey smiled, and Emma said, "Now, we measure."

Per her instruction, Molly and Abbey measured a pound of raw peanuts into a bowl and set out other ingredients: 2 cups of sugar, 1 cup of syrup, 1/2 cup of hot water, 2 tablespoons of oleo, 1 teaspoon of salt, 1 teaspoon of vanilla, and 1 teaspoon of baking soda.

Then they repeated the measures for a second batch and set it aside, so that it would be ready for later.

Emma now clipped a candy thermometer to the side of a two-quart pot and set the pot on the flame. She added the pre-measured sugar, syrup, and hot water. Then she instructed Molly and Abbey to take turns stirring until the mixture reached 250 degrees. That was the cue to add the peanuts, oleo, and salt and to stir, again, until the mixture would reach 310 degrees.

"That's when you have to be careful not to scorch it," Emma said. But then she retracted that to say, "Well, actually you do let it scorch j-u-s-t a little, for taste."

While Molly stirred, Emma put Christmas records on the record player, and the three of them talked.

As it was supposed to, the confection cooked and then scorched—just a little—and began to smell heavenly.

Everything up to this point had been calm and leisurely, and Molly assumed it would be like this all afternoon. But suddenly everything changed: the candy thermometer had reached 310 degrees.

Like lightning, Emma moved Molly aside, yanked the hot pot from the stove, and grabbed the vanilla and soda, which she poured in and then stirred, like mad. The mixture bubbled furiously. Still stirring down the bubbles, Emma poured the glob onto the buttered Formica tabletop. Before they could ask, Emma shoved two spoons into Molly's hand and two into Abbey's.

With fingers flying, Emma announced: "You have to pull it now, while it's hot! Once it gets cold, you can't do a thing!"

Pull it? thought Molly. *How can you pull something that's molten?* Up to now, Molly had envisioned pulled taffy, a cool concoction you could pull without searing your fingers off.

Molly watched as Emma demonstrated. Emma used her two spoons to separate the candy into smaller blobs. Then she attacked the first blob by pressing it down with the bowl of the spoon and pushing out, to virtually stretch the candy until it became as thin as it could be. With one done, Emma raced to another blob and stretched it. By now, Molly and Abbey understood the technique, and they joined in and set their spoons to work. Within a couple of minutes, the three ladies had "pulled" or thinned all of the blobs on the table. As they had worked, the candy had cooled and hardened until it could no longer be stretched.

They surveyed their work—a tabletop filled with dozens of patches of peanuts, all thinly coated and surrounded by crispy bits of delicious golden candy.

Emma popped a piece into her mouth and encouraged Molly and Abbey to do the same. It tasted wonderful! And it was delightfully tender. Nothing like the hard, thick peanut brittle they had eaten in the past.

"This is heavenly!" exclaimed Molly. "Let's make some more!"

Emma laughed her beautiful laugh, and as Abbey washed out the used pot, spoon, and measuring containers, Molly set another pot on the burner. Under Emma's watchful eye, Molly began to add the appropriate ingredients, and Abbey measured out another set of ingredients to be ready for the next batch.

The pace slowed, again, and as Abbey stirred, the mixture heated on the stove.

Every so often, with the Christmas music playing in the background, Emma would burst into song and draw them into a carol. "It's never too early for Christmas music!" she declared. "Jethro used to love Christmas!"

When she asked if Molly and Abbey had started their Christmas shopping, they each divulged their secret purchases and shared what they hoped someone would buy for them. Emma shared that she wanted a scarf she had seen at the dress shop on the Cherish square. "I hate buying that kind of thing for myself," she said, "but if someone were to buy it for me, I would be tickled pink!" Molly and Abbey exchanged a glance; of course they would tell Mac about it.

The mixture on the stove finally reached 250 degrees, and Molly added the appropriate ingredients and stirred. Then, when the magic 310-degree moment arrived, they all flew into action.

With each batch, their roles changed, in a synchronized fashion. One time, it was Molly's turn to wash the dishes and measure ingredients while Abbey took charge of the cooking. And the next time, Abbey washed and measured, and Molly cooked. Emma no longer had to remind them of the next step. She filled in as part of the assembly line and took her turn.

Whenever they were waiting for the ingredients to heat, they talked. Emma freely shared about Junior's illness and her earlier life. Although Abbey had known much of what she shared, it was all new to Molly. Molly tried to imagine Emma in the role of a full-time caregiver, and she admired what she had done for her husband. Molly wanted Emma to enjoy her time, now, free of those restricting responsibilities. And she imagined Emma enjoying fun times with Mac. Emma and Mac had each had a great burden lifted from them, and each deserved happiness in their future.

Molly wondered, however, how much Mac had told Emma about his life. Would there be secrets?

The hours in the candy-making basement passed quickly. And with every finished batch, Emma's festive tins began to fill.

Abbey asked Emma if doing two batches at a time might make things go faster, and Emma threw up her hands. "I did that once," she said, "and it nearly killed me. It wasn't enjoyable at all, and I kept getting confused about what I had added and not added. It took all of the fun out it, and it wasn't worth it," she said. "I even tried to double a batch while cooking it. That didn't work, either. It's much better to do things one at a time and enjoy the afternoon."

In the background, the chorus of *O Holy Night* soared, and the ladies sang with abandon. Soon enough, the sweet contents of the pot on the burner would reach 310 degrees.

An hour before all of the batches were finished, Mac showed up with Paul and Andy.

"Are you ladies ready for dinner, yet?" Mac asked.

Molly stifled a grin when Emma chided, "Not quite. You boys just settle. We'll let you know when we're done."

Mac reluctantly said, "Okay," and he and Andy and Paul moved to the recreation side of the room. Emma turned off the Christmas music so the guys could turn on the television.

But the sweet aroma flooding the basement tormented the hungry men. Molly knew it was inevitable that they would begin to pick through the filled tins.

"Get your fingers out of there!" commanded Emma. She looked furious. But then she belied it by leaving the lid off one tin and announcing that THIS was the testing tin. Andy grabbed it from her hands and led a chase around the room. He popped a piece into his mouth before the tin was torn from his hands by a protesting Paul and Mac.

"Wow!" Andy exclaimed. "This is the best peanut brittle I've ever eaten!"

After their first taste, the others agreed, and they began grabbing handfuls before passing the tin back to Andy.

Abbey informed them, "It's called *pulled* peanut brittle. And I'll never eat any other kind, again. It's wonderful, isn't it?"

"What do you do to make it like this?" Andy asked, while crunching another piece in his mouth.

But his answer had to wait. The pot on the stove had just reached 310 degrees, and there was no time for small talk.

At a bark from Emma, the men scattered like rabbits to the sofa, and the hot pot from the stove made its way to the Formica table where the women brandished their spoons.

Andy hovered at the edge of the kitchen, fascinated. Mac and Paul, however, kept their distance. Andy was rewarded when Emma let him pull a few pieces. He carefully scooted the candy he had pulled to one edge of the table and announced, "These are mine." Now, Paul and Mac wanted in on the act. "We'll make some," they volunteered. But Emma shooed them all—including Andy—back to the recreation room and the empty testing tin.

"We'll be going to dinner, soon," she declared. "We just have a few more batches to make."

The men pretended to watch television but could not ignore the growls of their stomachs.

When, at last, only one batch remained on the stove, Emma sorted through her various tins and awarded three tins to each of the ladies.

"One is for you," she announced, "and one is for your man. The other is to share or give away."

Molly and Abbey looked at each other. *Right!* They each knew the third tin would never make it as a giveaway.

CHAPTER THIRTY-SIX

DECEMBER

Opal had filled nearly every square of the December newsletter calendar. Between deadlines for contributing to the mitten tree and toys-for-the-poor, there were practices and performances for the children's Christmas program, the adult choir cantata, Christmas tree decorating, and a candlelight Christmas Eve service.

Everyone was busy. It always was, every Christmas.

Street decorations on the square drew townspeople to stop and shop. The nativity on the courthouse lawn proclaimed "Peace to all!" Red-hatted volunteers jangled bells on the corners for donations. And church message boards reminded shoppers of the reason for the season.

Andy tucked a copy of Opal's December poem inside his sermon notes to read to the congregation on Christmas Eve. Opal had cleverly captured the responsibility of believers regarding the Christmas message.

THERE SHOULD HAVE BEEN TRUMPETS!
by Opal Reese

There should have been trumpets
That first Christmas Eve.
There should have been trumpets
Down Bethlehem's streets.
There should have been trumpets
Announcing the King.
There should have been trumpets
When the angels took wing.

There should have been trumpets,
And not silent night.
There should have been trumpets
When the angels took flight.
There should have been trumpets
To herald the news,
To add to the chorus
Of sung hallelus.

There should have been trumpets
Like Gideon's horns.
There should have been trumpets
On the night Christ was born.
His birth showed the promise
Of Jericho's "falls;"
He came to tear down all
The enemy's walls.

I can't wait for the trumpets
When He comes again.
I can't wait for the trumpets,
And God's thrilling command.
I can just hear those trumpets—
That bright blast of the horn.
We'll rise in the skies on
That beautiful morn.

Today, let's have trumpets,
And not just jingle bells.
We need to have trumpets,
And dancing as well.
We need to have trumpets
To wake up the earth.
We need to BE trumpets
Proclaiming His worth!

In light of their name, Greg and Bonnie Easter might have been in the wrong business. But their Christmas tree farm was definitely the right place to get your Christmas tree.

An announcement in the Sunday church bulletin read:

MEET AT THE EASTER'S AT TEN ON SATURDAY TO PICK OUT THE CHURCH TREE.

"It's fun! Come with us on Saturday," Chelsea begged Siege. "The tree farm is amazing. We'll look for a big tree for the church, and the teens will pick out a small tree for their classroom. You could even get one for the veterinary office, if you want."

Remarkably, Siege had no morning calls. And now, he could see that Chelsea was right: there were acres of trees. The question was where to begin? Although it was cold, it was a bright, sunny day, perfect for wandering through the piney, man-made woods. Several of the youth and at least ten adults waited at the tree-farm gate, ready to begin the search.

As the unofficial leader of the tree search committee, Chelsea told everyone that she remembered a potential tree near the one they'd chosen, last year. She suggested they check there, first, to see if it was still standing. When they agreed, Chelsea flung her gray-striped muffler over her shoulder, hooked her arm into Siege's elbow, and called out, "This way!"

Siege liked seeing her in charge. She was a natural leader, and the teens and adults rallied to her call.

The section she led them to rose taller than the rest, with older trees that had grown too tall to fit into most homes. But these trees were not too tall for the church's high-ceilinged overflow room.

"It should be right about—here!" Chelsea said triumphantly.

Indeed, the tree before her looked magnificent. The group admired it, certain that their tree hunt was already over. But then came a quiet "uh-oh." Siege wondered what was wrong.

Danny Hart had noticed it, first. What had looked perfect from the front did not look so perfect from the back. The magnificent tree had been run into by a truck. A tan gash marked the encounter, and the needles around the trauma site were brown, instead of green.

"What a shame!" sighed Erica. "The tree at the church has to look nice from all sides since we can't just push it against a wall."

Siege saw that Chelsea was disappointed but not defeated. "Let's find another one!" she cried.

The teens immediately made it their mission—and they had the energy for it—to find another tree. While the adults strolled leisurely, the youth raced from row to row, hastily evaluating tree after tree. After about ten minutes, the call went up. Josie Fisher and her brother Jimmy were sure they had found it. They guarded their find while the others ran to urge the adults to pick up their pace.

"It's perfect!" panted Eric Mowry, as he danced around the slow pokes. "You'll see! Come on!"

The other teens called out, "We found it! We found it!" once the adults arrived.

But Chelsea called out an ominous "Whoa!" when she arrived. The excited teens grew quiet as Chelsea narrowed her eyes, cocked her head, and walked slowly around the tree the teens had picked. Then, as if she wasn't sure, she asked, "What do you think, Danny?"

Danny Hart also made a show of slowly and deliberately checking out the tree from all sides, putting up his hands as if estimating its height, and then backing away to eye it from top to bottom. He put his hands on his hips and blew out a little air, as if not quite sure.

"Come on!" one of the teens cried. "It's perfect, and you know it!"

Chelsea shushed them. She pursed her lips in a doubtful way, looked at Danny, and then back at the tree. Danny looked at Chelsea with a scowl. And then Chelsea grinned and abruptly said, "Yup!"

The teens cheered. Siege laughed. He wondered if it was like this, every year.

"Can we help cut it down?" the boys asked.

Chelsea shook her head. "Sorry, but that job is too big for you guys. Let's go find the tree for your classroom, instead. That one you can cut."

Siege overheard Jimmy Fisher whisper to his sister, "I saw Dr. Logan kiss Miss Mitchell, behind the Christmas tree we didn't take!" And Josie had whispered back, "So? They're engaged."

Siege smiled. *Yes, we're engaged!*

Danny, Stu, and a couple of other churchmen collected the ax, saw, and some rope from Junior Harris' truck. It didn't take long for them to fell the beautiful tree. As they were loading it onto the flatbed, the teens drug in their smaller tree, and Andy and Abbey pulled in a little Scotch pine to lash down, too. The smell of fresh-cut evergreen filled the air. Siege slipped in a three-foot ("for the office counter") spruce at the last moment.

People who passed the truck on its way to town waved and called out "Merry Christmas!"

It was no small effort to get the big tree through the church doors and into its tree stand. But the men seemed to be expert at it.

"We've done this for as long as I can remember," Stu told Siege.

The tree proved to be the perfect height, and its piney scent created the Christmassy atmosphere that filled the church each season.

After the morning service, the next day, dusty boxes of ornaments and lights emerged from storage, and ladders were set to help the brave reach the upper branches. Everyone seemed to know what was needed, and they picked up the familiar tasks with enthusiasm. A dozen poinsettias skirted the edge of the sanctuary platform, and carols blasted from a transistor radio as workers hung a garland over the top of the choir loft and situated electric candles and a little greenery on the window ledges.

Youngsters decorated their classrooms, under the direction of their teachers, and Siege helped a small contingency of men wrap greens around the outer stair railing and hang a great wreath over the outside front entrance.

Best of all was the sloppy-Joe-and-cookie lunch prepared by the senior Sunday school class for those who helped to decorate.

With the transformation complete, everyone admired their handiwork. Siege loved the finished product. *Christmas can now officially begin,* he thought.

The lights dimmed in the sanctuary for the children's Christmas program. Mary, Joseph, and the baby in the manger remained in the background under a small spotlight, and up front, various children prepared to sing and recite their parts.

The youngest started first: kindergarteners and first graders. As the children made their way onto the platform, their parents smiled, proudly. The little boys appeared deceptively angelic with their scrubbed faces and slicked back hair. Each one sported a green or red shirt and suspenders that held up pants with pockets, into which they all stuffed their hands. The little girls smiled in shiny curls that were tied back with bows, and their little red and green skirts puffed out on all sides above white tights and patent leather shoes.

"There's my Jenna!" Christy Wilson whispered loudly behind Andy and Abbey.

When gently prodded, five-year-old Jenna Wilson stepped forward to take her turn. A tiny, red pleated skirt, nearly perpendicular to her waist, lay on top of a tightly gathered crisp white crinoline. Her patent leather shoes, which capped off her perfectly white tights, sparkled in the spotlight, like her thickly lashed dark eyes.

"Isn't she a picture?" Christy sighed, and her husband, Butch, agreed with a papa grin.

"And she's smart as a whip," Butch whispered loudly into Andy's ear.

Gripping the hem of her skirt for support, and in proof of her father's assessment, Jenna stared intently at the microphone in front of her and began to recite the lines of the poem Opal Reese had penned for the program.

JUST LIKE ME
By Opal Reese

Jesus Christ was born one day,
JUST LIKE ME.
His bed was soft upon the hay,
NOT AT ALL LIKE ME.

His momma sang Him lullabies,
JUST LIKE ME;
And angels stopped to harmonize,
NOT AT ALL LIKE ME.

He cried and cooed and ate and wet,
JUST LIKE ME,
But shepherds came and bowed and went,
NOT AT ALL LIKE ME.

He held such promise at His birth,
JUST LIKE ME.
But He would save the whole wide earth—
AND THAT INCLUDED ME!

A burst of applause and laughter rose from the congregation (with Andy in the lead), because in addition to a flawless presentation—with perfect emphasis on every JUST LIKE ME—little Jenna's nervousness had gravitated to her grip on the hem of her skirt. As Jenna had spoken line after line, she had punctuated the poetry with a twist of her skirt. Then, with every JUST LIKE ME she had stuffed that handful into the top of her tights. By the end of the fourth stanza, the entire skirt and crinoline had disappeared, and Jenna's tights had ballooned about her waist!

With every nervous "stuff," Christy and Butch had slid down another inch in the pew. But oblivious to the audience snickers and her unwitting response to her stage fright, Jenna had finished with a bob in a perfect bow, just as she'd been taught, and she had stepped back into place with the other kindergartners.

"Nothing, the rest of the evening, is going to top that," Andy chuckled ever so softly to Abbey, making sure the Wilsons could not overhear.

Siege wondered if he and Chelsea would settle in Cherish. *Would Chelsea like that?* he wondered. He imagined that she would.

He drove her slowly to her home after the Christmas program. She had presents, there, for him to unwrap, and he had presents for her in the supply hold of his truck.

Snow had fallen; just enough to blanket everything with a bit of white.

Siege continued his contemplations. Cherish was a remarkable little town. A life-sized nativity glowed on the courthouse lawn. Street lamps bordering the square were wired with piney wreaths and tinseled stars that twinkled warmly in spite of the snow and cold. Store windows spotlighted various nostalgic Christmas scenes. The hardware window featured a grand red sleigh, drawn by a painted chestnut horse. The bed of the sleigh was piled with a profusion of gaily wrapped packages. Some spilled over onto the seat of the sleigh, and some were partially opened to reveal toy cows, pigs, and sheep, as well as tractors, hay wagons, silos, and barns.

The up-scale dress shop that faced Main Street was aglow with a living room scene: a well-dressed manikin family smilingly decorated their Christmas tree. Dad held the littlest wide-eyed child aloft so she could place the angel at the top. The little boy seemed to have just spied a flop-eared puppy that peeked from a box under the tree. And from another box, a flaxen-haired doll gazed through eyes that opened and closed.

The pharmacy window held candies and mints arranged in glass jars plastered with ribbons. Suckers and lollipops decorated a tiny tree situated between the legs of a giant panda bear.

Although it was closed tonight, a score of Christmas-shopping customers usually made a colorful display, too, behind the Star Diner's aerosol-frosted windows.

The brightest lights that Siege and Chelsea passed, however, illuminated the Cherish Playhouse. The ticket window was dark, but the marquee flashed, brightly, with the message: "We Wish You All a Merry Christmas and A Happy New Year!"

Yes, Siege thought. *I could live here the rest of my life.*

Andy and Abbey hurried from the Christmas service, so they could join the family at Molly and Paul's. They stopped at the parsonage to pick up Winston and to toss their pajamas and gifts into the car. Their sleeping bags were already in the trunk. The double-wide didn't have all of the extra rooms the farmhouse had offered. But it was family, and they could sleep on the living room floor for one night.

Andy was glad that his father and Emma would be there for the evening. It would be different, this year, but it would be good.

Emma belonged. And Mac was content. His children held no reservations about her. He wondered what the future held, and he liked to imagine Emma as part of it.

She knew about his past; he had told her the story. But she hadn't judged him for it. She had understood the forces that had squeezed Mac into a mold of guilt and pain. And she had cried with him about his losses. "I wish I had known Rachel before she died," she had said. "And I wish you would have known my Jethro." In her grief over Jethro, Emma had learned hurt, too. "We will always grieve our lost ones," she had said wisely. "And one day we'll see them, again. But we are still here, and our todays are important. Every new day is a present." Not long ago, Andy had said the same thing. It was time to live in the present and to move into the future.

Mac had once thought he had to prove himself. All of his life, he had fought to reach the top. In Herndon, he had been driven to be somebody. But here, with Emma and his children—in this little town—things were so different! In more ways than one, he had been reborn, here. He had never felt taller and more complete, than here and now.

It was here that he had made his peace with God. And now, a Christ-filled Spirit overflowed from his heart, and it powered his energies and his goals. He had always been so consumed with a guilt-driven past that he had never had anything to give to anyone else. But God had brought him forgiveness and freed him from his burden. After being dead for so long, Mac was finally alive! And his heart could now love and be loved.

So much has changed, he thought, *since I came to Harmony and Cherish.*

Somehow, two tins of pulled peanut brittle had survived until tonight. Andy was sure that Emma must have brought them. But unlike on the day the candy was being made, everyone now politely took one piece and passed it along. Restraint was easier, tonight, because there were also iced cut-out cookies, and fudge, and popcorn balls, and punch. Phillip took the most peanut brittle—this was the first time he had tasted it.

"Well, well!" he said. "Where has this stuff been, all my life!"

In the absence of the old farmhouse fireplace—where everyone had gathered in years past—the atmosphere in the double-wide living room had been set with the lights on the Christmas tree and some convincingly realistic electric candles on the tables. There were no real Christmas candles, this year; the memory of the fire was too fresh.

Piles of presents surrounded the tree, waiting to be opened before the evening's end. And carols played softly in the background. Mac and Emma had been led to the sofa, where they sat together holding hands and smiling. Phillip was in a better mood than he had been at Thanksgiving. (He and Paul had started a chess game, earlier, and it sat ready for them to finish, tomorrow.) And Emily flailed her arms in excitement at the tree lights.

Only Winston had trouble settling, and Andy decided it must be time for a trip outside. Andy hated to leave the warmth of the gathering, but he excused himself. He guessed it was time for him to stretch a bit, anyway. He and Abbey had been sitting on the floor.

When Andy stretched, Mac also yawned and stood. He patted Emma's hand and said, "I could use a bit of air and a stretch of the legs, too. I'll be back in a minute."

Andy had thought Mac was heading for the back bathroom, but instead, Mac followed Andy and Winston out to the porch.

"Beautiful night, isn't it?" Mac declared, and Andy agreed.

Andy carried Winston down the stairs and set him on the ground. (Winston didn't always navigate slippery things well, with his top-heavy build.)

Andy and Mac watched as Winston's square, pugged nose followed the path that Paul took every morning and evening to the barn. Moose joined him midway across the farmyard, and the two dogs bounced and wagged like long-lost playmates. The farm cats hugged a sheltered corner and scattered when they saw the dogs coming.

Andy chuckled to think the cats didn't know they had little to fear from his dog. Winston couldn't even face down his neighbor cat.

As Andy and Mac watched, Winston did his business and then snorted along the edge of the barn door. Moose already knew what the door smelled like, and he preferred to play. But Winston stolidly held him off.

Outside of Moose's playful bouncing, the night was calm.

Andy and his dad stood without a word, until Andy said quietly, "I like Emma, Dad."

Mac nodded with a smile. "Hmmm-huh."

"And," Andy continued, "I like who you are when you're with her. Emma brings out the best in you."

Mac was silent. Then he said softly, "I'm not the same person I was."

Andy nodded, now. "Hmmm-huh," he said. "God has a way of doing that. He did it for me, too."

Winston was now across the yard, checking out the fence around the chicken coop. Mac and Andy made their way in that direction.

"I can't believe God gave me a second chance," Mac said. "I know I don't deserve it."

Andy lifted his face to the sky and replied, "That's why they call it *grace*. None of us deserves it."

Andy wanted to say more but wasn't sure if he could. After a moment, he said, "I don't want you to take this the wrong way. It's not because I'm so wonderful or spiritually better in any way. But…" Andy tried not to choke up. Finally, he said, "Dad—I'm proud of you!"

Mac's breathing grew uneven. Andy had known this would touch him. Andy didn't look, so as not to hinder any tears that might form.

Winston finished his exploration and turned back toward the house. His pampered feet were getting cold. The men followed.

At the double-wide steps, Winston waited to be picked up, but Andy ignored him. Mac had slowed, and Andy sensed that his dad wasn't ready to go back inside, just yet.

Mac scuffed his toe in the snow, as if he was clearing the area under the step. And then he cleared his throat. "Son," he said, ever so quietly, "I'm proud of you, too." His voice caught, but he went on. "I couldn't have had a better son."

Now, it was Andy who wept. In the dark, where only God could see, Mac drew his son close. Andy had longed for years to hear his father's praise, and he had wondered if he would ever hear it.

If stars could talk, they would have said that tonight, there were no sweeter words or better Christmas presents between these two. Father and son had been able to give each other the greatest gift of Christmas: Love.

Back inside, Mac wiped his face on his sleeve, and he and Winston started through the kitchen on their way to the living room. Andy ducked into the back bathroom.

Andy stood in front of the mirror. Laughter sounded in the other room, and Andy marveled at it.

Was this the same family he had grown up with? What had happened to everyone? Whatever it was, it was wonderful.

Andy pictured Emily's eyes, bright in the lights of the Christmas tree, and he could hear Molly prompting her little one to rustle the shiny paper on the package that Emma had brought for her. He knew that Winston would be at Emily's feet. He heard his father laugh at something Emma said. Then Paul laughed, and then Abbey.

And in the background, washing over it all, were the strains of *Silent Night* on the record player.

Andy heard no hesitancy to share, no unkind digs that were intended to prompt angry responses, no growls about the cost of gifts. Those were the dark memories of Christmases past, when his parents had not known the true meaning of Christmas. Instead, tonight, he heard thoughtful promptings, and warm memories, and shared kindnesses between people who cared about one another.

The angry shouts that had swirled outside of his childhood closet could hardly be recalled, now. The pejorative "idiot boy" refrain seemed to belong to someone else. And there were no secrets pulling anyone back into a dark past.

All was calm. All was bright. All because of a child born 2,000 years ago who fulfilled a promise of hope and brought the power to change lives.

Thank you, God, Andy breathed. *Thank you for things that I once never realized I was missing.*

Thank you for coming into my life and for giving me Abbey. Thank you for keeping Molly close to me and for the joy of Emily. Thanks for my goofy bulldog. Thanks for our wonderful church and church family. Thank you for Mom and Grannie in heaven with You. And thank you for bringing Your peace and grace to my father.

You are truly a God of love and miracles—a Mighty God of renewal. Thank you for creating in all of us a new heart and a right spirit. I love You, Lord! Praise Your Holy Name, forever! Amen!

THE END

NOTES FROM THE AUTHOR

We all live in a battle-scarred world. But there is always hope, because our God has not abandoned His created ones, the ones He formed in His image and made for eternity. Only God, in the form of His Son, holds the answers we need for life. Only Christ offers grace and salvation to restore us to our original design. Only He can turn our hearts of stone into hearts of flesh and holiness. My prayer for you, my readers, and for myself and all those I love, is that our eyes would be opened to look on His face—to see Who He is and how much He loves us. Our God longs to make us whole. May we abandon our stubborn refusal to look up and, instead, reach out for His daily redemption!

Create in us a clean heart, O God!

ABOUT THE AUTHOR

In her fiction series about a pastor in a small Midwestern town named Cherish, Debby L. Johnston illustrates eternal truths and brings to life characters like the members of the churches that she and her husband, Scott, served in their forty-year ministry. Debby and Scott currently reside in Ohio. Visit Debby's author site at *www.DebbyLJohnston.com* and link from there to her Blog and Facebook Page.

Debby L. Johnston

CHERISH: CREATE IN ME A CLEAN HEART
READER'S DISCUSSION GUIDE

1. When Andy challenges his father's assertions that God is not loving, Mac sees for the first time how much God has given him. It is human nature to let the difficult things of our lives overshadow our many blessings. Name five blessings that God has brought into your life that you sometimes take for granted.
2. God often orchestrates our circumstances, to put us in the right spot to minister for Him, even when we may not be aware of it, at the time. In our story, Mac happens to

be at the farm at a time when he is most needed: in the rescue during the fire and in the work of keeping up the farm until Paul can take over, again. When has God put you in a circumstance that you later realized could have turned out differently—perhaps tragically—without you?

3. Mr. Tranor refused to call for help for his sow until it was too late. He tried to take care of things (perform a Caesarean operation) without the knowledge or ability to do so, and he suffered loss because of it. Have you or someone you know stubbornly "done it your way" and refused to call on God or others for help that was readily available?
4. After becoming a Christian, Mac is frustrated to find that he hasn't been instantly transformed into the perfect, holy person he expected to become. What does God expect of us as He works to perfect us, in our time on this earth? And what part does He play in that process?
5. The huge draft horse that suffered from constipation had to submit to a twist of chain on his lip while Siege and Andy helped him back to health. Has God ever had to use a "twitch" on you, to get you to hold still long enough for Him to restore you in your Christian walk?
6. Vera Bartlett suffered from an inability to break away from her abusing husband. Learn about domestic abuse in your community, and offer support and prayer for any domestic abuse shelters in your area.
7. Andy and Molly had to learn to forgive their parents for the mental abuse they suffered as children. Until the secret of Little Mac's death had been revealed, Andy and Molly had no idea what fueled their parents' dysfunction. Learning the truth helped them to not only deal with their own hurt but also the hurt of their father. When others hurt us, it is often because they carry hurt from

other sources in their lives that we don't know about. Pray that God will help you forgive someone who seems to be cruel without reason. Trust Christ to take care of their situation and bring healing.

8. Andy and Molly came to grips with their father dating Emma, even though it was a surprise to them. When someone we know has come through the redemption of Christ, it is important that we don't keep them locked in their past. We need to let God lead them into His new future. Pray for someone you know who is coming out of drug abuse, alcoholism, infidelity or some other difficulty. Pray that God will not only redeem them but also offer them His perfect future, prepared especially for them.
9. After Mac's argument with Phillip and then Andy, he sits through a storm that calms him. He calls out to God for forgiveness, and it feels as though God embraces him, even in the midst of thunder and lightning. Sometimes a display of God's power can be reassuring. Thank Him for His power, as well as His still, small comforts.
10. When Lizzie wandered into the cornfield, two unlikely dogs become heroes. God can use the least qualified people and the most insignificant things to bring about His purposes. He might even use you! The only thing He asks is that we make ourselves and our resources available. Ask God to help you be ready, with all you possess, when He needs you.
11. Andy is finally able to tell his father of his love for him and how proud he is of who he is becoming. And Mac finally says the words that Andy has waited for all of his life: that his father is proud of him. One day we will hear Christ say: *"Well done, good and faithful servant."* Live your life, today, in light of that anticipated praise!

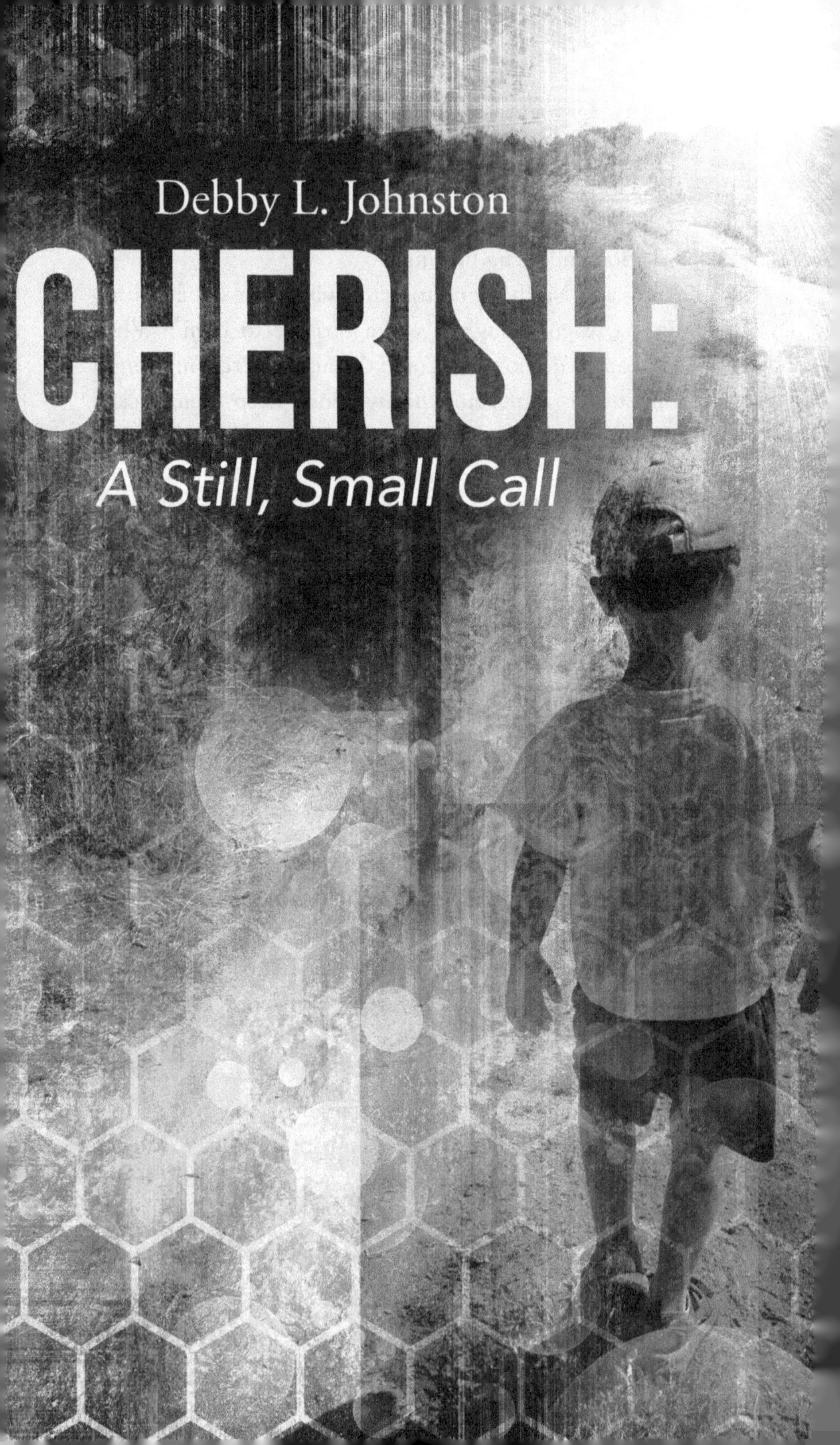
Debby L. Johnston
CHERISH:
A Still, Small Call

Book One—where the Cherish series begins!

Cherish: A Still, Small Call is the first book in author Debby L. Johnston's Christian fiction series about Reverend Andy Garrett and his family. Read the story of Andy's past—a surprising past. Get a peek at the difficulties of Andy's childhood, but also uncover his dramatic conversion and the positive influences of people like Grannie who prayed for him; the gorgeous ninth-grade teacher, Miss Randall, who spurred him to read; and a college friend named Bonnie who helped him to open the Bible. Learn how Andy met and pursued Abbey Preston, the love of his life. Then follow Andy's call to serve the Cherish First Baptist Church—the endearing small-town ministry that God had in mind for him all the time!

CHERISH:

Behold, I Knock

DLJ

"Second novel of the Cherish series"

Debby L. Johnston

Book Two—joys and tears bring you closer to Cherish and the Garrett family.

Cherish: Behold, I Knock continues the story begun in the first *Cherish* novel, about Reverend Andy Garrett, his family, his friends, and the working of God in the quaint rural community of Cherish. Andy grows as a minister, despite bats in the sanctuary, a deaf substitute pianist, a wild-haired and poetic church secretary, and a baptistry that boils over the night before a baptism. Andy also learns how his unchurched, bartending background was part of God's plan to change the life of a drug-addicted teen. Most of all, Andy finds an opportunity to share with his own parents the love of God and the truth of Christ's redemption. The story of *Cherish: Behold, I Knock* reveals a remarkable God at work in drawing the broken and the broken-hearted to Himself.

Irises, watercolor by Debby L. Johnston

ADDITIONAL POEMS BY DEBBY

The *Cherish* character of Opal Reese (the poetic church secretary) gives author Debby L. Johnston an opportunity to share some of her verse with readers, especially poems that are a bit tongue-in-cheek. Additional poems by Debby are included here. Some are light and others are more serious in tone.

"These are some of my favorites," Debby says. "Poetry is an extension of my quiet times with God, and I find the verses often say things that teach me, even as I write them. I hope they will be meaningful to you, too."

Other poems, paintings, and devotionals by Debby appear on her Facebook page (find a link on Debby's web page: *www.DebbyLJohnston.com*).

O TO BE…

O to be like a child, again,
And to wonder at a worm;
To see it crawl
With no legs at all
And to wriggle, stem to stern.

O to see a yellow butterfly
As it whispers to a petal
On a gentle date
Near a junkyard gate,
Beside an old rusty kettle.

O to trace a rainbowed sky
Once the sun tells the thunder goodbye;
And to pretend
Jeweled grasses all bend
To me, as to a breeze passing by.

O I believe in Who's child I am
And the wonders I've been told
Of fine, divine things—
Like seraphim's wings
And meandering streets paved in gold.

O I believe what I've always imagined—
That the Way is a Door
That Love opens wide
To let us inside
And invite us to come and explore!

O please, friend, do come, too,
And we'll adventure, together.
We'll greet the New Morn
As if Eden's reborn,
And we'll walk in the cool with Him, ever.

YOU ARE THERE!

I'm still amazed that You are there
And how easily You're found.
I would have thought the God of all
Would've made the search profound.

You're reflected everywhere—
Your handiwork astounds.
In all the world's great mysteries,
Your majesty is crowned.

You are there, You are there.
I lift my hands, I lift my prayer,
And Lord, You are there!
You are there, You are there.
I lift my hands, I lift my prayer,
I thank you, Lord, You are there.

I see You in a million stars,
I feel You in the breeze.
I smell You in the season's change,
And hear Your feathered symphonies.

And when Your Love came down, that day,
To take our death away,
You took a step upon a cross
That takes my breath away.

You are there, You are there.
I lift my hands, I lift my prayer,
I thank you, Lord, You are there!
You are there, You are there.
I lift my hands, I lift my prayer,
I thank you, Lord, You are there.

You could have stayed where the angels sing,
You could have stayed where Your praises ring,
But You came down and bled for me.
You are there! You are there!

You are there, You are there.
I lift my hands, I lift my prayer,
I thank you, Lord, You are there!
You are there, You are there.
I lift my hands, I lift my prayer,
I thank you, Lord, You are there.

I thank You, Lord, that You are there!

FOR EARTH SHALL BE HEAVEN

Thank you for roses,
For colors so bright.
Thank you for sunshine
And moonbeams at night.

Thank you for rainbows
And skies that are blue.
Thank you for friendships,
And thank you for You.

If heaven's more lovely
Than all of these things,
I covet the moments
That Your promise brings—

Of when earth shall be heaven
And heaven be mine,
And no more will sorrow
And evil combine.

Thank you for windows,
And thank you for doors.
Thank you for pathways
From my heart to Yours.

Thank you for healing,
Whenever there's pain,
And thank you for comfort
When all seems in vain.

At night, I dream of what heaven will be,
And what treasures You've said will be mine.
And one day the Lion will lie down with the Lamb
And earth and heaven be twined!

If heaven's more lovely
Than all of these things,
I covet the moments
That Your promise brings—

Of when earth shall be heaven
And heaven be mine,
And no more will sorrow
And evil combine.

Then earth shall be heaven
And heaven be mine,
And no more will sorrow
And evil combine.

SHEPHERD OF MY PRAYERS

Bring all my thoughts into Your fold;
Jealously guard them there.
And make my wayward heart lie down,
Thou Shepherd of my prayers.

Show me exactly where deep waters lie
And where it's safe to drink.
And where life's course rims rocky steeps,
Pasture me far from the brink.

Speak Thy Name, and I will hear;
And tether me to Thee.
And 'though the lion roars my name,
I pray You'll cherish me.

If all the meadows of this world
Were spread before my feet,
They would not even half compare
To all Your paths where I may leap.

RAMS' HORNS IN THE BREEZE

Surround me with Your holy band,
And guard me with Your sword,
And challenge all who seek to maim—
Repel them with Your Word.

Fight for me with clash of wings
And cherubim on high,
And with Your glory blind my foes
And lift Your banner high!

Help me know Your force is near;
Let me hear You in the trees,
To know the sound of battle gear
And rams' horns in the breeze.

Open the blindness of my eyes
To see Your bright array,
To count Your warriors on the hills
And Your watchers on my way.

For greater are they that guard my ways
Than those that clang and roar.
For the battle is already won—
With victory, evermore!

I SAW TEARS STREAM DOWN HIS CHEEKS

You ask why troubles do not crush me
And in grief's shadows I have peace?
It is because my Jesus gave a face to God,
And I saw tears stream down His cheeks.

I know God cares for me;
I know He cares and sees.
I know He knows
The hurts I feel.
I know it's true—
He died for me!
He's felt my deepest pain
In all His deepest agony,
And when I hurt, I know
He's there to cry with me.

And that's why troubles do not crush me
And in grief's shadows I have peace.
It is because my Jesus gave a face to God,
And I saw tears stream down His cheeks.

MARTHA'S REGRETS

She left all the housework.
(I've never done that.)

Mary just sat there.
(I could have done that.)

She eagerly listened.
(I would have done that.)

She spent time with Jesus.
(I should have done that.)

She fulfilled all MY wishes
While I did the dishes—
And now it's too late to go back!

PENNY RICH

When she took her tiny tokens—
Her two itty, bitty mites—
To increase the Temple treasury,
It made her budget tight.

With her couple copper coins, she
Made her simple sacrifice,
And giving up her weekly living,
Gave her tenth part, more than twice.

She thought she gave her gift unnoticed
(who would note a widow's mite?),
But to this day her gift is honored
More than gold in heaven's sight.

TOMBS OF THE GADARENE

Sometimes we see the face of hell in the eyes or acts of another.
And we see the naked reality of the lie the Serpent's shared.
And like Adam and Eve exposed, we run to hide—
To distance us from the horror of evil bared.

But if we go to the heights, the terror flies too.
If we go to the depths, its weight is like a stone.
Its bloody images haunt our waking and our dreams—
And chill our evening twilight zone.

Flee you to the hills, you Gadarene,
And live among the stinking tombs!
A madman, in agony so profound,
Puppeted mercilessly by horrid demon tunes.

Scream your epithets when innocence passes by;
Tear your clothes and beat your whip-scarred breast;
And whimper, helpless, in defeat, 'mid shrieks
And mutilated thrashings without hope of rest.

"What is hell?" the pompous windbags scoff,
Pooh-poohing what the tortured know so well.
And these rainless clouds who give no hope to rescue souls,
Like the blind leading the blind, march gaily into hell.

"Peace! Peace!" the pitiful begs in vain.
But no man can relieve his distress—
Except for one, who steps upon the shore
And is recognized with wild-eyed, hellish witness:

"What have you to do with me, Jesus, Most High God?"
In dread the craven demons whined and cried,
And quivered in fear at the feet of highest heaven's Lord,
Whose sentence could kill and would not be defied.
He who spoke "Peace!" to the thunderous storm on the sea,
Now roared in command over lesser things in Lordship, again.
And the demons beat their ignoble retreat into a drift of pigs
They drove, mad, to destruction to outrun their pain.

And as the squealing clamor faded and the herders mourned,
There remained in composure and awash in love,
A madman, curled in peace at His feet, sequestered from all harm,
Fully dwelt with healing restoration and the fanning of the Dove.

In the gaze of his Savior was the sense of all the hurt that had been.
Who else could have understood, could have stirred the deep within,
With healing that not only moved one God-ward, but plumbed the depths
To touch the putrid, metastic, murderous clutch of sin?

No one but He who would one day bear it all and die Himself, to save!
O blessed One, who else could beat the granted hate of hell
In pounding nails and beaten flesh and rawly twisted agonies,
And then descend the yawning darkness with a million souls expelled?

He who could feel all of that and grasp the strangling fear of living death
Could surely know my pain and earn my trust to raise me from my tombs!
I was a madman, tortured soul, without that miracle of hope to hold,
Until I claimed those mighty arms that paid to cover all my wounds.

O turn my nightmares into dreams, my torments into healing streams.
O bid my curse of the knowledge of hell be battled to retreat.
Grant Thou my soul to see Your form and hear Your "Peace, be still!"
So that I may slumber as a trusting child on the seas beneath Your feet.

Command Your watchers in the night to canopy their wings o'er me.
O light my shadows with Your peace and Your promises divine,
And may I waken to Your gentle things and innocence so kind,
As You walk the rest of the world with me and unravel the threads of time.

FIERCE ARE THE CHERUBIM

With wings outspread from tip to tip
To touch the walls of gold,
Two cherubim, molded fierce and bold,
Stood guard in The Presence of old.

They hovered not that God should fear—
No might need shelter Him;
Their presence was instead for sin,
To guard our dust from Him.

Our worship of the Holy Fire
By distance was required,
To come not near with lute and lyre,
But praise with outer choir.

And then, one night in Bethlehem,
Unseen but hovering,
They guarded God-turned-dusty-king—
While herald angels sing.

And as He grew, they prowled nearby—
Invisible, unheard,
Until, baptized with Dove and Word,
He desert angels stirred.

He could have called the cherubim
To annihilate His foes,
But in His pity, healing flowed,
And love was what He chose.

Where were the cherubim when Jesus died?
What chains restrained their claws?
What made the angels wait in awe
As sinners killed our God?

Was it the cherubim He flew
When from the grave He rose—
When lightning tore and soldiers froze
And death dropped 'neath His toes?

Once again, did the cherubim fly
(did He ride them through the sky?),
When on bright wings above, on high,
He passed from seeing eye?

'Twill be a steed that bears Him, when,
Again He claims His own.
And as we gather 'round His throne,
The cherubim will lie prone.

WOULD YOU BE SAFE?

Would you be "safe"
And never see His power?
Or submit to suffering
And share His heavy hour
When darkness draws to overwhelm
And evil's triumph stands?

For it is then, and only then—
When evil dances on the grave—
That the tomb is cracked!
And Life tears from the cave
To crush the Lie,
And Redemption is at hand.

LET YOUR BEAUTY

Let Your beauty shine through me
Like the crown of the lily in bloom,
That lifts its head in unassumed poise
Toward the yellow sun at noon.

Let Your love be felt through me
In a word to encourage a friend,
To lift their uncertainty up,
To coax their fears to end.

Let Your truth be on my lips
When deception covers the land,
And its drought dries up the springs
And misleads through quaking sands.

Let Your mercy plead through me
To spring the captives free,
When brutal justice bruises the poor
And the rod silences the meek.

May Your peace cry out before me,
As to the waves of long ago,
When the storm and rain clouds folded
Into rainbows at Your toes.

WHO ARE YOU, THEN?

What happens when
The party ends
And all the lights go dim?

O, my soul,
Who are you, then?

Do you know yourself in silence?
Have you ever been alone?
Do you know yourself in solitude?

O, soul,
Who are you, then?

With thoughts exposed,
With shadows lit,
With shames enlarged,

O, my soul,
Who are you, then?
Forever pain is the longest time,
And nowhere is a fog.
And empty is an awful thing!

O, soul,
Who are you, then?

No one to walk the moon with you,
Or search the lane of stars;
Alone, forever, is a long, long time.

O, soul,
Who are you, then?

But One has love that lasts:
Beyond the span of years,
Beyond the pale of loneliness.

O, soul,
Be open, then.

He gave His life to draw you in,
And He does seek you, still;
Come, now, while chance remains—

O, soul,
Come, run to Him.

No more alone beyond the Morn,
His love will make you His—
As a bride for a groom for eternity.

O, soul,
Come, fly to Him!

MORNING PRAYERS

Between the moon and morning,
Silver pearls of dew are formed.
The owls haunt the clearing,
And the deer slip through the corn.

There is no sound, no windy blow;
The stars all fade away.
The fingers of the yawning dawn
Stretch wide to paint the day.

Gold on gold, like lights of home,
And purple like a queen,
The curtain lifts, and as it folds,
The rooftops start to gleam.

These bounties ache my soul
And yearn me for that land,
Where beauty rides in splendor
In His forever hand.

Visit Debby's Blog at her Author Web Page—
www.DebbyLJohnston.com.

Printed in the United States
By Bookmasters